ALWAYS WITH YOU

HARMONY WEST

Copyright © 2023 by Harmony West

Cover Design © 2023 by Beholden Book Covers

Published by Westword Press

All rights reserved. No part of this book may be reproduced in any form or by any electronic or mechanical means, including information storage and retrieval systems, without written permission from the author.

This is a work of fiction. Names, characters, places, and incidents are the product of the author's imagination or are used fictitiously. Any resemblance to actual events, locales, or persons living or dead is purely coincidental and not intended by the author.

ISBN (paperback): 979-8-9881181-1-4

ISBN (ebook): 979-8-9881181-0-7

To Alex,
For being the reason I write love stories.
Thank you for helping make my dream come true.

CHAPTER ONE

THE FIRST BOY I ever loved might be a murderer.

At least, that's what everyone else believes. I know what happened to the girl they all think he killed, and he had nothing to do with it.

Not that he's on social media defending himself. He doesn't have a single account—no Instagram, no TikTok, no Snapchat, not even Facebook. I've been Googling *Miles Mariano* since he moved away in sixth grade, curious how he's changed. But I haven't caught a glimpse of him since we were twelve, not even in any of the press conferences since his sister went missing last year. Not a word from him asking people to help look for Sophie, to come forward with any information. Like he doesn't even miss her.

I hope he doesn't. I wish they would all stop missing her, and we can pretend she never existed at all.

The driver's side door of Jordan's BMW swings open and the sounds from Natalie's graduation party rush in. Laughter, splashes in the pool, Taylor Swift begging a boy not to go.

My heart flutters in my chest like it does every time I see him: the best thing that's ever happened to me.

The brief flash of light illuminates Jordan climbing in the backseat with me. He's massive—six-foot-four with wide shoulders and huge muscles from years playing football. His chestnut hair is perfectly styled, his obsession, and his blue eyes are nearly crystalline in the brightness. Then the light fades.

"You've been waiting for me?" His voice is low and rocks me like ocean waves.

"Where else would I be?"

I can just make out his grin in the darkness. "Then I'll make this worth the wait."

I'm in the tight tank top, tiny mini skirt, and push-up bra he bought me. I wear what I know he likes me in because it's not my clothes that give me confidence—it's Jordan. It's that look he gives me, like he's about to devour me. It's the brush of his palm against my neck, rough and calloused from football practices and bench presses, before he grips my hair and pulls me toward him, crushing his lips to mine.

I yank his letterman jacket off and toss it onto the floor. His hands are all over me, his tongue slipping into my mouth.

Six months in, and we're still like kids who only get candy on Halloween. We can't get enough of each other.

Jordan's the first guy I've ever been with. First boyfriend, first kiss, first time. When we got together, I kept track of how many times we kissed, how many times we had sex, but now I've lost count.

I never imagined my first would be *the* Jordan Goldman. The most popular senior at our school, the hottest guy in Beaumont, our town's golden boy. His mom is the mayor and his dad is a business tycoon. They run this town, and everyone here thinks Jordan can do no wrong.

They have no idea how right they are.

He tugs down my bra and shirt together and kisses from my neck to my breasts. "God, you're so pretty," he murmurs.

I could never get tired of hearing those words from his mouth. "I want you."

That makes him growl against my skin.

When his tongue circles my nipple, I gasp and reach for his hair, but he pins my hands down. He hates when I mess it up, but I don't care if my hair is a mess after. I want people to know exactly what I was doing with Jordan Goldman in his backseat.

One of his hands releases me and slides up my thigh and under my skirt. My legs are practically shaking with anticipation.

I am the luckiest girl in the world to be here with him. To be the girl he chose to give his heart to after another girl ripped it out.

His fingers stop at the edge of my thong. Trailing slowly, agonizingly slowly, to the spot between my thighs.

A hard *thud* of a fist on the window behind my head makes me yelp.

Jordan and I jump apart, me scrambling to tug my bra and shirt back into place. A hiss escapes his lips. "*Shit.*"

Is it the cops here to break up the party? Or have they finally come to ask me about what really happened the night Sophie disappeared?

A high-pitched laugh outside tells me exactly who it is. My heart rate slows.

"Hey, Coitus Interruptus," I say when I climb out of the car.

Natalie Shin keeps cackling, Liv Hernandez her shadow. Raven black hair to golden blonde, cherry red lips to pink matte, preppy to athleisure.

Natalie was one of Sophie's friends from the cheerleading squad, and she and I have been close since we started searching for Sophie last year.

Liv was Sophie's best friend, and she still hasn't warmed up to me. She's a badass, multi-sport athlete who's bound for Brown to major in STEM. I was the worst cheerleader on the squad—accepted only because Coach needed bodies—and I'm heading to USC in the fall with Jordan to major in . . . undecided. Liv and I don't exactly have a lot in common, but we do our best to fake a friendship for Natalie's sake. They've been dating since she asked Natalie to prom, so we're stuck together.

"Sorry. I couldn't resist." Natalie grins like she isn't sorry at all.

"Just wait until I get my revenge."

She turns to Jordan, looming over us and slipping his letterman jacket back on, the number fourteen a stark red against the white of his sleeve. The jacket stretches over his shoulders. He's still just as big as he was during football season.

"Did you bring more beer?" Natalie asks him.

"Was I supposed to?"

She throws her head back and groans. "You're my supplier, Mr. I-don't-even-need-a-fake-ID."

It's true. Somehow, Jordan has gotten beer twice without getting carded. Something about his intimidating height, bulky muscles, and charming smile convinces adults he's older than he is.

"If we need more, I'm on it." Jordan's fingers drift from my shoulder to my hand, sending tingles down my spine. "Coming?"

Of course I am. I don't want to be anywhere without him if I can help it.

"No, leave her here!" Natalie insists, grabbing my arm. "I miss my bestie."

When Jordan turns to me, I force a reassuring smile. I've spent Natalie's entire grad party so far waiting for my boyfriend in the back of his BMW. I should spend at least some time with my best friend at her own party before he gets back. "It's okay. I'll see you after."

"You sure—"

"Heyyy, buddy!" A shirtless Brett bounds over to us,

throwing an arm around Jordan. He's like an overgrown golden retriever, bouncing from place to place, tongue out, and if he had a tail, it'd be wagging. He's sweaty and red-faced, already drunk, but he's harmless. He's on the football team too, though I never bothered learning his position.

The only reason I even know Jordan's is because there's only one starting quarterback and everyone mentions it when they ask me how he's doing. *Best quarterback Beaumont High's seen in a long time!* I've never been interested in football before Jordan, but I don't really care what he's doing as long as I get to be the girl he catches in his arms and kisses when he wins.

"Did you bring booze?" Brett shouts in Jordan's ear.

"Getting it now."

Brett whoops and drops into the passenger seat. "I call shotgun!"

Jordan turns to me with a grin. "Before I go, I have something for you."

He reaches past Brett into the glove compartment, and before I can even try to guess what it could be, he pulls out a tiny, black velvet box.

My heart stops. Natalie gasps. She's thinking exactly what I'm thinking.

Engagement ring.

I smile so wide my cheeks hurt. If Jordan proposes, I will officially be living the fairytale romance I've only read about in books. I'll marry my high school sweetheart, and we'll live happily ever after.

It'll be like Sophie never existed. Never had him first.

When he opens the lid with a tiny *pop*, my heart bursts. It's a ring adorned with an amethyst stone. For my birthday in February.

I expect him to drop to one knee until he sees our faces and laughs. "I'm not proposing."

I try not to let the disappointment squeezing my heart show.

Brett laughs way too hard, and Liv mutters, "God, I hope not."

I flash her a look to shut the hell up. Then, before she can notice, I reign my emotions back in. You don't get people to like you by shooting them death glares, and Liv is the one person I still need to win over.

"It's just a promise ring," Jordan tells me. "Sorry, you're not getting a real ring until after college. This one just says I'm promising to stick around until that day comes."

Natalie watches with a huge grin across her face, while Liv examines her nails.

Jordan takes my hand. "You want it, right?" He towers over me, but the vulnerability in those gorgeous blue eyes makes him seem smaller. Like he's actually worried I might say no.

"Of course I do!"

He grins and slips the ring on my finger. Sealing my fate.

It's not the commitment of an engagement ring, but this has to mean he's chosen me over her. I never saw a promise ring on her finger.

"Wow, Jordan, thank you! It's gorgeous." I hold my hand up, and it feels like I'm looking at my future. Even my prom queen crown doesn't compare to this.

"Just like you," he says, voice warm and low.

From the passenger seat, Brett pretends to retch.

I ignore him. "You already gave me flowers, though. You didn't have to get me anything else."

Only Jordan Goldman gives his girlfriend white roses *and* a promise ring for graduation. I'm so lucky.

"I know, but I wanted to get you something special for graduation."

"You're literally the best boyfriend ever."

Liv groans. "Okay, can someone kill me now before I stab my eyes out?"

"I volunteer." I give her the most saccharine smile I can muster, and though everyone else laughs, Liv doesn't.

She glares, and I don't know . . . maybe she's even a little afraid.

Jordan sweeps me up in a kiss before getting in his car and squealing out of the driveway. I miss him as soon as he's out of sight. Natalie leads me by the hand through the crowd to get a vodka cranberry, and Liv shoves a red plastic cup in my hand, full to the brim.

Once the vodka cranberry kicks in, the three of us dance and snap selfies together on the deck, where the thud of the bass nearly drowns out all conversation.

I still can't believe we've graduated. I won't go back to school on Monday. Before Jordan, I lived for summer. I shuffled through the school year like a zombie, invisible and with only one girl I could sort of call a friend. Junior Year Madalyn would've been thrilled to be done with high school, but Senior Year Maddie is going to miss having everything she ever wanted.

When the track switches to a slow ballad and Liv's hands drift to Natalie's hips, I stumble off the deck to find my third cup. Or is it my fourth? Plus the shot Natalie handed me that Liv objected to as it was already burning its way down my throat.

Jordan texts me.

Me and Brett got the booze. Driving back now.

He has to drive out of town since everyone in Beaumont knows him, so it'll be at least another twenty-minute wait until he's back.

Drive fast. I miss you.

I always feel lost without Jordan by my side. He's the reason I'm at this party. The reason I'm friends with girls like Natalie and Liv. The reason I have clothes that actually make me look good. The reason everyone in this town knows my name.

Half these kids bullied me in elementary and middle school. The other half shunned me. And none of them remember it. I want to keep it that way. And the best way to do that is by being Maddie, Jordan Goldman's girlfriend.

I pass a giggling group of girls, their faces lit up in the darkness by the blue light of their phones. "Maddie!" Chelsea waves to me before wrapping me in a tight hug, her platinum blonde hair smothering me. "I'm going to miss cheer with you *so much!*"

I hug each of the cheer girls while we sniffle into each other's shoulders. In fifth grade, Chelsea was one of the girls who laughed hardest when Sophie made fun of my Goodwill sneakers at recess.

"I need another drink!" All this shouting is making my throat sore.

"Try the cooler!" She points past the pool, where a small group of grads who definitely weren't invited blow clouds of smoke into the night air.

Ten feet from the cooler, they break into a chorus of hyena laughter. Dark clothes, piercings, tattoos, and vapes among a sea of pastels, manicures, and vodka cranberries.

In the middle, a shock of long, blue hair. Ash.

Beneath her hood, her eyes and phone are trained on a guy with his back to me. When she spots me, she grimaces like I'm something rotten. She knew I'd be here, and she would've stayed away if this party didn't have the kind of weed and booze that only the rich kids can afford.

I dig out one of the last cans of beer from a cooler filled with half-melted ice. I hate Miller, but it'll have to do.

As soon as I'm taking a sip from my cup, Ash's group bursts out laughing again. At me?

Even though I shouldn't care what they think, I do. I want everyone to like me, even if I don't like them. I've been that girl nobody likes. I've been that girl with no friends. I don't want to be her again.

I turn, and too late, catch sight of the body flying toward me.

His back slams into me like a brick wall, spilling my beer down my shirt. I jump back and gasp.

Ash spits out a loud, braying laugh.

When the guy spins to face me, I realize he's not one of my classmates. He doesn't go to Beaumont at all. Still. Maybe it's the vodka, but something about him looks familiar.

When he flicks his dark hair out of his eyes, that's when I recognize him and my stomach flips.

Miles Mariano.

CHAPTER TWO

I'VE BEEN DAYDREAMING about this moment for years. The day the first boy to capture my heart returned to Beaumont.

In middle school, Miles was the only boy—the only person—who liked me. The only other kid who liked to read at recess. The boy in the library who helped me look for the next book in the *Heartland* series when I couldn't find it on the shelf. The boy who shoved a kid on the playground for stealing my bookmark and leaving me in tears on the swing set. The boy who became my first real, daydream-about-him-while-falling-asleep, ache-for-him-so-hard-it-hurts crush.

Then he punched his sister in sixth grade, and his parents divorced. He and his dad moved to Hartford; his sister and mom stayed in Beaumont. I may not have heard a word from him since, but I've heard plenty of rumors: how he kept throwing fists at classmates. Got detention after detention. Suspended three times. And finally, expelled for writing a hit list.

The angry, loner brother who didn't get along with his popular, cheerleader sister.

Now he's back. And he looks nothing like the boy he was when he left.

Back then, he had splotchy red acne, a mouth full of braces, and gangly arms he hadn't yet grown into. Now he's at least six inches taller, his skin has cleared, his teeth are straight, and his hair is a shade darker. Black hoodie, dark jeans, hands in his pockets. And burning-hot coals for eyes.

The sight of him makes my heart stutter.

He used to be the kid who got pushed around by middle school bullies. Now he's the guy who pushes back.

His eyes rake down my body, from the wet tank top plastered to my boobs, to the skirt that barely covers my ass, to the heels that have been making my feet ache for the past hour.

I expect some compliment Jordan might offer me. *Hot. Sexy.* Instead, his lip curls. "What the hell happened to you?"

It takes a second for the words to compute. They're sultry and deep and—

Not a compliment.

Luckily, the only ones watching us are Ash and her group of slacker friends. She's cackling and pointing her phone at us. Filming this whole embarrassing exchange. She's been waiting for a moment like this since I stopped being her friend.

"Excuse me?" I ask him.

"Don't tell me you're one of those girls now." His tone is flat, but his eyes aren't. There's a fiery intensity in them. Like I've somehow disappointed him after a single look. Like being *one of those girls* is a bad thing. Even though it's what made me Maddie, what made Jordan notice me, what made people finally start to like me.

"You know your sister was one of those girls, right?" I spit.

I almost clap a hand over my mouth, but he doesn't flinch. Not a single facial muscle twitches at the mention of his missing sister.

Now that he's standing in front of me for the first time in six years, I realize that I've been fantasizing about a person who no longer exists. That boy who was kind and sweet and stood up for me is gone.

He's been replaced with a guy who starts fights and crashes parties. A murder suspect.

Even if he didn't kill his sister, Miles could still be dangerous. Especially if he finds out what I've kept secret about the night his sister disappeared.

He steps toward me, and it takes everything in me not to back up. When his eyes dip down to my cleavage again, I cover myself, but the heat of his gaze sends a thrill through me.

"Were you friends with her?" he asks.

I don't know how to answer that. The truth is that I wasn't, but if I admit that to him, he might wonder how I'm friends with all of Sophie's friends and dating her boyfriend. I pick my words carefully. "I knew her."

His eyes finally leave mine to scan the party around us. We're attracting attention now as more and more people notice the accused murderer in their midst.

"What are you doing here, anyway?"

"Same as you," Miles tells me.

"Getting railed in the back of a BMW?"

His eyebrow quirks up, and he fights the smirk that pulls at a corner of his lips. "Only if you're up for an all-nighter."

I take a step back, even though the rumble of his voice, the temptation of his words, sends goosebumps down my skin. "Not with somebody who just spilled beer all over me."

"Like you don't love the attention." His words drip with disdain, and I don't know whether I want to slap him or cry.

He used to like me. Didn't he? Or did I imagine that? Maybe I built it up in my head for so long that I let myself think there was something between me and Miles that was never actually there.

I don't know how he felt about me when we were younger,

but I do know how he feels about me now. Somehow, in less than two minutes, he's decided he hates me.

"You don't know anything about me," I hiss.

He unzips his hoodie, shrugging out of it to reveal a black t-shirt underneath and the bulge of his biceps. I wonder what it would be like to be wrapped in his arms. A lump forms in my throat, and he tosses his hoodie at me. "Take this. Cover yourself up."

"Why? Never seen a pair of boobs in real life before? I can't control if you cum in your pants at the sight of me. That's your problem." Still, I shrug it on because more and more people are watching us now.

Miles's mouth morphs into a snarl. "Trust me. There are plenty of girls like you to go around."

I step toward him, unable to contain my fury anymore. "Yeah, but we all stay the hell away from guys who kill one of us."

"What are you doing here?" Liv has a forty-year-old smoker's voice, even though she hasn't smoked a day in her life, and it cuts through the tension between me and Miles like a machete.

Natalie loops her arm through mine, and somehow, there's more distance between me and Miles, but I'm not sure which one of us moved. I pull his hoodie closer, and it looks like I'm wearing nothing underneath. All I want is to get out of this soaked shirt and into something warm and dry so I can fling his hoodie back at him.

He shrugs. "Hanging out."

"Leave," Liv tells him.

But Miles doesn't move except to lock eyes with me. There's something about the intensity of his gaze that sends a shiver down my spine. "Sorry about the beer."

His apology throws me. He was just being a complete asshole two seconds ago.

"It's fine." It's the response I'd give to anyone else. Nice Maddie would never be mad at someone for accidentally spilling beer on her. She'd never cause a scene at a party.

But that's exactly what I'm doing, and all it took was seeing Miles again to completely unravel me.

"I said *leave!*" Liv snaps at him. The only time I've heard her yell like this is on the field. Now it's the only sound as a hush falls over the party.

Miles chuckles and backs away, hands in the pockets of his jeans. The first smile I've seen on his face since he ran into me, and it's . . . disarming. A half-smirk that turns my knees to jelly. "Nice seeing you again, Madalyn."

Even though I knew he remembered me, my name on his lips makes me freeze. My name isn't Madalyn anymore—it's Maddie. But I still want to hear him say it again.

Natalie gently nudges me toward the house. "Come on. Let's go find you a clean shirt."

The inside of Natalie's three-story Victorian is about ten degrees colder. Even with Miles's hoodie, the central AC blowing from the ducts sends goosebumps down my bare legs.

Up the stairs, I trip on the final step and Natalie steadies me. Liv huffs and storms past us. By the time Natalie and I get into her bedroom, Liv is already yanking open the second drawer on the mahogany dresser, filled with neatly folded tops.

I struggle to get my top off. Dressing was a lot easier before I started drinking. The first time I got drunk, Jordan nearly cried laughing while calling me his *little lightweight.*

I manage to get the tank top over my bra but can't get it off my arms. "I need help."

Natalie pulls my top off and helps me get the clean one on. She's tinier than me, so it's tight and the hem lands a couple of inches too high.

I slip Miles's hoodie back on to chase away the cold, and I hate that his overwhelming musky scent clings to every fiber.

His words play in a loop in my head. *What the hell happened to you? Don't tell me you're one of those girls now.*

"What the hell was he doing here?" Liv asks.

"I have no idea," Natalie says, voice small.

He never gave me a straight answer, but he was here for a reason. He wouldn't have shown up uninvited to a party where everyone suspects him of murder without one.

"Is he staying in town?" Liv says.

When I glance up, I realize she's asking me. "I don't know."

God, I hope he isn't. If tonight was any indication of what he's like to interact with on a day-to-day basis, I plan on staying the hell away from him.

Not to mention, if I talk to him again, who knows what secrets might spill out of my mouth.

"What did he say to you?" Natalie's biting her lip.

I shrug, cheeks burning. It's too embarrassing to admit to all of the insults he hurtled at me. "Nothing, really. He was just apologizing for spilling beer on me."

"You need to stay away from him," Liv snaps.

I know what she's getting at. "The police said she ran away," I remind her.

She rolls her eyes. "You know the police don't care. They wouldn't even search for her."

Natalie presses her lips together and folds her arms tight across her chest. She looks like she's about to cry. Months later and the wound from Sophie's sudden absence is still fresh. In nearly every one of Natalie's posts about her missing friend, she referred to Sophie as a sister. Liv was the best friend who cried on camera while being interviewed. She is not an easy topic of conversation.

Sophie went missing after a huge party at Jordan's house while his parents were out of town. The next morning, her mom reported her missing. Except she made the mistake of reporting Sophie missing three years earlier, when Sophie went to her dad's house without telling her mom where she'd be. Just days before she vanished, she turned eighteen—a legal adult free to leave without a word.

People have spread a lot of rumors about Sophie since she disappeared. Some say she ran away, others say she killed herself, others claim she was abducted. Some suggest she got into drugs and overdosed. Others say someone had a vendetta and did something about it.

When pretty girls go missing from sleepy small towns, where people are supposed to be safe, everyone wants answers.

It was Jordan, with the influence of his mayor mother and business mogul father, who put a three-day search together in Beaumont with local volunteers. Then after the TikTok about his missing girlfriend went viral, there was a circus of media and press.

Where Is This Missing Teen?

TikTok Boyfriend Goes Viral After Girlfriend's Disappearance.

Gen Z Is Going Crazy for This Heartbroken Boyfriend.

The police finally searched Sophie's home, her room, her devices. Aside from the phone she left behind, there wasn't any evidence of suspicious activity. With her history of running away, they stopped digging.

Police Rule Missing Teen a Runaway. No Evidence of Foul Play.

Sometimes, Even Prom Queens Want to Disappear.

"Why would Miles do something to his own sister?" I ask. Because even though I know about his violent streak, no one's ever been able to give a good reason for why he'd hurt Sophie.

Liv folds her arms and lowers her voice. "You don't know him like I do."

From somewhere downstairs, someone lets out a loud curse. "Cops!"

"Shit," Liv hisses.

Natalie grabs my hand. "We gotta go!"

We manage to stick together through the house, but in the

rush of bodies outside, Natalie's hand slips from mine and I lose them in the crowd.

A police cruiser sits in the driveway, blocking a few cars in, red and blue lights flickering across the dark grass.

My house is a couple of miles from Natalie's. Stumbling home drunk will suck, but it's better than being escorted by the police.

I sneak behind the cars and make a break for the road. A black sedan and a lifted Dodge pickup whiz by, and when I've made it a few stumbling steps down Maple, a car with a loud, rumbling engine slows beside me.

"Need a ride?"

Through the rolled-down window, I spot Miles behind the wheel of an old Mustang, giving me his infuriating smirk.

"So you can kidnap and kill me? No thanks."

He shakes his head, and I expect him to speed off, but instead, he jerks his car to a stop beside me. "Get in."

"Forget it. You want nothing to do with me. You made that very clear."

"Just get in before the cops pick you up or someone turns you into roadkill."

I hesitate. He makes a good point. My classmates are whipping by, most of them have been drinking, and I don't really want to get arrested or killed tonight.

"Have you been drinking?" I give a poorly timed hiccup.

"Nope. Not much of a drinker."

You don't know him like I do.

I hop in before I can change my mind.

CHAPTER THREE

I'M AN IDIOT. I'm literally in a car with an accused murderer. With a guy who wrote a freaking hit list. Why did I drink that fourth vodka cranberry? I'll never admit it to her, but I should've listened to Liv when she warned me not to take that last shot.

I scan the interior of Miles's Mustang. No guns, hammers, or axes in sight. No blindfolds or rope or duct tape. The floors and seats are surprisingly clean, actually. Nothing more than a few straw wrappers and loose change at my feet.

My hands curl into fists at how good he smells. Old Spice and mint. Gum maybe? No beer breath. No BO. Why do the biggest jerks smell the best?

Whatever. He's still got nothing on Jordan. No guy ever will. He has the face of an Abercrombie model and the body of Thor. Miles is more like . . . Loki.

I slip the hoodie off and hand it to him. I should thank him for the ride, thank him for the hoodie, but he's the reason I needed it in the first place and I don't actually want to talk to him. It's only a couple of miles to my house, so maybe we can sit in silence this entire car ride and then we can go our separate ways for good.

Miles takes the hoodie from me, our fingers brushing. The touch lurches through me like an electric shock, and I jerk my hand back.

Just like the first time we accidentally brushed hands in sixth grade, when he held out the next book in the *Heartland* series. I was going through my horse girl phase and racing through the books to figure out when Amy and Ty finally get together, but the next book wasn't on the shelf and the library system said it hadn't been checked out. I was embarrassingly near tears when Miles figured out what book I was looking for, and without a word, found it where someone had carelessly shoved it between random books in the U–Z section and handed it over. Our fingers brushed in the exchange, and it was like my fingers had never been touched before. Like they'd been dead and rotten on my hand until his touch brought them to life.

He tosses the hoodie carelessly behind him now. "Where we headed?"

"Straight until you hit the intersection, then a left onto Elm. It's only a few miles." Good. That's done. Now we don't have to talk anymore.

He isn't much of a getaway driver. Classmates fleeing Natalie's house pass us illegally, flying over the double yellow lines. A beat-up Toyota beeps as it passes us. You'd think a guy with a loud-ass Mustang would at least do the speed limit.

I fumble with my phone and predictive text helps me type out a drunken warning to Jordan.

> Don't come back to Natalies. Cops.
> Showed up

Natalie DMs me.

Oh my god are you ok?? Did you get away from the cops???

Yeah I'm fine. Where are you ?

With Liv. I'm staying at her grandparents' tonight!

Lol they don't care?

Nope they're both clueless and think I'm just her straight BFF!

When I glance up from my phone, Miles is watching me. I freeze under his gaze. He has the kind of eyes that are always ablaze with a ferocity that could melt you where you stand.

I'd say he got that look in his eyes because his sister disappeared. But he's always had those eyes.

I rub at my temples. "Your car's giving me a headache."

"No muffler."

"Why do guys think it's cool to have the loudest car on the road?"

"Less about being cool, more about being broke. Old one rotted off and can't afford a new one."

"Oh." I should've known Miles is the type of guy who doesn't give a shit what anyone else thinks is cool.

"You never told me what the hell happened to you."

My spine goes rigid. Here we go. I knew the five seconds of blissful silence were too good to last. "You never told me why you were at a party you obviously weren't invited to."

"I asked first."

I roll my eyes. Maybe he actually hasn't changed that much since sixth grade. "Nothing happened to me. I grew up. I changed. Everyone does."

He fixes his glare on the road ahead, fist squeezing the top of the steering wheel. "Not everyone."

"You have."

"No, I haven't." He sounds so sure of himself and I don't know how that's possible when he's completely wrong.

"Yes, you have. You're totally different. You're this angry asshole who slut-shames girls for daring to look hot at a party." I haven't spoken my mind this freely since . . . I don't remember when. But I guess that's because I don't care if Miles likes me. No one likes him, so why should I care about his opinion?

"First of all, I've always been the angry asshole. That hasn't changed."

"That's not true. You were always nice to me."

Miles snorts. "Not anyone else."

Now that I think about it, I can't recall a single other person he was ever nice to in middle school. Maybe that's why I thought he loved me and why I fell in love with him. It was us against the world.

"Second of all," he continues. "When the hell did I slut-shame you?"

"Um. When you took one look at me, at my outfit, and asked what the hell happened to me."

He narrows his eyes. "That has nothing to do with you looking hot at a party. You're just a completely different person. You're trying to be someone else. You're not even trying to be yourself anymore."

He's right, but becoming a completely different person is the best decision I ever made. He makes it sound like the worst thing I've done. "You have no idea who I am."

"I know who you used to be. A sweet, smart girl who couldn't stop reading and had an amazing mind."

An amazing mind. I didn't think anyone saw me that way back then. I didn't think anyone saw me at all. I was invisible.

"You needed to stand up for yourself more," he concedes, "but you were never anyone's clone."

I hold up my ring, where my promise ring tells me otherwise. "I'm not anyone's clone. I'm special."

I'm the only girl who gets to be with Jordan Goldman. That makes me more special than any girl in this town. More special than his sister.

His mouth twists into a sneer. "A ring makes you special?"

I drop my hand back into my lap and cover it for a second. But I refuse to let Miles Mariano make me feel ashamed about anything. "A promise ring from my boyfriend does, yeah."

"Having a boyfriend and a promise ring doesn't make you special."

"Yeah? What does then?"

"*You*. You make yourself special. By being you, when no one else can be."

I fold my arms. I want to fling open the door and leap out. I don't care if it hurts. It can't hurt worse than sitting in this car with Miles. "Yeah, well, no one liked her."

I don't have to remind him, though. He remembers.

"You know you don't have to change who you are to make people like you, right? You can just be you, and if that's not good enough for them, they can fuck off."

Of course he would say that. "Maybe that works for someone like you who obviously doesn't care what people think."

"Why should I?"

"I don't know, so maybe people don't think you killed your own sister?" If anyone should care what other people think, it's Miles.

His jaw feathers and I feel this inexplicable urge to reach out and touch it. Draw my finger across his jawline and down the smooth slope of his neck. I force myself to look away from him.

"That's what you think?" he asks.

"No," I admit.

"So why'd you say that at the party?"

"Because you were pissing me off. You still are."

He shakes his head. "I don't care if people think I'm Satan. I care about finding Soph. That's all I care about."

"Is that why you were at Natalie's party?"

He smacks his turn signal. "Yeah. Drunk people like to tell their secrets. And someone's keeping one about my sister."

My heart stops. He can't know. That's impossible. If he knew, he wouldn't be sitting in this car with me, having this conversation.

No, he's just upset that he still doesn't have answers, months later. He wants to blame someone else for Sophie's disappearance instead of the person actually responsible—Sophie herself.

I swallow and let out a slow breath to calm myself. "But why now? It's been months. You weren't even at any of the search parties."

"I wanted to be there," he snaps. "My parents didn't want me involved in the searches because they didn't want me to . . ." His eyes drift from mine back to the road, throat bobbing. ". . . find anything."

They didn't want him to find his sister's dead body. "Oh."

Of course they didn't. Who would be able to erase something like that from their memory? Yet everyone uses his absence from the searches against him. Points at his absence as evidence of his guilt.

"Then Dad just . . . lost it. So I couldn't come back." The fury is gone from Miles's voice now. All that's left is a hollow void.

"What do you mean?"

He shifts uncomfortably and his eyes flick to me, like he's still not sure he can trust me. Like he doesn't want anything to do with me, and I'm the last person he wants to open up to. "Not really any of your business, is it?"

"Fine. Forget I asked. Let's just sit here in awkward silence until you drop me off."

At first, I think he's actually going to take me up on it. The silent seconds tick by until he sighs. "He was drinking every night. Then every day. At first, I was keeping him going. To work, the grocery store, whatever. Then I was keeping him alive. That's why I haven't been back."

I can't even imagine that kind of burden. Mom and I have always been close, closer than most mothers and daughters, but she's always been my mother. She takes care of me, not the other way around.

"Is he doing better now? Is that why you could come back?"

Miles gives a mirthless chuckle. "A lot harder to drink your-self to death when you're locked up, so yeah. I guess you could say he's doing better."

At first when he said he's not much of a drinker, I didn't believe him. But now I know it's the truth. He doesn't want to follow in his father's footsteps. "Why is he locked up?"

"DUI." Miles grips the steering wheel with both hands now, squeezing the life out of it. "He could've killed a kid. He could've done to somebody else what somebody did to us."

Sophie's disappearance didn't just mean Miles lost his sister—he lost his dad too. To alcohol first, then to jail. For the first time since we laid eyes on each other again, I feel bad for him.

My phone pings with a text. A smile still pulls at my lips every time I get a notification from Jordan.

> Damn. See you tomorrow then. Text me when you make it home.

I should've gone with him to get beer. I could be with him right now instead of trapped in a car with Miles Mariano.

We finally get to the intersection and turn left onto Elm Street.

"So are you living with your mom?" I ask.

"My gran. Gotta get my GED and work while I'm here. Part of the deal."

Right. He has to get his GED since he was kicked out before he could get a diploma. "Are you going to college in the fall?"

"Nah. Not for me."

"Is that because they won't admit anyone who got expelled from high school for writing a hit list?"

He rolls his eyes, totally fed up with me now. "I didn't write a hit list."

"That's not what I heard."

"It was a suspect list. All the people who had a motive to want Soph gone. Somebody saw the list and got the wrong idea."

I roll my window down further, but the warm summer breeze against my skin does nothing to stop the sweat beading on my neck. "You don't think she ran away?"

"I know she didn't. And even if she did, she would've been back by now." He shakes his head. "She had her enemies. Someone was out to get her."

How could Sophie Mariano have enemies? She was the most popular girl in Beaumont. The girl everyone liked. No one ever said a bad word about her.

I'm the only one who ever hated her.

"Whoever they are," he says, "I'm going to find them."

I need Miles to fail. I need Sophie to stay gone because if she comes back, Jordan might choose her, and then I'll lose everything that matters to me.

I need to know who made it onto that list.

We're coming up on my house. Thank god. I can't breathe in this car. "It's right up here on the left. You can just stop down the street."

Mom and I live in one side of a duplex. Trees and shrubbery separate us from our closest and nosiest neighbor, Tess, so even she doesn't know when I sneak out. I take advantage of the privacy and peace by crawling out my window to read on the roof. It's not big—nothing compared to Natalie's house or Jordan's—but I love it.

Instead of dropping me off on the sidewalk, Miles pulls into the driveway. The engine groans as he comes to a stop.

I grit my teeth. "I told you to stop down the street."

To my surprise, he turns the headlights and engine off. Oh god. Does he think because he gave me a ride home, I owe him something? Now he deserves a blowjob?

I type out a text to Jordan.

> I'm home I misss you sooo much see you tomorrow

I unbuckle my seatbelt and fumble with the door handle. "Thanks for the ride."

Miles opens his door, and in the harsh glare of the overhead light, I can finally see the deep brown of his irises. The color of soil darkened by a summer rain.

"Um. What are you doing?" I ask.

He points to the other side of the duplex. "My gran lives over there."

It takes me a second, but eventually, all the pieces click into place. Miles said he moved in with his—"Right. Mabel is your grandma."

"Yup."

Mabel is our landlord and lives in the other side of our duplex. She's also my boss and owner of the sole diner in town.

I have two doors in my room—one that leads into our hallway, and another that leads to the attic and Mabel's side of the duplex. If I wanted to, I could walk through my room and into the guest bedroom on her side.

The one Miles will be staying in.

Miles Mariano is living in my house. We're sharing a wall. A door. Every night as I sleep, there will only be a few feet between us.

Between me and the first boy I ever loved.

Between me and the boy accused of murder.

He flashes me a grin that makes my heart hammer and backs toward the house with his hands in his pockets. "Night, neighbor."

CHAPTER FOUR

MOM IS asleep on the couch when I sneak in the front door, thank god. Even with Natalie's shirt on, she might be able to smell the alcohol on me. She works so hard at Bloody Mary's Inn, she rarely makes it past nine o'clock most nights before she's passed out. Everyone who stops in Beaumont on their way to bigger, better places wants to stay at Bloody Mary's, known for both the drink and its spooky decor.

Mom got pregnant with me in her senior year of college, and when my father found out, he broke up with her and signed his rights away. Somehow, she managed to balance prenatal appointments, classes, studying, and working part-time. We wound up in Beaumont when her parents in Hartford wouldn't let their unmarried daughter with a newborn move back home, and we ended up living in a room at the inn for a few months before she found the duplex for rent. It's just been her and me ever since.

Though not for Tess's lack of trying. She's been begging to set Mom up since my bike had training wheels.

I head for the stairs up to my room, exhaustion hitting me

like a wave. But as soon as the first step creaks, Mom's voice calls out, "Hon? Is that you?"

Damn. So close. Hopefully she won't sniff the vodka I'm sweating through my pores. "Yeah, Mom, just me. No burglars."

She bounds out of the living room. She's like that—one minute she's passed out cold, the next she's the Energizer Bunny. "And you weren't going to celebrate with me? On *graduation night*?"

"You were asleep!"

She gives her trademark, exaggerated jaw drop and slaps a hand to her chest. "Me? I would never fall asleep while my daughter is at a party, especially when there's still ice cream in the house."

I gasp. "There's ice cream?"

I really should drink some water first before bed anyway, so I don't wake up with a hangover.

"Did you drink?"

"No," I say quickly. I never used to lie to Mom, but ever since I became Maddie, there's been more and more lies and secrets between us.

Mom folds her arms, eyes narrowing. "Drugs? Satanic rituals?"

I laugh. "Oh my god, Mom, no."

"Then you can have ice cream."

I nearly let out a sigh of relief. I love my mom, but she doesn't need to know everything.

She gives my shoulder a playful shove. "So? How does it feel to be a high school graduate? Is it everything you dreamed it would be?"

Before Sophie disappeared, today would've felt like an enormous relief. Instead, I mostly just feel nostalgic for all the years I didn't get to spend with Jordan and Natalie and Liv and the cheer girls. For all the memories I didn't get to make until senior year. I wish I had more time to keep being Maddie, football star Jordan Goldman's girlfriend.

"Yep. Everything I dreamed."

Mom's eyes fall to my hand and she snatches it with a gasp, eyes wide. "Another gift from Jordan?"

I beam. "Yeah, he gave it to me tonight."

The second we were official, Jordan showered me in gifts. We ran out of vases for all the bouquets of white roses, and Mom bought a Fitbit after she kept eating all the dark chocolate he gave me. Still, nothing compares to this ring.

She twists and turns my hand and sighs wistfully. "It's so beautiful. Jordan did a great job. I wish I had a boyfriend buying *me* pretty jewelry."

"Like you didn't have twenty guys showering you in gifts when you were my age." Liv called Mom a *MILF* once, and I made her swear to never say that again.

Mom waves me off.

"George asked you out last week," I remind her with a peevish smile.

She heads for the kitchen and pulls out two bowls from the cupboard. "You should be grateful I didn't say yes. He's closer to your age than mine."

"Why should I be grateful? The town's not going to gossip about me if you date him."

"Ha! You underestimate them." Mom drops two spoons in our bowls with a loud clatter and spins around, smile wide. "I can't keep it in any longer. I have a secret!"

"Tell me!"

"Guess who's the new executive manager of the inn!"

I gasp, and we jump and squeal. Mom has been working toward this since her first day at the inn. She started as a housekeeper, and now she'll be running the place.

"Bad news, though." She abruptly stops jumping and pouts.

"That means more shifts and more hours on-call. But I'm still going to make time for my favorite kid before she abandons me to party in college."

I try not to flinch at the mention of college. Now that I'm not friends with Ash, the only thing Mom and I argue about is my future. "I'm your only kid," I remind her. "And I'm actually going to college to learn."

She scoffs. "You wouldn't abandon your only mother to *learn*."

Our original plan was community college so I could graduate with no—or at least manageable—debt, then the summer publishing course at Columbia, and finally my dream career in book publishing in New York, where Mom could visit me in the city and attend Broadway plays.

But after applications went out and acceptances came in, I got into the same school as Jordan, the University of Southern California. They recruited him, so there was no way he could turn it down, and there was no way I could turn him down when he suggested we go together.

USC is too expensive, kid. What about community college like we talked about?

But you've always wanted to work with books. I don't understand why you're changing your mind now.

Book publishing was my escape—my ticket out of Beaumont. Back when I was Madalyn. But now I'm Maddie, and she doesn't need a ticket out. Not when she has a golden ticket.

Jordan is my future now, and his future lies in Beaumont. He'll help his father run his businesses until he takes over. Maybe he'll even follow in his mother's footsteps and become mayor. Jordan is the kind of guy who can do it all, and I'm the kind of girl who will stand by his side while he does. That's the only place I want to be.

Mom opens up the freezer. "Now. Ice cream to celebrate!"

"With chocolate syrup?"

"Hello? How many years have you lived with me? Do you really need to ask?"

In my room, I scramble to get in my pajamas as quickly as possible because all I want is to curl up on my pillow and sleep for twelve hours. I haven't been this exhausted since the days of ground searches for a girl I knew we'd never find.

I don't know if I'll actually be able to sleep, though. How can I when Miles is on the other side of my wall?

What's he doing right now? Listening to music? Playing video games? Jerking off? I can't hear anything, but I keep glancing at one of the two flimsy doors that separate us. I hope he's sleeping.

Does he sleep in boxers or naked? I shake the image out of my mind.

Just as I'm tugging my silk shorts up, there's a creak behind the door to the attic. Then the doorknob twists.

My heart leaps into my throat, but before I can scream at the ghost entering my room, Miles steps inside.

He's in my room. *Miles Mariano* is in my room.

I've spent hours daydreaming about him in here with me. Fantasizing about the two of us lying in my bed, him above me. Brushing my hair behind my ear. Kissing me, all over. Making me feel things no one else ever has.

Now I have a boyfriend, our entire town hates him, and he's the last person I want in my room.

His eyes drop to my bare legs, and all it takes is that one look to set my whole body on fire.

I throw my skirt as hard as I can at his head, but he simply catches it.

He unravels it with a look of approval. "Is this my payment for the ride home?"

"Gross. No, it was supposed to be a warning to get the hell out of my room."

He shrugs and tosses my skirt across his shoulder like a dishrag. "Didn't know this was your room."

But he doesn't leave. Instead, he takes in the two bookshelves shoved against the walls, overflowing with books. It's my greatest secret. The one part of being Madalyn I couldn't give up.

At least, it's been my secret. Until now.

"You really like barging into places you're not invited," I tell him.

He ignores me. "Lots of books. Glad to see you're still reading. At least you're not a complete disappointment."

"That makes one of us," I snap.

He doesn't take the bait.

I want to be the girl Jordan wants, and I know that girl doesn't hole up in her room and read for days on end, but when I'm not spending my nights with him, all I want is to curl up with a good book.

Still, I don't want him to remember I was the girl who spent recess reading on the swings because she had no friends. The girl who tried not to stare when other girls giggled together and braided each other's hair. The girl who was only ever noticed by one person, one boy. Miles. Who saw in her what she saw in him—a lonely heart that didn't know how to ask for love.

It's all Miles's fault, really. He's the reason I started reading at recess in the first place. Though we never spoke the challenge out loud, we were competing with each other in sixth grade for the most points in our reading program. Which meant reading as many books as possible, as fast as possible. All I knew was that I needed to win. I needed all the hours I was pouring into reading, all the hours I was spending alone and lonely, to mean something.

That's when a group of girls blocked the sun shining on my copy of the first *Percy Jackson* book, one girl standing closest to my swing with a sneer on her face. I instantly recognized the gently upturned nose, the soft chin, the round, pine-green eyes, and the cocoa brown hair that fell in perfect waves even back then.

Sophie Mariano. Miles's older sister by eleven months, so we all ended up in the same grade. Unfortunately for me. "Why do you read at recess? That's so weird," she said.

The girls around her laughed and the humiliation brought tears to my eyes. Normally, I was invisible. They ignored me because I pretended not to hear when they called me weird. I was jealous of Miles because even though he was bullied worse, he always had angry words to spit back. I was only ever frozen in fear.

But this time, Sophie saw me. And she wanted to make sure everyone else did too.

I quickly pretended to be reading again, hoping they'd go away. The words were blurry on the page.

"She doesn't have any friends, so she has to read books," another girl sneered.

"That's so sad." Sophie cackled, and the other girls joined in.

A tear slipped out. Then another. I tried to wipe at my face quickly, discreetly, so they wouldn't know they were getting to me.

"Look!" Sophie crowed, and I knew she was pointing at me. "Her face is turning red—"

Then a scuffle of feet in the wood chips, and Sophie was on the ground clutching her eye. Miles standing over her.

Her friends were horrified, screeching and sobbing, saying he punched her.

"What's your problem?" Sophie snarled at him, but her words were watery with the pain.

"You. Leave her alone."

After that, I didn't see Miles again. I didn't even have a chance to thank him.

A few days later, summer break started, and the next year, the girls only talked shit about me behind my back, not to my face. I wasn't sure which was worse.

"Not organized alphabetically," Miles says now, examining my bookshelf. "Not by genre or color or size. You organizing them by favorites or just throwing them on the shelf at random?"

I organize my bookshelf by spice level. Not that Miles needs to know that. "Um. Yeah, by favorites," I say. "Don't tell anyone, by the way."

"Why don't you want anyone to know you read?" Miles says it like I just asked him not to tell anyone I like cheese.

Before I can think better of it, I blurt, "Because assholes like your sister used to make fun of me for it."

Shit. You can't call a missing girl an asshole, even if she was one.

But Miles doesn't stomp out of the room or yell at me. Instead, he laughs. An actual, genuine laugh. The kind of laugh that makes something swell in my chest. That makes me want to say whatever I have to so he'll keep laughing and I can hang on to this feeling forever.

"Damn," he says. "I've missed people being honest about her instead of acting like she was a damn angel all the time. Like they don't even think of her as a real person anymore."

"That's shitty," I tell him because that's all I can think to say.

"It was shitty of her to make you feel bad about this." Yeah, it was. And then she made me feel bad about my whole life, just by existing. "She was a really angry kid—we both were—

and she took it out on the people around her. Including you. But she's not like that anymore."

I almost snort. Freshman year, Sophie dropped her mean-girl attitude to put on a nice-girl act. I didn't buy her fake smiles and compliments for a second. I knew she'd stab anyone in the back when she had the chance. But this time, she'd do it with a smile.

A silence falls between us. His eyes roam over the books the way mine do at the bookstore or the library. With reverence. With the hope that you're about to find the next book of your heart.

His finger skims a spine, and I've never been jealous of a book before. "*A Lover's Choice?*"

Here we go. I should've known a nice moment with Miles Mariano wouldn't last. "Don't talk shit about romance because I don't want to hear it. I wouldn't make fun of what you read, even if it's boring and doesn't have any smut."

"Wasn't going to," he says simply. "I read books about people getting their heads chopped off. Who am I to judge?"

"Exactly." Although a slight chill races down my spine. If Miles is so worried that something bad happened to his sister, why would he be reading books like that?

"What I read isn't boring, but it definitely could use more smut." He plucks a thick paperback off the shelf. Oh no, that one includes a threesome and bondage in a secluded cabin. "You should let me borrow one."

I snatch the book from him and slide it back into place. "No, I don't trust anyone with my books. They don't leave this room."

"Then they won't." He grabs another. A traditionally published rom-com with an illustrated couple on the cover and beginner-level spice. At least it's a better introduction than the reverse harem book. He sets it down on top of my bookshelf. "I'll come back and read them right in here."

I scoff. He's got to be joking. "You're not coming back in my room."

"I won't come back in your room unless I'm invited," he amends, and I hate the way that look in his eyes heats up every part of my body from my head to my toes.

"You'll never be invited."

He grins. A real one this time. Not his smirk or sly half-smile. This one is confident and shows off all his perfect teeth. Like he knows something I don't. "We'll see about that."

The hangover isn't the worst I've ever had, but my head pounds hard enough that I consider calling in sick before remembering we need the money. Airline tickets, textbooks, moving bins, and a new laptop won't come cheap.

I slump beside the cash register, chin in one hand while our neighbor, Tess, rattles off her order because she's too impatient to wait for me to get to her table. Her voice is so raspy, she may have chronic laryngitis. "You doin' all right, hon?"

"I'm fine." I force a smile because if I don't convince her it's true, she'll tell Mom how rough I looked this morning.

"How's Jordan doin'? Bet he's gettin' real excited about playing for a college team, huh?"

"Yep. Really excited," I say. "Two waffles coming up."

I take the order back to Mabel in the kitchen, where she's cooking everything alone. She sweeps one of the few graying strands of hair behind her ear.

Mabel named the place Mariano's, which always confuses people because they expect Italian food, but it's just a diner serving the standard American diet. Depending on my shift, I either leave smelling like pancakes or fries and can't seem to get rid of the smell no matter how much I scrub.

"I've got an order for Tess," I tell her.

"Waffles with extra butter and syrup. Got it." Mabel's voice grates, like a spatula scraping a metal pan.

I grab two steaming plates of scrambled eggs and fried potatoes from the dispatching counter and take them out to Table 7—a red booth by the door—grab extra napkins for Table 2 with the messy toddler, and pour a cup of coffee for Tess, even though the last thing she needs is caffeine.

Behind the cashier's counter, I check my phone. Another hour before the end of my shift. I might drop before then.

A barrage of DMs from Natalie waits for me.

Did you see that video Ashley posted??

Omg she posted it on tiktok AND reels

It's honestly kind of creepy

Um. You seriously need to watch the second video. And you owe me an explanation??

I told her to take it down but she's ignoring me

And apparently so are you!!

You're not still asleep are you?? Don't you have work today?

MADDIE! ANSWER YOUR PHONE!

When I click on the first TikTok, I keep the volume low so Mabel doesn't catch me on my phone—rule number one—and watch the camera focus on Miles.

He's standing a few feet from Ash's group, hands buried in his pockets. Attention fixed on someone in the crowd. A loner living up to his reputation.

Then the camera follows his gaze, directed toward the deck. Where I'm dancing with Natalie and Liv. When I leave the deck, Miles's eyes follow me. All the way to the cooler.

And just before I can catch him watching me, Ash closes the distance between them and backhands his arm so he turns to face her. "Why don't you go ask her out?"

She knows I'm with Jordan. Was she trying to set Miles up for rejection? Is she that cruel?

One of the guys jokes that Miles is going to die a virgin, and when they all burst into laughter, Ash shoves him in my direction.

Our collision at the party was no accident.

Yet he didn't blame Ash. He apologized to me like it was his fault, no one else's.

Even with the volume down, you can't miss Ash's cackle. Miles takes his hoodie off and hands it to me. When Liv and Natalie show up, the video ends.

Ash captioned it: *love in the air*

My heart pounds. I hate her.

The comments are all a version of: *Sophie's brother is so creepy.*

Why tf is he staring at her like that?

Maddie better watch her back.

Omg tell me she got the HELL away from him!!

They're all reading way too much into Miles's stare. He recognized me, that's all.

When I click on the second TikTok, my stomach drops.

The video was taken from behind Miles's Mustang, his brake lights on as he came to a stop.

And me, stumbling and drunk, getting into his car.

Ash was in the Toyota that passed us. This TikTok she captioned with: *Where are the love birds headed next?*

God, how much of last night did Ash spend trailing me? Watching my every move, just waiting to capture the moment my skirt got caught in my underwear or I tripped over my own feet so she could mock me all over social media?

The comments are flooded with speculation about what exactly Miles and I did together after I climbed into his passenger seat.

Natalie left two comments.

Ashley can you take this down?

We don't need this drama. High school is over.

Ash hates being called Ashley. But Natalie wouldn't know that.

One person hasn't liked or commented on either video.

Jordan.

Maybe he still hasn't seen them.

He won't take the comments or Ash's captions seriously. He knows I would never, ever cheat on him. I love him too much, and I'm well aware I've got the best guy there is. But these are still videos of Miles Mariano, his ex-girlfriend's loner brother who may or may not have something to do with his own sister's disappearance, surveying his drunk girlfriend, giving her his hoodie, and driving her home.

"Order up!"

Mabel's shout makes me jump. I ditch my phone under the counter before she sees and grab the plates for Table 1. Just as I'm setting the massive helpings of eggs, bacon, and toast down in front of George and his white-haired father, George Senior, who co-own the only auto body shop in town, I spot a familiar shock of blue hair through the window.

A woman is waiting at the counter, but she's more focused on getting her four-year-old to listen to her than paying her check, so I make a break for it.

Outside, I shield my eyes against the sunlight and call out to Ash, who halts in the middle of her typical Black-Friday-holiday-shopping stride. Her eyes are rimmed with dark liner, lashes coated with thick mascara, and her nails painted blue to match her hair. Even in seventy-degree weather, she's in jeans and a navy hoodie with the sleeves rolled past her elbows.

"Hey, Mads. What's up?"

I cringe at the nickname Ash gave me when she moved to Beaumont in the middle of seventh grade. Back then, Ash was new enough that she didn't know no one liked me. We both needed a friend, and no one else was lining up for the position. I asked if she wanted to be my partner for a science project, she said yes, and that was that. She dragged me to parties I didn't want to go to and ditched me while she went to smoke weed. She pushed me to join her once, and when I coughed so hard I thought I might crack a rib, she laughed at me. If I told her I had to work or grab dinner with Mom when she asked to hang out, she'd scoff and call me a bad friend. She made fun of my A cups in seventh grade and told me I looked like a slut when I grew C cups the next year and dared to show a hint of cleavage.

I don't know if we ever really liked each other, but we needed each other because we didn't have anyone else.

Now, Ash is the last person I want to ask for a favor. Which is exactly why she took those videos.

"Can you take those TikToks down?"

She tilts her head in mock confusion. "Which ones? The one where you put on a murderer's clothes, or the one where you got in his car?"

I don't bother asking why she pushed Miles or why she filmed any of it. Ash has always hated the girl who has what she wants and does whatever it takes to knock her down from her pedestal.

She can't stand that Jordan chose me. But she's not his type. He doesn't like his girls sociopathic.

"Both of them."

Ash takes a step forward and lowers her head and voice conspiratorially. "Oh shit. Did you actually cheat on Jordan?"

The suggestion is so ridiculous, I laugh. After I started dating Jordan, she called me one of those pathetic girls who revolves her whole life around her boyfriend. So she should know I'd never do anything to jeopardize my relationship with him.

"Of course not," I tell her. "But those videos just . . . They might make Jordan worry for no reason. Just—please take them down."

Ash folds her arms across her chest. "Why should I take them down if nothing happened?"

"Hey, prom queen!" Natalie's soprano voice sails to us from across the street.

She's glamorous as usual—sleek black hair sheared into a short bob, diamond studs in her ears, dangling necklace, and jangling silver bracelets that make her look like she belongs in a fashion magazine, not small-town America.

She's pulling a reluctant Liv behind her, dressed in her typical dark yoga pants and cropped sweater that shows the slightest sliver of her midriff.

When Natalie notices Ash, she stops short. "Oh."

Loudly, Ash says, "If you're so scared about your boyfriend seeing a couple of innocent videos, maybe you *do* have something to hide."

Natalie's glance flicks over to me. She doesn't say anything, but for a second, I swear I glimpse a flash of doubt.

"I don't. Whatever. Keep the videos up, I don't care."

All Ash ever wants is a reaction. I won't give her one.

She backs away, waving her vape in the air. "See ya around, *Maddie*."

Liv grabs my arm and pulls me into the diner's shadow, demanding, "What the hell were you thinking getting into Miles's car?" at the same time Natalie says, "Um. You have *a lot* to tell me!"

"I wasn't thinking," I whisper, shaking off Liv's grip. "I was drunk, panicking, and he offered me a ride home." I turn to Natalie. "*Nothing* happened. Obviously."

"But did you see that other video?" Natalie insists. "The one of him staring at you? Didn't that freak you out? It creeped me out, and I wasn't even the one being watched."

"It's not a crime to stare at somebody. He recognized me from middle school, that's it."

"Yeah, okay." Natalie smiles and rolls her eyes. "He thought you were cute and couldn't stop staring." She nudges me, playful, until she cringes. "Jordan's going to *flip*."

My heart thuds harder. "What? Why?"

"His drunk girlfriend got in a car with another guy." She laughs. "He's not exactly going to be happy about that."

"Not just another guy," Liv adds. "His missing girlfriend's asshole brother."

"Ex-girlfriend," I correct.

"What did you two even talk about?" Natalie asks.

I shrug. "Nothing really. School, college."

"That's it? You didn't talk about Sophie at all?"

Of course we did. No one in this town can go a single day without talking about her. "I really need to get back inside."

"Okay, but you better talk to Jordan as soon as your shift's over," Natalie says.

"I don't think he's even watched the videos. Besides, he would know nothing happened," I insist. "Me and Jordan are end-game."

I don't miss Liv's eye-roll.

"*I* know you are, and *you* know you are," Natalie says. "And I'm sure Jordan does too, but . . . ever since Sophie, he's bound to worry about losing you too."

I haven't even thought about that. I don't want to imagine the horror that Jordan would feel, watching his tipsy girlfriend getting into an accused murderer's car after a party.

If he watches those videos, I'll be responsible for eliciting that fear in him.

"I need coffee," Natalie announces and leads the way into Mariano's.

Mabel is behind the register.

She's pissed.

"And what do you think you're doing?" she snaps.

"Sorry!" I hurry behind the counter to take over. Three people are waiting in line to pay. "There was an emergency."

"I don't see any blood." She searches the diner and says to herself, "And where the hell is *he*?"

Natalie and Liv find an open booth by the wall of windows and hold hands across the table. I manage to get through the three people waiting in line to pay and then a fourth person steps up to the counter, leaning his elbows so far across it, his hands rest beside my waist.

Miles.

Does he feel the heat of Liv's glare on his back?

In the stark light of day, I notice a few freckles—one at the corner of his eye, one along his hairline, another on his jaw.

I can't help but stare. He's really here, back in Beaumont. I didn't dream everything that happened last night. I almost want to reach out and touch him, make sure he's real.

He's wearing a tattered denim jacket like he just stepped out of an 80s movie.

"Nice jacket."

"Soph got it for me a couple years ago. Supposed to be a gag gift. Joke's on her. I look hot as hell."

I hate that he's right.

"So. You my new boss?" Why does his voice have to sound like that? Low and scraping, like teeth against my skin. Lighting every inch of me on fire.

"What are you—"

"Hey!" Mabel barks behind us. "You were supposed to be here ten minutes ago!"

"Tell that to my alarm."

She holds up a finger. "Rule number one: no one's a smart ass in my diner."

"I thought rule number one was no phones while you're on shift?" I ask.

Miles laughs, melodic and low, before I realize my innocent question sounded like mouthing off.

"What did I just say?" Mabel snaps.

When Miles saunters around the counter, she shoves a black apron at him. "She'll train you on register."

That's the last thing I want to do. It's bad enough that I have to share a house with him. Now he's invading my job too? "My shift's over in an hour," I remind Mabel.

"If it takes him more than an hour to learn how to work a register, I don't want him here." She disappears back into the kitchen.

"That's family love right there." Miles slips off his jacket to replace it with the apron.

"You need to find a different job," I hiss.

His eyebrows furrow. "Why?"

"Because I don't want to be stuck with you for six to eight hours in a row, four days a week."

"Aww, really? I just *love* being around you. Almost as fun as getting a root canal."

I grit my teeth. If we're both working here, one of us won't survive.

Beneath the sleeve of his t-shirt, I glimpse a small tattoo peeking out. *Smiles*. Weird tattoo for a guy who definitely prefers frowns.

"Is that a reminder to smile or something?" I ask, pointing at it.

Miles lifts his sleeve as if he forgot about the ink permanently etched into his skin. "Nah. When Mom would call for me or Soph, she'd always start with the other person's name first. *S—Miles! Mi—Sophie!* So we told her to just start calling us Smiles and we'd both show up." He shrugs and drops his sleeve. "Pretty stupid, but Soph told me to get it for my eighteenth birthday, and since she wasn't around to talk me out of it, I got it."

Sophie is so selfish for doing what she did, knowing her brother would have to celebrate his birthday without her. Her disappearance led to a domino effect she never bothered to anticipate—a brother kicked out of school, a father in jail, an entire town grieving.

He nods to the register and steps into my space, arm brushing mine before I jerk away from him. "Guess you better show me how this works."

From her table by the window, Natalie shoots me a sympathetic smile before turning her attention back to the menu.

But Liv keeps staring at Miles.

Like she could kill him.

CHAPTER FIVE

AFTER MY SHIFT ENDS, I run to Jordan's house, my legs and feet already aching from spending hours bustling around the diner. He lives on the other side of town, on Hunter Road, where the McMansions sit acres apart.

His regal colonial is surrounded by a towering stone and wrought iron fence. A castle in our town of bungalows and cottages. The house towers over the nearby trees, the concrete driveway encircles a perfectly manicured flower garden with a fountain at its center, and the sprinkler system keeps the grass a lush green.

His house is the kind of quiet that feels like walking into a museum, where your shoes squeak against the floors and every cough echoes off the walls and towering ceilings.

I hope to sneak past Jordan's mom, but she's striding out of the kitchen, the clack of her heels echoing down the hall.

"Hi, darling." She grabs her Chanel purse and flashes me her blindingly white, mayoral smile. Stark against her fake-tanned, Botoxed face. "I was just on my way out. Jordan is up in his room."

I give her my biggest, brightest smile and hope she likes me more than Sophie. "Thanks, Mrs. Goldman."

Since the night Sophie went missing, Jordan has been banned from throwing parties. But that hasn't stopped the two of us from hanging out in this giant house unchaperoned. When it's just us, I feel like the queen of a castle.

I rush upstairs and in through his open door. Trophies are displayed on shelves and dressers, and awards hang on his walls, some of them dating all the way back to elementary school. Tee-ball trophies, memorabilia for the records he's broken, his winning touchdowns. No matter where Jordan looks, he sees his victories.

His room isn't the chaotic mess I assume most guys live in—the corners of his bed are neatly tucked, the surfaces wiped free of dust with pungent disinfectant, all his dirty clothes tossed in a hamper. The result of their housekeeper's hard work.

He's shirtless and standing in front of his closet, hair wet. Every tanned, muscled inch of him is perfect. Normally he'd flex for me, but today, he glances over his shoulder when the door creaks. Then turns back around.

"Hey." His voice is flat, and my chest squeezes so hard it hurts.

He saw the videos.

I hurry toward him and brush my fingers against his arm. Not sure if touching him will make things better or worse.

When he shakes me off, I have my answer.

"Why did you leave the party with Miles Mariano last night?" Jordan spits Miles's name out like a curse. The hangers screech as he flips through his shirts, but I can barely hear them as my heart thuds in my ears.

"Jordan, nothing happened. I swear. I just needed a ride home."

He's never refused to look at me for this long before. I'm not used to feeling invisible around him. Panic makes my heart pound harder, my skin warm, my blood boil. Jordan's never been angry with me before. Never. I can't handle it.

"Then why did you keep it a secret?" he asks.

Because if I told him Miles Mariano gave me a ride home, he'd panic. Assume that would be the last time he'd ever see me because Miles was going to kill me. And he'd think of Sophie. The last thing I ever want to do is remind Jordan about her. The girl who broke his heart when she left him behind. Who shattered him so thoroughly, we never talk about her. Never even say her name.

During the days we were actively searching for her, Jordan would shut down every time I said her name out loud. Either he'd tear up or his jaw would clench, and I quickly learned that if I wanted Jordan, I needed to bury Sophie.

"I didn't think it was a big deal," I tell him. "Someone offered me a ride home and I took it. We were only in the car for a couple of minutes."

"Not just *someone*." His voice is quaking with anger now. "Miles Mariano. You know people say he's a murderer, right?"

"But they don't know that. I knew him. He wouldn't hurt his own sister." I don't know that for sure, but it's what Jordan needs to hear.

I wish I could tell him what I know. That Sophie is perfectly fine. She ran away because she didn't appreciate how good she had it here. Because she wanted even more attention than she was already getting.

But if I tell him how I know, he'll never speak to me again. Not for keeping this secret for so long.

Jordan finds a polo shirt and yanks it on. The sleeves of his shirt stretch over his shoulders, and I'm sad to see the muscles along his arms and abdomen covered up. He must be getting ready for his summer job at the country club. He doesn't need the money, but the only thing more important to his family than money is connections.

"You know him that well, huh? Did you hook up with him?"

"What? No!"

Jordan shakes his head, jaw clenched so tight it might snap. "I've been cheated on before. I don't need to be with someone who just wants to waste my time."

Who would cheat on a guy like Jordan? Was it Sophie?

I take his hand, hoping it's the right move. Yes, I might be attracted to Miles. I can't deny that. But that doesn't mean I'd act on it. The only person I want is Jordan. He's the perfect boyfriend. He treats me like a queen. The life I want isn't complete without him. "You know I love you. I'd never do that to you. I'd have to be an idiot to cheat on you, Jordan."

He keeps his gaze locked on our joined fingers. Where the amethyst on my promise ring glints.

"You're the only person I want to be with," I tell him. "You know that, don't you?"

The tight muscles in his face slowly relax, and finally, Jordan's bright blue eyes land on me and it's like magic. The relief makes my knees weak.

He pulls me to him and buries his chin in my hair, his stubble scraping my skin. "Yeah," he mumbles. "I know."

I grab his face and kiss him with everything I have, an apology and a truce.

After a few seconds, he pulls back, thumb on my chin. "If something like that happens again, I want to hear it from you. Not find out from a video some random girl posts."

"I can do that."

"Just stay away from Miles Mariano," he says. I want to tell him I plan on it, but I'm not sure how that's possible now that he's living in my duplex and working with me at the diner. "And don't keep secrets from me, okay?"

"I won't."

No new secrets.

Jordan kisses me and threads his hands into my hair,

pulling me against him so hard, our bodies meld into one. Heat thrums from my head to my toes.

His tongue parts my lips, and his groan fills my mouth. *This is the reaction I'm used to getting from Jordan when we're alone.*

He backs me up, up, up until I thud against the wall. The next second, he's grabbing my wrists and pinning my hands above my head. The anticipation of his mouth on my skin sends an electric bolt down my spine. Sex with Jordan has always been amazing, but there's something more intense about the way his eyes devour me this time.

Is this makeup sex? Natalie said there's no better feeling than sex after a fight.

Miles is forgotten. Sophie is forgotten. Those stupid TikToks, Ash, everything else is forgotten. Nothing exists right now but us.

With one hand, he keeps mine pinned to the wall. The other drifts up my thigh and squeezes my ass. He drops his mouth to my neck, sucking so hard I know he'll leave a mark. His mark.

I'm taken. I'm his. Exactly what I've always wanted.

Jordan yanks my shirt up and covers my face with it. Not being able to see where he is, what he's going to do next, always makes me squirm. He loves to watch me squirm.

He tugs each cup of my bra down, then kisses my nipple. Then the other. His tongue swirls around them, and then he sucks one into his mouth and I gasp, arching into him. He sucks them both, back and forth, until I'm whimpering, putty in his arms.

His face is suddenly next to my ear. "You want me." It's not a question.

He pulls my shorts down, slips a finger inside my panties, and growls at the slickness waiting for him. I tremble. His finger slides inside me, slowly at first as I stretch around him. God, I want him so bad.

Slowly, he nearly pulls his finger out of me, then plunges back in, palming me at the same time. I groan, and my knees start to buckle. I don't know how much longer I'll be able to stay upright.

Thank god his mom is out of the house. He doesn't have to muffle my moans.

Just as I'm about to tell Jordan to take me to the bed, he pulls out of me and spins me around, flattening me against the wall. He's hard against my ass, and his hand slips back inside my panties, finger circling my clit and slipping in and out of me. Deliciously torturous.

Around. In. Out. Around. In. Out.

I want to scream, beg.

"Jordan," I groan. "I need you."

"Finally." He picks me up and drops me onto the bed, pulling off my shirt and bra. Then he rips my panties off and tosses them onto the floor.

I sit up on my knees and wrench his shirt off. God, he's gorgeous. Made from marble, carved from stone. I sweep my hands over the tanned skin, the hard muscles. I'll never stop wanting him.

While he takes his pants off, I fumble in his bedside drawer for a condom.

"Put it on," he tells me. He sits back against the headboard, arm draped lazily over his head.

So I do, taking my time to roll the condom down slowly, stroking to make him drop his head and groan.

Jordan pushes me back. The anticipation builds while he settles between my legs and grinds against me, pleasure rippling through every muscle.

Slowly, he slides into me. Even with the warmup from his finger, I still feel the stretch. I clench around him involuntarily and he groans, a wide grin across his face. "*Fuck.*"

He dips down to kiss me, swallowing my moans as he eases in and out of me.

I suck his neck, hard enough to leave a hickey. "Faster," I breathe, and that's all it takes.

Jordan braces himself on his fists and thrusts in and out of me. Hard. Harder. Faster. Faster. I claw at his back, wrap my legs tight around his hips to keep him in place. My breasts bounce up and down with every smack of skin on skin.

"Tell me you love me," he pants.

"I love you." The words come out breathless, desperate.

He's perfect. We're perfect. Everything about my life is perfect. Except for one thing.

One person.

Somehow, even though she disappeared months ago, she's still causing me trouble. Still the cloud looming over my head, the shadow in every corner.

When I leave a hickey on Jordan's neck, I wonder if she's left her mark in that exact spot. When my nails scrape down his back, I wonder if hers were sharper. When he stares at my face while pumping into me, I wonder if he wishes it were her face gazing back.

His eyes roll up to the ceiling while he's pumping so hard, my head hits the board. *Thud, thud, thud.*

My heart is pounding. That familiar ache between my legs building, building—

Suddenly, Jordan slams into me and stills, groaning in my ear. "*Fuck,* baby."

I grin. I love when he calls me baby.

He rolls off me, chest rising and falling, sweat glistening across his forehead. I roll onto my side, brushing my fingers down his cheek, when I notice something there.

A small white mark the shape of a half-moon. A tiny scar.

I press the pad of my thumb against it. "How did you get this?"

"Hmm?" He's still out of breath, half-delirious from pleasure.

"This scar."

His face clouds for a second before his eyes light up. He covers my hand with his, keeping it pressed against his cheek. "No one's ever noticed that before," he murmurs, adoration across every inch of his face.

I grin so hard it hurts. "I guess no one's ever loved you like I do."

"No, they haven't." He brushes a strand of hair behind my ear. "You're special."

Some scars are so small, only the person who loves you most will find them.

After dinner, Mom scrapes the last of the vanilla ice cream into our bowls. "Can you believe we made a gallon of ice cream last two whole days?"

"It's a new record for us." I check my phone again. Still nothing from Jordan.

I texted him when I got home and expected one soon after, when he should've gotten to the country club. Then I sent one right before Mom and I grabbed dinner from Mariano's.

Radio silence. Which is weird for Jordan. I usually don't go more than an hour without hearing from him.

My mind immediately jumps to the worst possibilities. An accident on the way there. On the way home.

Sophie getting in contact with him. Calling him or texting him about how much she's missed him, how she's coming back to Beaumont so they can be together again.

They dated from sophomore year until she disappeared

right before the start of our senior year—they have more history. Sure, he put a promise ring on my finger, but that was when he thought she wasn't coming back.

I open TikTok and search for jordanthegoldman. His pinned TikTok was his first to go viral: the one he made about Sophie a week after she disappeared.

I've watched it enough times to have his words memorized.

She's the love of my life.

If you know anything about where my girlfriend is, please call the police.

Sophie, if you're watching this, please come home. I love you so much.

Then there's the loud sniff, the way he pinches his nose and ducks his head at the end before anyone can catch the tears pooling in his eyes.

The comments range from *I hope you find her!* and *How can I join the search?* to *I wish I had a boyfriend who loved me this much.*

Sophie can't come back to Beaumont. If Jordan chooses her over me, my heart will shatter. My entire life will unravel.

No, everything's fine between me and Jordan. He literally just told me how special I am to him, like, five hours ago. He gave me a promise ring yesterday. And Sophie is gone.

There's a knock on the screen door.

Miles stands on the other side, a glass pan in his hands. His jeans barely hang onto his hips and the denim at his knees is ripped. He's still wearing that stupid denim jacket, the sleeves rolled up to his elbows. Why do bare forearms have to be so sexy? A lump forms in my throat. What is he doing here?

"Hon?" Mom says. "Can you get the door?"

"Oh. Right." When I open the door, Miles doesn't come in, but he holds the pan out to me. I keep my voice low so Mom doesn't hear me. "What the hell are you doing here?"

"Just take this." Our fingers brush when he thrusts the pan into my hands and I ignore the bolt of electricity that thrums through me. To Mom, he says, "Gran wanted me to bring over brownies."

Yeah, right. More like he's trying to poison me with brownies. Mabel has lived next to us for eighteen years and she's never once brought us dessert. If she's cooking or baking, it's happening at the diner, not at home.

Mom appears at my side, swiping a loose lock of hair behind her ear. "That was nice of Mabel."

I can practically feel the chill coming off her. Mom is usually bubbly and friendly, offering water to passing joggers and inviting anyone who stops by in for a Pop-Tart or a coffee. But I guess she draws the line at accused murderers when it comes to neighborly hospitality.

"What's the occasion?" I ask him.

"Bribery, probably."

"What do we need a bribe for?"

He shrugs, bored but his dark gaze somehow still lights me on fire. "Because I'm your new neighbor."

"You're right. We're definitely owed apology brownies for that."

This time, he doesn't snipe back. Instead, a hint of a smirk pulls at his lips. Like he might actually get a tiny bit of enjoyment out of our verbal sparring.

Mom grabs the doorknob. "Tell her we say thank you."

Then she shuts the door in his face.

I set the pan down on the counter, and Mom asks, "Do you know him?"

I definitely can't tell her about Natalie's party or how he drove me home. "He works at the diner with me. And we went to elementary and middle school together."

"Oh" is all she says.

"What?"

She sighs. "Just . . . be careful, kid. He's Sophie Mariano's brother."

As if I could live in this town and not know that. But I didn't think Mom was like everyone else—assuming Miles is guilty of a crime without any proof.

Part of me wants to defend him, except I don't have any proof of his innocence, either.

Mom retrieves a brownie, takes a bite, and groans. "That's *good.*"

I check my phone. A Snapchat notification. I'm about to swipe it away when I notice someone added me.

The account looks brand new. Default avatar, a Snapchat score of three, and nothing posted to their stories. But they found me by Quick Add and their username is madyoungfan.

Mad Young. As in short for Maddie Young? Or they meant *mad, young fan.*

Weird coincidence. It's probably just a bot.

They sent me a message too.

i know what you did

I roll my eyes. Whoever madyoungfan is, I know exactly what this is about—the stupid rumor that I cheated on Jordan with Miles. The person behind this account is probably one of the thousand other girls who would love to date him.

Another message appears.

dont you feel guilty

It's probably Ash. She's still trying to make me feel like crap for those videos, even though I didn't do anything wrong.

I'm tempted to tell her off, but I take the high road and simply hit Block.

Mom and I curl up on the couch with our bowls of brownies topped with ice cream and *The Golden Girls* until there's a knock at the door. "Who is it?" Mom yells.

"It's Tess, hon!"

Mom sighs and heaves herself off the couch.

"Good luck," I murmur. No one goes into a conversation with Tess and expects to get out less than an hour later.

Tess announces she got a new kitten, and I tune them out for *The Golden Girls* until I catch a familiar name.

". . . can't believe Mabel's lettin' that Mariano boy work at her diner! I hardly even wanna go there anymore!"

"Tess, she's home. She could hear you."

Not to mention Miles could too.

"Well, somebody ought to let her know no one wants him here!"

When my phone flashes in the dark, my heart leaps, hoping for Jordan's name across the screen.

Instead, it's another Snapchat add.

madyoung.fan this time.

In my chats awaits a promise.

you wont get rid of me

CHAPTER SIX

WHEN I SHOW up at Natalie's house, she's poolside in her bikini and FaceTiming with Liv.

"Oh good! Say hi to Maddie!"

"Hi, Maddie." Liv makes a halfhearted attempt at enthusiasm. "I've gotta go. My abuela needs me."

She ends the call just as Natalie is blowing a kiss at the screen.

My best friend pats the sunlounger beside her, already adorned with a beach towel. I strip off my green sundress so I'm down to my swimsuit and lather on the sunscreen Natalie keeps by her side.

Jordan still hasn't texted me. He hasn't been on social media at all either. No posts, no comments, no likes. But if something bad happened to him, wouldn't his parents call me?

Maybe he lost his phone somewhere. He got to the country club and it dropped out of his pocket, or it got run over by a golf cart or fell in a pond. There's a perfectly reasonable explanation.

I force a smile for my selfie with Natalie and use a filter that erases the pores and blemishes from our skin before I post it. Then I post a story of the pool with my bare legs featured—a thirst trap Jordan will never be able to resist.

I have another message from madyoung.fan, but I clear the conversation from my chats without reading it. I'm a graduate now. I don't need to deal with this dumb high school drama anymore.

Natalie glistens in the sunlight while every exposed bit of my skin is slathered in sticky sunscreen. She slips her sunglasses off. Her nose is a bit crooked from when she broke it during cheerleading practice. She took a wild elbow to the face while I held up Chelsea by the foot. On the bleachers, I watched the blood pour from Natalie's nose beside me and held her hand even while her blood hit my skin and Coach instructed her to tilt her head forward, not back. And for the first time, I didn't like this part of Sophie's—*my*—life.

On my way to the gym for tryouts months earlier, I nearly ran into Ash, and she glared at my tiny pink shorts.

"Why are you trying so hard to be like her?" she demanded.

"I don't know what you're talking about."

"You'll never be her, you know."

"I'm not trying to be her."

Jordan was the one who told me I'd look hot in the uniform. He wrapped an arm around my waist and said, "I'd love to have my girl cheering me on."

After that, I had to join.

"So guess what?" Natalie says.

"What?"

"I got approved to volunteer at the animal shelter." She beams.

"That's amazing! I didn't even know you applied. When are you starting at the vet clinic?"

"On Monday. And I'm hoping to volunteer at the zoo too. It's only an hour drive."

Natalie has known she wants to be a vet since she was six. She's been on a path toward her dream ever since—AP courses all through high school, advanced biology sophomore year, daily tutoring when she struggled with AP physics, and now a summer full of volunteering and shadowing a veterinarian until she heads to UMass-Amherst as a pre-veterinary science major in the fall.

"I don't think simultaneously volunteering at three different places is physically possible."

Natalie grins. "You know that's never stopped me."

Nothing could ever stop Natalie. I may have only become friends with her in the six months since I've been dating Jordan, but I've quickly learned exactly how Type A she is.

"I bet Joyce is disappointed," I joke. Joyce Shin is the mom who lets her teenager throw parties as long as we make sure no one drives home drunk. The mom who encourages her daughter to study less and enjoy her youth more because, as a consultant who travels constantly, she hasn't enjoyed a day of her life since she graduated college.

Natalie's dad, on the other hand, harps on her from South Korea about why her A- wasn't an A+.

"She doesn't understand why I'm not spending my whole summer in the pool. She said someone needs to use it."

"I volunteer." I elbow her. "Just make sure you squeeze in time for your best friend this summer."

"I'll pencil you in," she says. "So was Jordan upset about those videos?"

"He was at first," I admit. "But we're fine now."

At least, I hope we are.

She gives a small grimace. "I bet Jordan hates that Miles is living in your house now. That must be so creepy for you."

I stiffen. "You know those are all just rumors, right? We have no idea what happened to her." I don't have to say her name. There's only one *her* we could be talking about.

"We know he definitely punched her in the face. We all saw the black eye. And I know people in Hartford who went to school with him. The rumors about all the fights and suspensions are true."

I shrug. Miles may be trouble, but that doesn't make him a killer.

A notification on Natalie's phone distracts her, and I click my own phone screen because I need a distraction too. Something to make me forget about my new neighbor and how the mere mention of his name makes my heart beat faster.

I have a new Instagram follower.

madyoungfan. The same handle as whoever added me on Snapchat.

No profile picture, no posts to their feed or story, no followers. Only following one account.

Mine.

I have a message request too.

tell natalie i say hi

What the hell?

How do they know I'm here? *Shit.* They must've seen the selfie I posted of us. Or the story of my bare legs poolside. I practically invited madyoungfan over.

I scan Natalie's yard, heart hammering, but there's nothing out of the ordinary. No one lurking in the woods, no one watching us from the driveway.

"What are you looking for?" Natalie asks.

"Uh. I don't know. I just got this really creepy DM." I show her my phone.

When she reads the message, she frowns. "Who is this person?"

"No idea. They added me on Snapchat too, but they're anonymous."

"You should block them."

"I blocked them last night. They just made a different account."

I wish Jordan was here so he could hug me and reassure me. Tell me that it doesn't matter what creepy messages and empty threats some random person online sends my way, he'll protect me.

Another DM follows.

My heart stops. Spiders trickle down my spine, down the fine hairs along my arms and legs.

This time, they've sent me a photo. Of a girl on the sidewalk in a green sundress, sandals, and a braid. Earbuds in, blissfully unaware of anything or anyone around her.

A picture of me.

Someone was watching me on my way to Natalie's.

How did I not feel their eyes on me? How did I not notice?

I want to rip out those earbuds and tell the girl in the picture—*me*—to turn around. To see who is behind her.

"What's wrong?" Natalie asks. When I show her the photo, she frowns like it's a picture of someone picking their nose. Not a creepy photo someone snapped of me when I had no idea I was being watched. "Who do you think took that?"

"I'm guessing it's Ash."

Natalie's thin, dark eyebrows come together. "Why her?"

"Her DMs said she knows what I did and asked if I feel guilty. I'm sure she was talking about those videos. Still accusing me of cheating on Jordan." I roll my eyes, but part of me is picturing a looming, dangerous man in the shadows.

"That makes sense. I'm sure she's hoping you two break up." Natalie locks her screen and slides her sunglasses on before leaning back. "Girls like that always hate girls like us."

Does Natalie even know that Ash and I used to be friends? If she doesn't, I'm not going to be the one to tell her.

The girl who was Ash's best friend doesn't exist anymore.

I navigate to my own Instagram profile. Before I left my house, I took a selfie in my green dress with my spaghetti straps showing and mentioned I couldn't wait to see my bestie. Is that how they knew where I'd be?

I delete the story.

"Do you think I should tell someone?"

"What for?" Natalie yawns and stretches like a cat in the sun.

"Um. Because it's pretty creepy."

"Not really. Everyone takes pictures of random people in public."

"What about the DMs, though? And why do they seem to only be going after me?"

"They made the account like an hour ago. You're probably just the unlucky first target. I seriously doubt you have anything to worry about. They'll get bored and move on to someone else by tomorrow."

tell natalie i say hi

If she doesn't feel threatened, why should I?

Maybe Natalie's right. Maybe I have nothing to worry about.

On my way to work, I keep trying to listen to a fantasy romance audiobook, but there are too many distractions. Natalie sending me a bunch of texts venting about some rude girl who answered the phone when she called the zoo. Mom asking how much I have saved for a laptop and college supplies because we might need a new fridge. Jordan not responding to any of my messages or checking his social media. And DMs from the burner account that I'm too creeped out to open.

I can't stand the silence from Jordan any longer. I call him. The phone rings. And rings.

He's never not answered when I've called.

On the seventh ring, I hit End. But I need to talk to him. To at least know he's okay.

I find his home phone number in my contacts and hit Call.

"Hello?" His mom's alto is that of a friendly customer service representative.

"Hi, Mrs. Goldman. It's Maddie. Is Jordan there?"

"Oh, I'm sorry, darling. He just hopped in the shower. I can tell him to give you a call when he gets out?"

So he's fine. Alive and well. I should be relieved.

Instead, a piece of me cracks. He hasn't been forced to leave my texts and calls unanswered—he's chosen to. "Thanks. That'd be great."

I thought I reassured Jordan that nothing happened between me and Miles. But maybe his radio silence for more than twenty-four hours means he's doubting me, just like Natalie did.

Or Sophie's coming back. Or she told him where she is and he's planning to go be with her.

Either way, he's probably been spending the past twenty-four hours thinking about breaking up with me and that's why he's not talking to me. He's trying to figure out how and when to break things off.

The thought alone makes my chest give a hard, painful squeeze. We can't break up now. Not when he's just given me a promise ring. Not when we're attending the same university across the country in a few months. Not when we'll be sharing an apartment. Not when we're planning our whole future together. Not when we're perfect for each other.

Inside Mariano's, I'm hit with the smell of burnt toast. Only two tables and a stool are occupied, and all five customers are watching Mabel and Miles argue behind the counter.

Strands of graying brown hair are already slipping out of

Mabel's short ponytail, like she's finishing up a twelve-hour shift and didn't just open an hour ago. Miles has his apron looped lazily over his neck, untied. Hardened muscle and a hint of his tattoo peek out from under his black shirt sleeve, his face a blank mask of boredom.

Mabel waves a slice of charred toast in the air in front of him. "How hard is it to cook bread?"

"I'm telling you, your toaster's fried."

The man on the stool with gray hair and drooping jowls calls, "Toasters don't fry, son. Toasters . . . well, they toast."

Miles drags a hand down his face.

Mabel flings the burnt toast onto a plate. "I should hire *him!*"

"Um." I slip on my apron, not sure I actually want to get involved in this. "I can make the toast."

"Oh good," Mabel says, thrusting the plate into my hands. To be fair, the toast is rock-hard. "We need you."

Before she can disappear back into the kitchen, I tell her, "Thanks for the brownies. They were delicious. Mom already finished them."

Mabel's eyebrows furrow. "What brownies?"

I turn back to Miles, who's now halfheartedly wiping down the counter and looking like he'd have more fun getting stuck in traffic.

"Uh, never mind. Someone left brownies for us and Mom assumed it was you."

Mabel purses her lips. "You shouldn't be eating food that's just left sitting around when you don't know who made it. Who knows what's in it." With that, she heads back to the kitchen and barks an order at us to get to work.

I pop two fresh slices of bread in the toaster. "You made those brownies?"

Miles shrugs. He's still staring at the counter while he wipes it down, and I can't help but feel grateful his eyes aren't on me. "I might've."

"So why were you trying to bribe us?"

"Not you. Just your mom. I'd bribe you with a book."

My face warms. There's something almost unsettling about how well he still knows me. "Why were you trying to bribe my mom then?"

"Figured she'd have to hate me a little less if she had brownies."

"She doesn't hate you," I say automatically, even though I'm not totally sure that's true.

He snorts. "Everyone in this town does." He leans his arms on the counter and smirks at me. "So they were delicious, huh?"

"They were okay." I bite back the smile tugging at the corners of my lips.

"Guess I'll just have to make another batch."

"I can't imagine you baking." I try to picture Miles, the guy with the dark hair, tattoo, denim jacket, and missing sister spending his evenings covered in flour. But I can't. I can't reconcile that version of him with the one I know, with the one everyone else sees.

"Just picture me with nothing but an apron on and you can imagine it."

My face starts to burn, even as I say, "Ew, no, I'm not picturing that."

But now that he's put the image in my head, I can't stop myself. And the more I tell myself *not* to think about Miles naked underneath his apron, the more the image burns into my brain.

"Baking was kind of a family thing," he explains. "Dad was always into it and that was pretty much the only time Soph and I ever got along."

He probably shouldn't admit stuff like that out loud where

other people can hear him. They already think he killed his sister. He doesn't need to give them another reason to believe he did.

The morning rush will start any minute, so I check my phone one last time. Still nothing from Jordan. His silence is making me crazy. So is my online troll's chattiness. I have six new notifications from them.

"What's up?" Miles's low, sensual voice is entirely too close.

When I glance at him, his hand is braced on the counter, the other hanging loosely at his side. The smooth planes of his face are relaxed, but his eyes . . . god, those eyes. Why can't I make eye contact with him without wanting to melt into a puddle?

"I'm fine," I say quickly and stuff my phone under the counter.

"Right. That's why you look like your dog died."

I don't want to tell him about my boyfriend troubles or my online troll, so I opt for a part of the truth instead. "I'm thinking about getting a second job. I really need the money for college, but I don't think anyone in town is hiring."

"Be friendlier while you're on the clock and you'll make better tips."

"I'm very friendly," I snap.

"Yeah, you've definitely welcomed me back with open arms."

"Just wait until you see the parade I put together."

When the morning rush hits, I work the register while Miles runs plates and takes orders. I don't know why Mabel insists on putting him and our diners through this. She should keep him in the back to cook. He knows his way around the kitchen, at least. But they'd probably kill each other.

A pimply sophomore gives Miles his order. "Can you make sure my bacon is crispy, but not too crispy? Like just on the side of crisp."

Miles rolls his eyes, a pen tucked behind his ear and another spinning between his fingers. "I—"

"And I want my eggs scrambled with just a *hint* of brown."

"Man—"

"And can you make my pancakes into squares? That's how my great-grandma used to make them. And I want home fries, but—"

"Dude, if my gran doesn't kill you for this order, I will."

A white-haired woman pipes up. "Maybe you shouldn't be threatening your customers, young man!"

Miles narrows his eyes at her. "Maybe you should mind your own damn business."

Her mouth falls open like he just told her to drop dead. At least working here has gotten way more entertaining with Miles around.

When he passes me to deliver the order to Mabel, he mumbles, "Kill me."

Ten minutes later, he still hasn't returned, so I leave the register to take orders. Did he sneak out the back for a break or to make a break for it?

I'm wiping down a table covered in breadcrumbs and ketchup from the chaos of three boys aged two to five when Miles returns, two steaming plates in hand. He drops the plates with a clatter in front of the sophomore, who eagerly grabs a slice of bacon and tosses it in his mouth.

"Holy shit, that's good!" Bits of bacon spray past his lips. "Tell your gran I said thanks."

"I'm the one who made this shit for you. So you better leave the biggest tip of your life."

I cover my laugh with a fake cough.

An hour later, during a rare lull when no new customers walk in, no one spills anything, and Miles doesn't need help figuring out which pattern to hit the register buttons in, I take my apron off and shove it under the counter.

I peek into the kitchen and ask Mabel, "Can I take my break now?"

"Hang on a second." Mabel steps away from the stove to fix her attention on me.

Never a good sign.

She folds her arms. Am I about to get fired? I've been here since my sophomore year, and she just told me this morning that she needs me. I can't get laid off for ditching my post for a five-minute confrontation with Ash. I can't lose this job. I need the money.

"I've got a favor to ask," Mabel says. "Could you tutor Miles?"

That's possibly the last thing I expected. "Tutor him?"

"He didn't graduate, so he's gotta get his GED." She rolls her eyes. "He mostly just needs someone to study with. Keep him on track. I'll pay ya, of course."

My knee-jerk reaction is to tell Mabel *hell no* and go back the way I came. Miles either makes me want to pull my hair out or slap him, so I don't exactly want to spend more time with him than I already have to. But I can't turn down the cash. "Um…okay. Sure."

"Thanks. I really appreciate this." Mabel turns back to the grill. "Go ahead and take your break. You've got ten minutes. Or until Tess shows up because I'm not dealing with her."

Behind the register, Miles sits on the stool with a paperback cracked open. Seeing him read makes my heart flutter.

"I'm taking my break," I tell him, grab my phone, and sit at one of the three umbrella tables outside to scroll through Jordan's eerily quiet Instagram feed.

Nearly all his recent posts feature me. Selfies he snapped of us, selfies I sent him privately that he decided were "too beautiful not to share," posed photos someone else took. Even in the photos without me, he mentions me in his captions. *Wish @maddieo5young was here.*

My favorite photo of us is also the one with the most likes. Jordan at his most handsome in a pressed black suit and red tie to match my crimson, floor-length dress. The one that caught everyone's attention.

I wasn't trying to copy Sophie—I just look really good in red.

I sent a selfie in that gown to Jordan from the dressing room and he messaged back immediately: *That's the one.*

In the picture Jordan's mom snapped of us with her DSLR before prom, we're smiling at the camera exactly like a prom king and queen would. His arm is around me like it always is. The gesture doesn't just tell me he loves me—it tells me he's not going to let anything bad happen to me. Whatever happened to Sophie, if anything happened to her, I won't suffer the same fate. Not with Jordan around.

But what if he chooses not to be around me anymore?

The most recent comment on the post is from Ash: *yuck.*

When I click on his followers, I notice Jordan and I have a new mutual follower. madyoungfan.

Shit. I double-check his photos of us, looking for any comments from the profile. But there aren't any.

Yet.

What if they're planning on targeting Jordan next?

My phone buzzes with a new notification. A DM from madyoungfan. This time, I open it.

The blurry photo is of a girl hurrying down the sidewalk in a damp green dress, sandals, and a braid.

It's me.

It's *me.*

That road, the bottom of that carriage driveway . . . I was leaving Natalie's house.

Did they wait outside in the bushes the entire time, just to take a paparazzi shot when I was leaving?

When I scroll up, the first photo has already been deleted. Heart thudding, I take a screenshot of the second photo.

A few minutes later, the photo disappears and they send me another. My chest squeezes so hard I can't breathe.

This time, I'm in gray vans, denim shorts, and an orange crop top, light brown hair drifting halfway down my back. Me on my way to work this morning.

"What's that?"

My head barely misses slamming into Miles's nose.

He jumps back and laughs at me. "What? Did I catch you watching porn?"

"No."

His smile falters. "What's wrong?"

"It's not a big deal," I say, even though it feels like one. "Someone's just trolling me on Instagram."

The crease between his eyebrows smooths. Because trolling is something that happens to everyone, especially when you're popular enough. Just have to suck it up and deal with it, right?

"So not everyone's a fan?" His voice is flat. "Must be hard."

My hands tighten around my phone so I don't smack him. "More like a superfan. They've been sending me creepy DMs and taking photos of me."

I expect him to brush it off again. Mock me. Tell me this is what I get for becoming *one of those girls*. Instead, he sits down beside me. "Can I see?"

"I guess." I slide my phone over to him.

He reads the DMs and checks out the photo that madyoungfan hasn't deleted yet. His frown deepens, and when his gaze finally returns to mine, his irises have morphed into burning-hot coals.

An intensity that scares me.

"I'll take you to the police station."

"The police station? No." What are the police going to do

about a few creepy DMs and pictures? "I don't want to tell anyone about this. It's nothing."

I should've kept my mouth shut after telling Natalie. She was the voice of reason—none of this is actually *dangerous*. It's weird and creepy, but you can't arrest someone for that.

His deep brown irises catch a glint of sunlight, turning his gaze to a warm, delicious honey. Then he leans closer to me than he's ever been. "It's not nothing," he insists. "This shit happened to my sister. Right before she disappeared."

CHAPTER SEVEN

MILES DRIVES US TO CREEKVIEW, the nearest town with a police department.

During a school shooting drill, we discovered it would take nearly forty minutes for the police from Creekview to get to us. Very reassuring.

The police station is smaller than I expect. All wood paneling and cheap chairs next to a sad, drooping fern. Behind the counter is a woman chewing a piece of gum open-mouthed. Her badge says *Callahan*.

I wait for Miles to explain why we're here, but his lips are pressed together, hands tucked in his pockets. He's letting me do the talking, even though he's the one who wanted to come here.

"Hi. Um. I'd like to make a report," I tell her.

Officer Callahan blinks at me as if she didn't realize we walked through the door. Her face is round, hair pulled up in a disheveled bun, crow's feet at the edge of her eyes.

"Okay." She speaks slowly, as if she thinks we made a wrong turn on our way to the mall. "On what?"

"Someone's been . . ." I fumble for the right word. ". . . harassing me."

"She has a stalker," Miles corrects.

I want to deny it, tell him it's not that serious. Before I can, Callahan quirks an eyebrow and leans forward, elbows on the counter in front of her. "Uh-huh. And why do you think this person is . . . stalking you?"

Miles glares at her. But I get her reaction, the subtle disbelief. Because it's not like I'm famous. Not even TikTok- or Instagram-famous. Normal people in small towns don't have stalkers.

"I'm not sure. But they've been following me." I set my phone down on the counter, screen up. "They've been trolling me online. And they've been taking pictures of me."

I expect Officer Callahan to gape or her eyes to widen, but her face doesn't change. She grabs my phone, already opened to my DMs with madyoungfan. She slips on a pair of glasses and holds the screen out at arm's length.

"Who took these pictures?"

I shrug. "I have no idea. I don't know who's doing this. They're anonymous."

Her eyebrow goes up again and she returns her gaze to the screen, scrolling with her index finger like she's never used a smartphone before. "But you've seen someone following you?"

"I haven't seen them," I admit. "That's why I don't know who they are."

Miles leans against the counter. "But obviously someone *is* following her if they're taking these pictures."

Officer Callahan removes her glasses and lays my phone down in front of her. Leans back and sighs. "There's nothing we can do. If they make a threat or try to extort something from you, come back. If you find out who this person is and they show up at, say, your house or your school or your job, then you'll want to call it in." She points at my phone. "But there's nothing we can do with that."

Miles plants his palms on the counter. "You don't understand. This happened to my sister before she disappeared. Sophie Mariano."

But Callahan's face doesn't show a hint of surprise. She already knows who his sister is. Who he is.

Miles pulls his phone out and swipes through screenshots. The Instagram DMs are from an account called sophiemarianofan. They look like they could've been sent to me.

you look nice today

talk to me

i can see you

Then he swipes through photos of Sophie walking into the grocery store, sitting in her car, running in the park. The legs of a thousand spiders trickle from my neck down the length of my spine.

Since Jordan's party, I've assumed Sophie ran away. But I never considered she was running from someone.

Did Sophie's stalker make her want to leave Beaumont? Or did they do something to her before she could?

If they did something to her, they could be planning to do the same thing to me.

The nearly identical handles alone should get Callahan to sit up straighter, to take me seriously, but she remains disinterested. "And do you know who was . . . stalking your sister?"

Miles glares at her. "Nope. Thought that fell under your jurisdiction."

"I wasn't on that case."

"Gee, maybe you should pass on the information to someone who is then."

Callahan redirects her attention to me. "Best I can do for you is to suggest you make your accounts private. You kids share way too much sensitive information on social media.

Block that account. Most people are just looking to get you riled up." She smacks her cinnamon gum in her mouth. "Best bet? Get off social media altogether. Read a book. Go to the movies. You all share every second of your lives, then act surprised when somebody takes advantage."

Silence falls over us. Miles meets my gaze, his brows furrowed and jaw clenched.

Why does it sound like she's blaming me for being stalked?

"So there's nothing you can do?" If this person could be the reason Sophie disappeared, the police should at least do *something*. "What if they hurt me?"

Whoever they are, they're willing to follow me around town taking photos of me. What else are they willing to do?

Callahan folds her arms. "Well, unfortunately, we can't arrest a social media profile."

Before I can say another word, Miles spits, "This is bullshit. You ignored my sister and look what happened. And now you're gonna ignore someone else dealing with the same fuc—"

"All right." Callahan stands, directing her glare at him. "Time to go."

I snatch my phone from the counter and tug on Miles's arm when it's clear he's not about to go anywhere.

Outside, I collapse into the passenger seat of his car, the leather burning my thighs. "This is why I didn't want to come here. I knew they couldn't do anything."

I need to figure out who's behind the account myself.

But I have no idea how.

I could start with Ash. She laughed the loudest when the beer spilled down my top at Natalie's party, and she posted those videos of me and Miles. And she's probably still bitter that I ditched her for better friends.

Miles slides into the driver's seat. "They can. They just don't want to."

"Who else knows that Sophie was being stalked?" This is

what Miles meant when he said Sophie had her enemies. *Someone was out to get her.*

Now they're out to get me.

"No one besides my parents, Gran, and Deedee. She didn't want to tell anyone else because she didn't know who to trust."

If Miles is right, she didn't even tell her best friend or her boyfriend. There was a whole other part of her life they didn't know about. What else did she keep from them? How well did any of us really know Sophie Mariano?

"Who's Deedee?"

"My mom's mom. She lives up on a ranch in New Hampshire."

I already know the answer, but I have to ask it anyway. "Do you think whoever was stalking Sophie . . . did something to her?"

Miles hesitates. Like speaking the words out loud could make them true. "Yeah, I do. No one believed her either. And now she's gone."

That could be my fate. I could be the next Beaumont girl to disappear.

Miles leans past me and reaches into the glove compartment, the back of his hand brushing the bare skin of my knee. I jerk away, but my traitorous body aches for his touch like a magnet.

He presses warm metal into my palm. A pocketknife.

"Try it."

"Okay?" I run my finger along the back of the handle until the blade springs out.

When I sheathe the knife and try to hand it back, Miles closes my fingers over it. My skin burns where he touches me, but for once, I don't pull away.

"Don't tell anyone you have this. No one. Not until we figure out who this is."

My heart thumps. Because going to the police, carrying a

pocketknife, Miles volunteering to help . . . makes all of this real. "We?"

"I'll help you track them down," Miles promises.

"Why would you want to help me? You can't stand me."

He lets the words settle between us and doesn't deny them. I try to ignore the way his silence stings. "Because if we find them, we'll find my sister."

CHAPTER EIGHT

THE NEXT MORNING, Mom pulls me along by the arm toward Mariano's. "We're going to be *late!*"

"You mean *I'm* going to be late. I'm the one who has to be at work in three minutes."

"But I'm going to be late for the good coffee. You know Mabel stops making the good stuff after eight."

"You got coffee after eight *one time*. You don't know that it's always that bad."

"And I don't want to find out. So we need to *hurry*."

It's way too early for the sun to be baking us like this, and I need at least three cups of coffee to deal with Mom's energy. Sleep didn't come easy last night when all I could do was stare at my phone in the dark, at the latest DMs from my stalker.

Natalie messages me.

Are you working this morning?

I want the good coffee but I don't want to be around S's brother

And Mabel scares me

> Running to work with Mom now

> But you might only find my dead body if I'm late

> Run faster so I can get my coffee! Long day today

Inside Mariano's, we're hit with the sweet smell of coffee, home fries, and syrup. Mom distracts Mabel with a ridiculous coffee order while I scurry around back to slip on my apron and start taking orders like I got here right on time, five minutes ago.

"Can I get some whipped cream on top? Ooh and some dark chocolate?"

"Because rotting your teeth with coffee isn't enough." Mabel rolls her eyes as she pours a cup of black coffee for Mom and points to a basket with packets of sugar.

George has been joined at his two-person table by Tess, a someone-save-me expression on his face.

". . . heard he got caught with one of those homemade *bombs*," Tess croaks. "In his locker! The kid's dangerous, that's all I'm sayin'. Shouldn't be here. If he'd do somethin' like that to his own sister, who's to say he's not gonna do it to somebody else?"

I set two mugs of coffee down in front of them a little too hard, hot liquid sloshing dangerously close to the rim.

"Oh hey, hon!" Tess gives my arm a squeeze. She leans toward me, and in her usual failed attempt at a whisper, crows, "Glad it's you this mornin' and not that boy."

The bell chimes when the door swings open. Natalie hurries over to me with a grin. "I need my coffee to go. First day at the vet clinic!"

"Congrats, hon!" Tess rasps.

I promise Tess and George I'll be back in a minute, and George fixes me with a pleading gaze that begs me to make it the shortest minute of my life.

Natalie plops onto a stool while I pour her coffee in a styrofoam cup. "Are we watching *Friends* or *Riverdale* tonight?" she asks.

In November, when we were both feeling burnt out and stressed from college applications, essays, tests, and cheerleading, Natalie and I started streaming Netflix together at eleven every night when our brains were fried and couldn't absorb any more facts about infinitesimals or electromagnetic radiation. Now we spend at least one night a week watching a show together and falling asleep before we hang up.

"*Friends.*"

From near the register, Mom groans. "This coffee is *so good.* Did you know adding five packets of sugar makes black coffee taste *a lot* better?" She stands on her toes to call into the kitchen, "You know what would make this coffee even better? Whipped cream!"

Tess has moved to sit with Mrs. Wallis and two other women with short white hair. Sharing the same gossip with them. "—I swear, Mabel's gonna start losin' business if she keeps that boy on."

Natalie drops some cash on the counter for me, including a tip because that's Natalie.

"Good luck today," I tell her.

She flashes me a dazzling smile on her way out the door until she passes Miles, pushing his way inside. He holds the door open for her and she doesn't bother with a thank you.

Tess finally falls silent, and that's enough to make me happy to see him.

Wait. *Am* I happy to see him? No. He's still a huge jerk. Baking some brownies and agreeing to help track down my stalker doesn't change that. None of it has been for me, anyway.

He made brownies for Mom and he wants to track down my stalker so he can find Sophie. If she wasn't missing, he wouldn't care.

Mom's good humor slips away when she notices Miles, and she gives me a peck on the cheek. "I gotta get to work. I have to be there bright and early tomorrow for a reunion, so I'll probably stay the night at the inn. Will you be okay alone tonight?"

"Mom, I'm eighteen. And Mabel will literally be in the same house."

"I don't care if you're fifty. You'll still be my kid, and that gives me the right to worry about you forever."

"Busy morning." Miles slips his apron over his head, voice low and gravelly like he just rolled out of bed. I hate the way it makes goosebumps prickle along my skin. He gives a wide yawn that he doesn't bother covering up.

Mom actually scowls at him for a second before forcing a smile in my direction, telling me to have a good day, and bustling out the door.

Instead of asking me to move, Miles reaches across me to grab the coffee pot. In the few inches of space between us, the fresh scent of his shampoo floods my nose, and for just a second, I want to bury my face in it, feel the damp strands of his hair between my fingers—

I push away from him, snatch my notepad off the counter, and hurry to George's table to take his order. Before Miles can see my face flush.

I miss Jordan so much, it's driving me insane. Driving me to think crazy thoughts about *Miles Mariano*, of all people.

After my shift, I'm going to Jordan's house. I don't care if he doesn't want to talk to me. I'm getting to the bottom of this.

In the lull between the lunch and dinner rushes, Miles and I hunker down at a round table. He brought a bunch of GED study guides from the library, along with notebooks, pens, highlighters, and a laptop. I set up my ancient laptop and the charger it has to be plugged into at all times.

Since we went to the police station yesterday, I've gotten a few new DMs from my stalker.

talking to the cops about me?

dont do it again

youll regret it

How do they know? Did they follow me and Miles out of Beaumont all the way to Creekview? I didn't think to check the rearview mirror, but wouldn't Miles have noticed if a car had been following us that far? Unless he wasn't paying attention either.

"You work on the Pythagorean theorem," I tell him, "while I try to figure out who the stalker is." Although how I'm going to do that, I have no idea.

He nods at my laptop, already whirring like an airplane about to take off. "Did you do the login thing already?"

"What login thing?"

He rolls his eyes and I'm about to tell him I can search for my stalker on my own, but then he scoots his chair closer with a loud scrape, drawing the attention of a few diners. My blood thrums in my ears at his nearness.

Miles holds out his palm, and even though I hate when anyone else has my phone, I hand it over. He opens up Instagram, hits Add Account, and types in madyoungfan. Then taps *forgotten password*.

And there it is. The email address behind the fake account.

I can't help it—I gasp. Why didn't I think of that? It seems so obvious now.

sophiemarianofan@gmail.com.

The hope in my chest deflates. "That doesn't help us at all."

"It's something." Miles slides back over to his laptop. "Confirms what we suspected—it's the same person who stalked

Soph. Now we just have to figure out who would do this to both of you."

One name rings through my mind: Ash. The girl with a motive to go after both of us. She wanted Jordan, but Sophie stood in her way. Now I'm in her way.

While Miles types like a hacker on his laptop, I search Sophie's handle on Instagram.

She could've run away to put as much space between her and her stalker as possible before they acted on their threats. Or maybe they attacked her that night and she escaped. Whatever happened to her, if she ran away, if she's still alive, she might know who the stalker is.

But to figure out what she knows, we have to find her.

I never go on Sophie's social media because I hate remembering that she and Jordan were together, that he loved her. I want to be the only girl, and a red-hot knife pierces my gut every time I'm reminded that I never will be.

Even her handle—sophiebaby—sends an electric pulse through my chest. *Baby* is such a common endearment that I shouldn't be possessive of it, but it's the one Jordan uses for me. The name he calls me by almost exclusively. And she had it first.

I hate that my stalker has made her disappearance my problem.

Sophie was—is—next-level gorgeous. The kind of beauty I'll never be able to compete with. Cocoa brown hair that cascades down her back in natural waves. Slender figure, perfect skin, and the kind of bright green eyes a girl would kill for.

In the final months before her disappearance, her posts grew increasingly rare. She went from posting nearly every day to once a week until she stopped entirely. She posted on June thirteenth, a photo dump of the highlights of junior year, and didn't post again until August fifth.

Her last post is a selfie, beaming at the camera and dolled up in preparation for Jordan's party that night.

All of the most recent comments, on every picture, are from people who never knew her.

Never forgotten

we miss u sweet girl

Please come home, Sophie. We miss your light. <3

You are so beautiful. Hope you're able to come back soon

rip beautiful queen

They already assume she's dead.

There are comments from Liv, Natalie, and Jordan on nearly every post too.

Liv: *Miss you.*

Natalie: *Please come home!! We miss you so much! Cheer isn't the same without you. :(*

Jordan: *I love you, baby. Please just let us know you're safe.*

Jordan calling Sophie *baby* burns into my retinas. But he left that comment months before he and I started dating. I can't hold that against him, even if I hate that he ever loved her.

"Why aren't you studying?" Mabel's booming voice makes us both jump.

"Holy shit, Gran," Miles hisses.

She reaches over, shuts his laptop, then grabs it. "I'm paying you to keep him on track," she tells me. "Not to play around online."

"Right. Sorry." I flush and abandon my laptop. I read out the first math problem I find: "Twenty is thirty-two percent of what number?"

We run through it while Mabel looms over us, hands on her hips.

"Looks like sixty-two point five." His answer satisfies her, and as soon as she's gone, he murmurs, "Couldn't find anything on that email."

"Where's your sister's phone? Maybe we can look through it. I'm sure there's some clue in her DMs."

He shakes his head. "Trust me. I've looked; the cops have looked. There's nothing to find."

"Do the police still have it?"

"No, they gave it back to my mom."

"Can you ask her for it?"

"She doesn't like to hand over any of Soph's stuff. She's kept her room like a shrine."

This is feeling more and more impossible by the second. "So now what?"

"We need to narrow down the search," Miles says.

"How do we do that?"

"We know they've got a type." He waves his fists in the air in the worst impression of a cheerleader. "So who would do something like this to you? Someone who knows you and Soph."

I snort. "Um. Everyone in Beaumont knows us." Everybody knows the popular girl. That's the whole point.

Miles rolls his eyes. "Jesus, you're insufferable now."

For once, I bite my tongue. We need to stay on track, not spiral into another bickering match. "I do think I've narrowed it down to someone."

He raises an eyebrow. "Who?"

"Ash Jones. She was basically my only friend for a while, and we didn't exactly end our friendship on good terms. She's the one who posted those TikToks of us."

"What TikToks?"

I open the app, and of course, Ash still has them up. I show him the one of me getting into his Mustang first.

"Okay. This girl's a creep." When I show him the other TikTok of him watching me, his jaw hardens and he scrolls through the comments. "People are morons. For the record, I wasn't pulling a Joe Goldberg. I was thinking, 'That girl looks familiar.' But everything about you is different, so I wasn't sure if it was you at first."

"I know. If anybody is the creep in this situation, it's Ash. She was obviously keeping tabs on me all night."

"So it could be her," he concedes. "But why would she go after my sister?"

"Um. Well. She told me herself she hated Sophie and all her friends."

While I was on shift, she sat on a stool at the counter, staring daggers at the booth where Sophie, Jordan, Natalie, Liv, Chelsea, and Brett were laughing. *God, I hate them*, she said. *The worst people are the ones who are handed everything and think they've earned it.*

There are two types of jealous girls. Those who want what someone else has and go after it—girls like me. And those who want what someone else has and destroy the person who has it. Girls like Ash.

Miles leans back and his chair squeaks. "What about your friend? Natalie Shin, right? She cheered with Soph."

"No way. Natalie's a sweetheart." I might've taken prom queen from her, but she knows that wasn't in my control. And what reason could she have for going after Sophie? Natalie doesn't like guys, so she couldn't have wanted to date Jordan. She has no motive for any of this. "I was with her when I read one of the DMs from my stalker, so she couldn't have sent it."

Miles slumps back, mulling it over. "All right." He grabs his phone. "What's your number?"

"What?"

"I don't have your number. If I find anything, I'll need to text you."

"Right." I don't exactly want him to have my number—I can only imagine the vitriol he'll send to me at two a.m., informing me of all my flaws, but I pull out my phone and show him my number anyway. "No prank calls."

He adds my number to his Contacts. "The prank calls will be nonstop. What's Ash's Instagram handle?"

While he scrolls through her posts, I get a notification and brace myself.

But it's not my stalker this time.

It's Jordan.

A smile blooms across my face so wide my cheeks hurt.

Hey, baby. Come home. I've got a surprise for you.

CHAPTER NINE

EVEN THOUGH HE called me baby and his text sounded normal, I'm still a bundle of nerves when I get home. I half expect Jordan to be sitting outside my house, waiting to break up with me. But only his car is outside. His shiny BMW sticks out like a sore thumb next to the garage with a bent door and Miles's rusted old Mustang.

Before I reach the front door, the hairs on the back of my neck stand up.

Someone's watching me.

But when I whip around, no one's there. Nothing but the empty street.

Stop. You're being paranoid.

Just as I'm scrambling onto the porch, the front door swings open with a groan.

Jordan hovers in the doorway. He's in a navy shirt that stretches over his biceps and a pair of dark wash jeans he only ever pulls out for special occasions. His hair is styled to perfection because that's exactly what Jordan is—perfection.

He grins and I run to him. When I kiss him, I throw my arms around his neck and press my body against his. "I missed you so much!" I catch a whiff of tomato sauce coming from inside. "Something smells good."

He takes my hand and leads me inside, where the scent of vanilla mixes with the food. Jordan has kept all the lights off and lit vanilla candles around the kitchen, three placed on the countertops, one in the middle of the table.

Two plates are set across from each other, both piled with spaghetti noodles and tomato sauce, house salads in bowls on the side with parmesan cheese grated on top. Flutes of champagne drip onto the wood like they've been sitting there for a while.

He did all this for me. My chest swells.

"Jordan!" I jump into his arms, grinning so wide it hurts.

He spins me around in a bone-snapping hug. "Welcome home, baby."

When he releases me, I scramble for the right words to express my gratitude, but nothing seems like enough. So I settle for: "This is *amazing*."

"I'm glad you like it." His grin widens.

"What's the occasion?"

"No occasion. Just wanted to show my girl how special she is to me." He pulls out my chair and even pushes it in for me after I take a seat. I pinch myself, and I'm relieved when I don't wake up. "And one more surprise."

He holds out a box of dark chocolates. I force a smile because gifts are about the gesture, not the gift itself. Dark chocolate grosses me out, but Mom will eat them. "Aww, thank you."

Jordan takes the seat across from me, smile stretched wide across his face. His letterman jacket is draped across the back of his chair. He's never cooked for me before. I could melt. My favorite book boyfriends have nothing on Jordan.

When I find myself hoping he's never cooked for Sophie, I push the image of her pretty, perfect face out of my head.

Jordan waits for me to take a bite of salad before he digs into his own food.

Everything is perfect.

Almost.

Everything except the one nagging question I can't shake off: Why would Jordan ignore me for three days and then go to all this trouble? Why act like I don't exist only to shower me in romance the next second?

I shouldn't be upset with him. It was three days. What's the big deal? I'm just being insecure. I've spent the past seventy-two hours imagining Sophie got back into contact with him, that they were calling and texting about their plans to reunite, but I can't be upset with Jordan just because I've let my imagination get the best of me.

He picks up his flute of champagne and holds it out to me until I do the same. "Cheers." He taps his flute against mine and we sip, the bubbles tickling my throat.

I want to memorize the sight of the glass meeting his lips, the bob of his throat when he swallows. I want to burn the image of his face into my brain like a brand so I never forget even the smallest detail. The pale blue irises, the slight cleft to his chin, the soft plush of his lips, the white scar so tiny on his cheek that only the best girlfriend would spot it, would remember precisely where it is. Could trace it in the dark.

"How long have you been planning this?" I ask.

"Not long. I got the key from your mom earlier."

I smile and twirl the noodles around my fork. A text pings from my phone, quickly followed by two more, and my heart stops for a moment.

I meet Jordan's gaze for a flash of a second, and he watches me, waiting for me to check my phone.

When I do, the tension in my shoulders dissolves. It's not my stalker. It's Natalie.

How's it going with Jordan?

What was the surprise??

Please tell me it wasn't his

She sends an eggplant emoji, and I lock the screen without replying.

Jordan nods to my phone. "Who was that?"

"Natalie."

I take a sip of my champagne. He must've gotten a strong bottle because a headache is already blooming in my temple.

He slowly returns his attention to his pasta, cutting the noodles. "I was thinking we could do something tomorrow."

"I'd love that! I have to work for a few hours in the afternoon, but I'll be free after."

"Awesome. Can I use your phone quick? I'll check the weather."

"Sure." I unlock it before handing it over.

He clicks and swipes. "It'll be warm tomorrow. Clear skies." When he hands the phone back, he flashes me his trophy-winning grin. "Looks like we're all clear."

"What are we doing tomorrow?" Images of a picnic, a date at the drive-in theater, a late-night swim in his pool all run through my mind. Each of them ending with Jordan on top of me, driving pleasure through every muscle.

"That's another surprise." He stuffs a huge bite of spaghetti in his mouth. "So have you seen Miles around since the party?"

We both know nothing happened between me and Miles, but considering he's the source of our last argument, this seems like dangerous territory.

"Um. Yeah," I admit. "He moved in with Mabel. She's his—"

"Grandma," Jordan says, voice flat. Right. Of course he knows that. "Why did he move in with her?"

The lettuce crunches beneath the prongs of my fork. "Mabel got him a job at the diner."

"Wait. He's working with you too?" His frown deepens.

"Yeah." I shrug. My head is lighter, the champagne churning the contents of my stomach. "It's not a big deal. He kind of sucks at his job, and nobody really wants him there, but—"

Jordan shakes his head. "I don't trust that guy. I don't like the way he was looking at you in that video." Is this Jordan being protective or jealous?

"I'll be fine." I flash him a reassuring smile.

"How can you be so sure?" His stunning blue eyes have gone stormy.

Maybe he's right. Maybe I can't be so sure that I'll be fine. Not anymore.

I can't keep this secret from him. Not like Sophie did. "Actually . . . I have to tell you something."

He sets his fork down and fixes his eyes on me. I love when I get his full attention. There's nothing I'd rather do than bask in it. I'm the girl he cares about. The girl he loves. The girl he wants to spend the rest of his life with.

I spit the words out in a rush: "Someone's been stalking me. I went to the police, but they didn't help."

He frowns. "Stalking you? Who?"

"No idea." I show him the account and then the DMs.

When he leans closer and squints at the screen, he says, "Wait. What the fuck? That's you."

"They've been taking pictures of me. They're following you too." Then I add quickly, "On Instagram. Not in real life."

At least, not that I know of.

"Really?" He pulls his phone out to check. "I haven't been online in a couple days."

"I noticed," I admit. "I missed you."

Jordan gently bumps his knee against mine under the table.

"I missed you too. I told Dad I wanted to come back early to surprise you."

"Come back early? From where?"

He tilts his head. "From our trip? I told you about it."

I rack my brain, trying to think of a single time he told me about a trip, but none come to mind. I shake my head. "I don't think you did."

"I definitely did." He puffs his bottom lip out in mock disappointment. "Guess I'm not important enough to listen to."

I know he's joking, but the words still make panic bubble in my stomach. I bet Sophie never forgot anything Jordan told her. Especially not something as important as a trip with his dad.

I want to ask where they went, what they did, but that would only pour salt in the wound.

I can't believe I spent the past three days worrying over nothing.

"You are," I insist. "You're the most important."

He leans across the table and kisses me, chasing away the hollow ache inside me that his absence left.

When Jordan is with me, I'm whole again.

"Don't worry about this creep," he says. "I'm not going to let anything happen to you."

On the couch behind me, Jordan snores softly. Morning rays shine through the windows, and Metallica plays in Mabel's kitchen. She's been at Mariano's for hours by now and I've never heard her play music in her life, so it must be Miles.

I force the image of him flipping pancakes in nothing but an apron out of my head.

Jordan squeezes me tighter. Wrapped in his arms, I feel his strength, protection. I'm so lucky I have him. Especially now, with a crazy person out there following me.

I need water. My head pounds and my mouth is dry, like I spent last night throwing back shots. I didn't realize how much alcohol is in champagne.

Before I can extricate myself from Jordan's arms, he pulls me in closer. He's awake now, growing hard against my ass. Fingers slipping under my shirt, teasing my nipple. The water can wait.

When my nipple peaks beneath his touch, he "Mmm"s against my back. He uses both hands to palm my breasts, massaging, and I arch into his touch.

"God, Maddie," he groans.

I love making him say my name like that.

He flips me on my back, stuffing his head under my shirt. He kisses, licks, and sucks my breasts, eliciting all the gasps and moans he wants to hear. His hand slips down my shorts and panties, rubbing exactly where I want him.

Once he slips a finger in and feels the wetness waiting for him, he growls, "I need you *now*," and flips me on my stomach.

There's the crinkle of the condom and then he's sliding, slow and hot, inside me. I let out a groan at the stretch.

The warmth of his body envelops me as he lays on top of me. "You're so tight," he murmurs.

He thrusts, slowly, gently. The slow build of pleasure is excruciating and I dig my nails into the couch, unable to keep my moans contained.

On the other side of the wall, the scream of guitars and clash of drums grows louder. To drown out the sounds of me and Jordan having sex.

Maybe I'll feel guilty or embarrassed about it later, but right now, I can't bring myself to care about anything other than the throbbing need mounting inside me.

I wish Jordan would rub between my legs, so I do it myself. When he notices, he says, "Good girl."

The slap of his skin against mine grows louder as he moves

faster and faster inside me. Then he hauls my hips up and slaps my ass before plunging back in, making me gasp and clutch at the armrest.

His fingers grip my hips so hard, I know there will be marks there later, but I don't care. Not when he finally brings a hand around to rub between my legs.

That familiar, magical pleasure is climbing. I'm so close.

"Come on, baby," Jordan murmurs. "Make him hear how loud you moan for me."

I freeze. Jordan wants Miles to hear us?

He picks up speed, thrusting in and out of me faster, faster. I cry out. This angle is so deep. I try to stifle my sounds by pressing my face into the armrest.

He lets out the groan that I've come to recognize before slamming into me one last time, throbbing over and over until he pulls out.

I collapse onto the couch while Jordan heads for the bathroom. He slaps my ass before he goes. "Want to grab us some waters?"

I do. I definitely need to hydrate now.

On wobbly legs, I head for the kitchen, but when I step over the threshold, something crunches beneath my bare foot. I yelp and leap back.

My phone. Smashed on the floor. The entire screen spiderwebs, and I can't tell if that's from me stepping on it or if the damage was done last night, an accident lost to the recesses of my memory.

I hopelessly attempt to turn my phone on, but of course, it doesn't.

Shit. We can't afford a new one. Not on top of school supplies, textbooks, a new laptop, a plane ticket . . .

I groan, toss the useless phone onto the table, and grab two waters out of the fridge. When Jordan returns, water splashed on his face, I ask, "Do you remember me breaking my phone last night?"

He laughs. "You don't? I knew you were drunk, but I didn't think you were *that* drunk." He examines the wreckage of my phone. "I keep forgetting you're such a lightweight. You finished your glass, started stumbling around, and your phone slipped. I think you might've stepped on it at some point. I'm just glad you didn't burn the house down."

Mom is going to kill me. Thank god she isn't here to witness my hangover, broken phone, or the boyfriend who slept over.

"Do you have any old phones lying around that I can use until I can afford a new one?" Though I have no idea when that will be.

Jordan drops the phone back on the table. "Screw that, I'll just get you a new one."

Relief floods my chest. "I don't need a new one. Just a working one until I can save up." I kiss him. "Thank you."

His arms circle my hips. "You kidding? You're getting a new phone. Nothing less than the best for my girl."

He really is the perfect boyfriend.

CHAPTER TEN

MY FAVORITE PLACE in the world is the spot on my roof right outside my window. This is where I read, where I stargaze, where I send voice messages and FaceTime my friends and Jordan when I don't want to be overheard. Except now, when I don't have a phone.

Beside me, plastic squeaks. I jump and nearly drop the book in my lap.

Miles climbs out onto the roof. He's wearing distressed jeans and a black hoodie, the hood pulled over his head like it's not the middle of June.

He pauses when he sees me, and I think maybe he's about to go back the way he came. "Didn't know anybody was out here."

"Well. I am."

He shrugs, then swaggers over and plops down beside me, leaving mere inches of space between us.

My heart hammers, a sheen of sweat pricking up along my palms and back. "Do you have to sit so close?"

"Where's the boyfriend?" He scans the driveway below us.

"He had to work."

"Aww, before he made you come? Bummer."

I snap my book shut. "You have no idea what you're talking about."

"Did you take an acting class from Pornhub?"

"What—"

He smirks. "Those fake moans were almost convincing."

God, my face is on fire. If I touched my cheek right now, I'd burn my hand. "I wasn't faking anything."

"Definitely didn't bother trying to fake an orgasm."

I clutch my hands into fists. "So you're telling me you've made all your girlfriends come?"

If he actually thinks that, he's full of shit.

"Never had a girlfriend."

"Fine, friends with benefits, then. Fuck buddies. Whatever you call them."

"Never been with anyone like that." He actually looks serious. I would've assumed a guy like Miles would be sleeping around as much as he could.

I'm done talking about this. Miles doesn't need to know anything about my sex life and I don't want to know anything about his. I crack my book open again, hoping he'll take the hint.

"Come to my mom's house with me."

I look back up at him. His face gives nothing away. "What? Why?"

He stands and holds out a hand. "Got something there you'll want to see. My mom works nights at the hospital, though. So we gotta keep it down."

I don't take his hand. "Keep what down? I'm not doing anything or going anywhere with you. I have a boyfriend."

"Relax. I don't want to fuck you." His eyes are flat, and he tucks his hands back in his pockets.

It shouldn't offend me, but it does. Worse, it disappoints me. "Then what do you want me to see?"

"Mom took my backpack after I got kicked out. Notebook's got that list I was telling you about. You want to see it or not?"

The hit list. No—suspect list. If I can get my hands on a list of people obsessed with Sophie enough to follow her around town and harass her, I can figure out who on that list might want to do the same to me.

When we get to the single-story ranch house, Miles ascends the narrow concrete steps and fumbles with his key at the door. Tree branches nearly overhang the roof, and shrubbery crawls up toward the windows. In the corner of the yard, a push-mower is collecting cobwebs despite the grass tickling my ankles.

I wait at the bottom of the stairs because now that I'm here, the last thing I want to do is go inside that house.

Sophie's room is in there. Miles said his mom left it untouched, like she's hoping she'll wake up one morning and Sophie will magically be back in her bed. Like nothing's changed.

There's something about knowing my room could end up the same way that makes me want to stay the hell away from it.

Before Miles can get the door unlocked, it jerks open.

His mother is Sophie in twenty years. The same shade of brown hair, the same pale green eyes. Except her nose is long and narrow. She sighs through it. "How much money does your father need?"

"Not sure. Here to grab my backpack."

Her eyes narrow. "What for?"

"Because that's where my drugs are stashed."

"Miles Mar—"

"We need something from my notebook." He leans against the doorframe, arms crossed.

His mom's eyebrow quirks at the mention of *we*, and she peers around him. The moment her gaze lands on me, her demeanor turns icy. "What are you doing here?"

I freeze. I can feel my eyes bulging, but I can't help it. Miles faces me too, just as confused as I am. I've seen her from a distance at the search and on the news, but I've never actually spoken to her, so I'm not sure how she could already hate me.

"I brought her to see the list."

"I don't care. I don't want her on my property. You need to leave."

He stops her from closing the door in his face with a smack of his palm. "The same asshole who was stalking Soph is stalking her."

Miles waits for his mother to put the pieces together. To realize I may be the key to figuring out what happened to her daughter.

But her face doesn't change. If anything, her mouth morphs from pucker to snarl. "I'm sure they are."

She's just like Officer Callahan, but worse. Callahan obviously didn't believe me either, but at least she half-pretended to take me seriously.

Miles's mom thinks I'm lying through my teeth. Somehow making all of this up.

She disappears back inside without inviting me in. I drop down onto the bottom step and wait for Miles to return with his backpack. He plops it on the ground between his feet and pulls out a notebook.

"What'd you do to her?" he asks. "Shit in her front yard?"

I shrug. "No idea. Why's she pissed at you? For getting expelled?"

He gives a nearly imperceptible shake of his head. "Long story."

He opens up his notebook to the last page. A two-column list of scrawled names, so small and sloppy they're almost illegible. His shoulder bumps into mine when he moves closer so we can scan the page together. Even when I pull away, I can still feel the heat of his touch.

I wish he smelled like sweat for once instead of the usual musk of his cologne. The scent so intoxicating it reminds me of the days when Jordan and I first started dating, and every time I got a whiff of his Axe, all I wanted was for him to wrap me in his arms so I could breathe him in.

"Why are all the cheerleaders on your list?" I ask.

Miles has included last year's senior cheerleaders and this year's. Natalie, Rachel, Chelsea—

"Soph was captain. They might've wanted her spot."

"You really think any of those girls covet the role of cheer captain so much they'd *kill* for it?" I clap a hand over my mouth. I just implied someone killed his sister.

Even if that is what happened to her, for my sake, I need to hold onto hope that she's still alive.

"Um. I mean . . . I didn't mean that she's—"

Miles shakes his head, dismissing my fumble. "Not really, no. But I was grasping at straws. Wrote every possibility I could think of."

I grab the list to examine it again and start crossing off names. It definitely can't be Natalie or Jordan. When I find Liv's name on the list, I point to it. "You think Liv could've done something to Sophie? But they were best friends."

He shrugs. "Told you, wrote down anyone I could think of."

This list is a dead-end. Too many names, and everyone on this list knows both of us. It could be anyone.

When I reach the name scrawled at the bottom, my blood runs cold.

Maddie.

I swallow the lump in my throat. What has he heard about me that's so awful, he put my name on this list?

He's always called me Madalyn. He doesn't know about my new nickname.

I fold the list up and hand it back to him. I'm going to keep it that way.

A bouquet of white roses from Jordan is waiting for me when I get to the diner. I grin through the first twenty minutes of my shift, even after Mabel grumbles that this isn't a post office and Miles gives the flowers a lingering side-eye.

Natalie strides into Mariano's, scans the diner until she finds me taking an order, and marches over. Her dark eyes are framed by thick lashes, her eyelids shimmer with a pop of gold, and she wears a necklace and hoops in her ears to match. It's barely ten a.m. and she already looks glamorous.

"Where were you the other night? We were supposed to watch *Friends.*"

I scribble the last of the order and head for the kitchen. "Oh shit, sorry! Jordan made me dinner, and we got a little tipsy and I broke my phone."

"You realize I was forced to watch a tennis match with Liv because I didn't have a good excuse to get out of it. You owe me one, Maddie."

"I do. I'll make it up to you, I swear."

Miles sets a donut and napkin on the counter in front of her. "Give her a free donut."

Natalie grimaces at him, but as soon as he's in the kitchen and out of sight, she grabs up the donut with a little smile. "I have to head to the vet clinic, but get your phone fixed and text me so we can hang out."

After the lunch rush dies down, Miles and I finally get a break to stuff our faces. He makes us burgers and fries, and I don't say it out loud, but the burgers are even better than Mabel's. Which is pretty much the highest compliment a person can give. It's infuriating—it's almost impossible to hate someone who feeds you good food.

His hair is a mess from running his hand through it whenever somebody gets on his nerves. He stretches his arms over his head and yawns, the cotton growing taut around his shoulders and riding up to reveal the lean muscle at his biceps. He's doing it on purpose.

Through a mouthful of beef and bread, I tell him, "I hate to say it, but you need to become a chef or something."

He snorts. "Yeah, okay."

"Seriously. You're actually . . . good at it." Getting the compliment out is like dragging a dagger down my tongue. "You should ask Mabel to move you to the grill."

"Nah."

"Why not?"

"Both of us back there? Only one would survive, and it wouldn't be me."

"Break's over!" Mabel shouts from behind the register. "Get studying!"

I stuff a handful of fries in my mouth with a sigh. "What do you want to work on today? English, math, science, or social studies?"

Miles pulls out his giant GED study guides and drops them on the table with a thud. "Gee, they all sound *so fun*."

"Fine. I'll pick for you. English." I flip open to a prompt. "Write your response while I go give Table 4 their check."

As soon as one of the three elderly men at Table 4 is handing over the cash, Miles's mom marches in. She pauses when she makes eye contact with me, then pulls her purse closer and heads for the counter.

She catches sight of Miles but doesn't say anything to him. He doesn't say anything to her either.

I hurry to the register. Before I can ask what she wants, she rattles out an order. "Black coffee. To go."

"Uh, sure. That'll be—"

She thrusts out her cash, and after I hand over her change, I pour coffee in a to-go cup at lightning speed. "Can I get you anything—"

"That'll be all." She snatches the cup and I return to my seat across from Miles. She pauses at our table and stares down her nose at the books strewn across the surface. "What's this?"

"Studying for my GED," Miles mumbles.

"And you?" she asks me.

"Um. Uh . . . I'm his . . . tutor."

She gives a curt nod. "Well. Good luck." Then she's out the door.

The air curled into a tight ball in my chest whooshes out. "I can't tell if it's me she hates or you."

But it must be me. What kind of mother hates her child? Even one accused of murdering his sister. She can't believe that.

Can she?

"Me." His voice is low, and he keeps his eyes on his notebook, even though he's only written a single sentence and his pen isn't moving.

"Why?"

His dark eyes could burn through concrete. He leans toward me and the sun shining through the window behind us lights up the freckle at his hairline and the one at his jaw. My fingers ache to skim them, to feel how soft his skin is.

"Because." Miles inhales a slow breath through his nose. "The night Soph disappeared . . . she texted me to go with her to her boyfriend's party. I told her no." His Adam's apple bobs. "I didn't want to drive half an hour to hang out at some shitty party, and I didn't want her to go because her stalker might be there. Thought if she was scared enough, she wouldn't go without me. But she went. I called her and she told me she was with friends. So . . . I thought she was safe."

My heart sinks. This is why he's never defended himself against the accusations—he blames himself too. All this time, he's been carrying around this weight. Blaming himself for something he didn't do, a disappearance he didn't cause. While the whole world has been pointing a finger at him too.

"Mom hasn't looked at me the same since she found out about the texts. She blames me for Soph disappearing."

His own mom blames him. I scoot closer until our knees brush, and for once, I don't pull away. "Your mom shouldn't blame you for that. It's not your fault."

"Yeah, it is. I wasn't there when my sister needed me. I was a shitty brother. Broke up our parents' marriage. Our whole family."

I shake my head and think about taking his hand to comfort him. But Jordan would explode if he found out. "You're not to blame for that either. You were a kid. Your parents' marriage is between them. That's it."

He's everyone's scapegoat. The one everyone dumps their blame on to clear their own conscience.

"I should've been there to protect her." His voice turns gravelly, a catch in his throat.

He blinks hard, once, twice. Seeing him close to tears makes everything inside me melt.

"If someone did something to her, they are the only person to blame. Don't listen to the people who blame you to make themselves feel better."

He nods, but I know he doesn't believe it. Not yet.

"And we still don't know what happened. She could've left voluntarily."

"Yeah. Maybe." He doesn't look convinced, and a small, crazy part of me wants to close the little space left between us, press my lips against his, and hope it makes him feel better.

Someone taps on the diner window behind me.

I jump, and when I spin around in my chair, my heart drops at the familiar, hulking figure with chestnut hair and sparkling blue eyes.

Jordan grins at me and waves. Then he holds up a rectangular white box with a picture of a phone on the front.

When I stand, Jordan notices Miles in the seat beside me and the smile slides off his face.

"Wait. *He's* your boyfriend?" Miles's face has gone stormy.

But I don't have time to deal with Miles right now because Jordan is walking away.

I race outside. "Wait!"

Jordan spins, eyes darting around to see if we have an audience before pulling me into the small space between Mariano's and Sweet Tooth.

"I thought you said you were working," he hisses. No remnants of the jubilance from moments ago.

"I am." My voice comes out whiny, pleading. "I had a lunch shift and now I'm tutoring Miles."

Jordan's thick eyebrows shoot up. "You're *tutoring* him now?"

I shrink back. Jordan reserves his yelling for the football field, not for me. "I need the money."

"You don't need anything—you have me. Just tell me what you need, and I'll get it."

I'd love to take him up on his offer—quit my job and do nothing but spend my entire summer with him. But Mom would never allow it. She's the single parent who worked her ass off to get where she is, and she won't let us be the Goldmans' charity case.

"That's so sweet. But I can't. You know how Mom is. If I make a commitment, I have to stick with it, and I told Mabel I'd do her this favor."

"This is bullshit. You'd just rather spend time with that loser than with your boyfriend."

I reach for his arm, but he steps back. "That's not true—"

"Then quit."

My brain is scrambling, trying to figure out what's going on in Jordan's head. Would he react this way if I was tutoring any guy? Or is this all because of *who* I'm tutoring? "We're just going to sit in the diner and study."

"No."

The word throws me. So simple, so final. Not a request but an order.

Behind us, the bell to the diner clangs and Miles leans back against the wall. "What's the problem, Jordan?"

He scowls at Miles before facing me again and lowering his voice so Miles won't overhear. "I saw those videos. He watches you all night and the next day you have a stalker?" Jordan grips my arm, a bit too hard. Trying to get me to see reason. "That's not some coincidence, Maddie."

For a split second, I wonder if he's right. Miles *was* staring at me at the party. And the stalking started the next day. He knows where I live. He could easily watch to see when I come and go.

But why would he tell me about Sophie being stalked? Why would he show me the evidence? Why drive me to the police station? Why give me a knife? Why offer to help me?

He wants to track down the stalker, find his sister, and clear his name. It can't be Miles.

"I don't want you to do this," Jordan says. "I don't want you around him."

"Jordan—"

He throws his hands up. "Fine! Forget it. Have fun teaching that asshole algebra all summer."

I catch his arm before he can storm away and he shakes me off. He's never done that before.

My heart squeezes painfully and tears bloom in my eyes. He

can't walk away now. Not before I fix things between us. I need Jordan. I'm not Maddie without him.

"Here." Jordan thrusts the new phone at me. "I've already got it all set up with your old SIM card. You're on my family's plan, so you don't have to worry about a bill."

He knows we can't afford a new phone or an expensive plan. So he took care of it. "Thank you," I whisper. I want to melt into a puddle of gratitude. Throw my arms around him and kiss him.

But I won't be able to stomach the rejection if he pulls away. The thought alone nauseates me.

He leans down, voice low. "Don't trust him, Maddie."

He gives Miles one last glare before stomping off. We just had a fight. Jordan and I *just had a fight*. What the hell do I do now? My heart is smashed to pieces and scattered all over the sidewalk at my feet.

Do I go after him or give him time to cool off? I don't know what the right move is.

Ever since Miles came back to Beaumont, things have been off between us. I just want things to go back to the way they were. Jordan and Maddie. The perfect couple.

Miles strolls over, hands in his pockets. He leans back against the wall of Mariano's, and I wonder what he has against standing upright. "So you're the girl who started dating Jordan the second my sister went missing."

I bristle at the accusation. The last thing I need right now is shit from Miles Mariano, of all people. "It wasn't like that. I was there for him when he needed somebody, and we started dating a couple of months later."

Miles doesn't need to know that only a month in, after our first Friday night victory, Jordan swept me up in his arms right there on the football field, called me his lucky charm, and told me he loved me. Our whole relationship has been an explosion of love, and I still feel like shrapnel.

Jordan obviously didn't have this kind of relationship with Sophie or she never would've left.

Miles snorts. "A couple of months. Dude must've been real heartbroken when he moved on from my sister five seconds after she was gone."

"He was the one posting flyers of her all around town," I snap. "He was the one spreading the word about her disappearance online. He was the one who put the search together when the police didn't want to. He's the reason your sister's story even made it to the news. He can't be expected to pine after her forever—he's allowed to move on. But that doesn't mean he didn't care about her when she was still around."

I hate that he did. Hate that Sophie ever meant that much to him. But it's how I know he'd never hurt her.

Miles crosses his arms. His jaw is tight, the edge hard and dangerous. "It's not him you have to defend."

My heart pounds in my ears and I take a step back, bumping into cool, unforgiving stone.

"You're the Maddie my mom suspects. That's why she didn't want you at her house."

Something inside me wrenches. "Why would your mom think it was me?" I try to make my voice sound angry, strong, but it comes out the opposite.

"Maybe because you tried to take my sister's place as soon as she was gone." Miles moves toward me, closing the space between us fast. Too fast. "She disappears, and the next day, you're suddenly a cheerleader. Friends with her friends. Dating her boyfriend. Sounds a little suspicious, doesn't it?"

My heart pounds. I've been the Marianos' prime suspect this whole time. "You're kidding me, right? The guy literally everyone suspects is going to accuse *me*?" The rage shakes my voice. I don't know whether I want to scream or cry.

There's no space between us now. He's towering over me,

eyes dark as night. No one has ever hated me as much as he does.

For the first time, I think maybe Miles Mariano could kill.

"I never did anything to Sophie," I insist. "And I'm being stalked too. Obviously if anyone is behind her disappearance, it's whoever was harassing her for months. Not me."

His jaw is still tight. He doesn't want to believe me, but he has no choice. There's no way I could fake my own stalking. I couldn't have taken those pictures of myself.

"I'm sorry your sister's missing. I hope she ran away from whoever this creep is and she's safe somewhere. But right now, the same thing is happening to me and I'm not safe. And you're the only one who knows enough about all of this to help me."

Miles backs away, giving me space again, and I want to gulp down air after holding my breath the whole time he was near me.

He lets my words sink in for a full minute. Part of him knows he should believe me. Wants to believe I'm still the girl he always thought I was. Another part sees the cheerleader in front of him, in her tiny shorts and dyed hair, and doubts whether he knows anything about her at all.

Finally, he says, "You're seriously dating *Jordan*?"

"Yes. We didn't start dating right away. We—"

Miles holds up a hand. "Doesn't matter. Just didn't think you'd end up with a guy like him."

"Why? Because he's too good for me?" Because Jordan is the popular, rich, gorgeous jock and Miles thinks I'm still the lonely loser he knew in middle school.

He snorts. "The roid-raging, future frat boy with a drinking problem? No. You're too good for him. At least, you used to be."

I twist the promise ring on my finger. Miles has no idea what he's talking about. "What does that say about your sister?"

"Soph was too good for him too."

No, she was nowhere near good enough for Jordan. That's why he's with me.

"You believe me now, right?" I ask.

Miles lowers his voice. "You swear you don't know anything about what happened to my sister?"

I could tell him now. About the last conversation I had with Sophie.

But I can't bring myself to form the words.

"I swear I don't know anything."

CHAPTER ELEVEN

IN MY ROOM, I finish setting up my new phone. Even though I don't want my stalker to have access to me again, I need to be able to communicate with Mom and Jordan and Natalie and Miles . . . and maybe the police.

Plus, I've been going through social media withdrawals. I tap through stories and scroll through my feeds, liking posts I missed.

Until I get a notification.

Dread swallows me. I click and the image from my stalker churns the acid in my stomach.

A white house with blue trim, taken from the opposite side of the road. A duplex.

My house.

i know where you live

They're not just following me around town or sending me ominous DMs now—they've tracked down my address.

What if . . . they're out there right now?

I race to the window, heart thundering in my ears—

But the yard and street are vacant. Nothing but grass, trees, an asphalt road, and a concrete sidewalk.

The knowledge does nothing to calm my pounding heart. Because they're out there somewhere. Watching and waiting for their opportunity.

I planned to sit on my roof and read, but that's not happening now.

Mom is still at work, and Mabel and Miles are at the diner closing up. I'm all alone.

With shaking hands, I message Miles. The first time I've ever texted him, and this is what I'm sharing.

> Look what my stalker sent me.

I send him a screenshot, and his reply comes two minutes later.

> Fuck.
>
> Should be home soon.
>
> But I can leave now if you're alone.

Even though I don't want to be alone, I text back:

> That's okay. I think they're gone.

Besides, Mom should be back any minute, so I won't be alone for long.

I fold and put away my clean clothes from the basket at my feet, except . . . one of my thongs is missing. The lacy, black pair Jordan bought me at Victoria's Secret. I search through every drawer, but they're not here.

A blush creeps up my cheeks. *Please* tell me they didn't get mixed into Mom's laundry.

I check in the dryer downstairs. Empty. Then I check the washer, the laundry basket, and Mom's dresser drawers. But they aren't anywhere.

Maybe they got eaten up by the dryer. They must be in the same place where everyone's missing socks end up.

When I'm back in my room, the corner of the bed catches my eye. I made my bed like I do every morning, but the corner looks rumpled. I don't remember sitting on it when I got home. Did I?

I must have.

To kill time and distract myself until Mom gets home, I wake my laptop and open up tab number ten to scroll through Reddit—the corner of the internet filled with amateur sleuths and their endless true crime conspiracy theories. Everyone has something to say about Sophie's case.

Legal adults have the right to disappear if they want. Sophie was eighteen.

There's no way this girl is still alive. If she really did run away, what teenage girl would leave her phone behind? And would she really not leave a note for her parents at least?

100% she overdosed and people at that party hid her body. it's a huge coverup.

She's been missing nearly a year. The odds that she's still alive are slim to none.

Then there are the people who claim they've seen her. Most of the stories nothing more than disgusting ploys for attention.

Saw her at a gas station here in Florida!! Offered to help her but she denied who she was and told me to f off. Really rude actually.

this girl is being trafficked in arizona. she was in a hotel parking lot last night. could be anywhere by now tho. cops won't do anything of course. we can give all the tips we want but they don't believe any of them anymore.

I'm 90% sure I saw Sophie at a ranch in New Hampshire. It's a refuge and rehabilitation kind of place. Women and girls can go there to escape homelessness, abusers, drugs, that kind of thing. Anyway, I went there for a while and I'm pretty sure it was her, but her hair was shorter and she dyed it blonde. It looked like her face, though.

She's in New York. Best place to blend in is in a city with 8 million people, right? She was at my favorite pizza place the other day. Her hair was a mess and she looked so different! Lots of scabs on her face, bags under her eyes, real skinny. She's definitely on something.

This isn't getting me anywhere.

They might not want to talk about her, but Natalie and Liv may be able to tell me a lot more about who might've wanted Sophie gone.

Above my head, the attic creaks. Our duplex is old, and something's always creaking or groaning. When I was younger, I was convinced we had a ghost, and Mom said the house was "settling." How many years does a house need to settle?

I finger the knife in the shallow front pocket of my shorts and breathe slowly before my pulse can quicken.

We don't have a ghost. No one is in our attic. This stalking shit is just messing with my head.

When I notice I have a new email, I'm grateful for the distraction.

Until I see who it's from.

From: madyoungfan@gmail.com

To: maddie05young@gmail.com

i know what you did

be careful who you push too far next

At Sweet Tooth, Liv orders a gluten-free, sugar-free slice of chocolate cake while Natalie and I order sugar cookies and chocolate mousse.

"Normally, I wouldn't recommend coffee after two p.m., but you look like you need it," Liv tells me.

I rub my eyelids, careful not to mess up my makeup. "I didn't sleep great last night."

My stalker's thinly veiled threat kept circulating in my mind. Even when I could no longer keep my eyes open, my mind wouldn't shut off.

be careful who you push too far next

They can't possibly know about that night. Sophie and I were alone.

Then there was yesterday's fight with Jordan that kept replaying in my head.

"We can tell." Liv shovels cake into her mouth and I bite back a snide comment.

My phone buzzes. A text from Jordan.

Want to come over?

A *whoosh* of air escapes my lungs. I guess he's forgiven me for our fight yesterday. Thank god.

There's nothing I want more than to be with Jordan, let him wrap me in his arms, and forget about all of this. But I need to talk to Natalie and Liv first.

Girls day. Rain check?

What are you girls up to?

Indulging our sweet tooths.

Natalie launches into a story about her job at the vet clinic that involves a woman wanting a pawprint stamp from her dead cat. I try not to yawn or let my mind wander to what I really want to discuss: Sophie. ". . . so we literally had to pull out a *frozen cat*, and trust me, getting a pawprint from a frozen cat is a lot harder than it sounds—"

Liv groans at something over my shoulder. "Really? You couldn't go five minutes without your boyfriend?"

Behind me, Jordan is striding into the bakery, waving to us with an easy grin.

"I didn't invite him," I mutter to Liv, even though I don't owe her an explanation, and I'm glad he's here.

His arrival does throw a wrench in my plan to ask Natalie and Liv about Sophie, though. I don't want to rock the boat with Jordan again, and I know bringing her up will do just that.

He takes the empty seat beside me and drapes his arm over the back of my chair, a few beads of sweat at his hairline.

"You're just in time to hear my frozen cat story!" Natalie tells him.

"Great, that's what I came here for." Jordan turns my head by the chin and kisses me, deep and possessive, and it's almost like our fight outside of Mariano's never happened. He tastes sickly sweet.

"Have you been drinking?" I ask.

Jordan only ever drinks at parties, with the exception of the flask he snuck to graduation. A wicked grin spreads across his face. He pulls out his silver flask and gives it a little shake before slipping it back beneath his letterman jacket. "Just a little Jack Daniels."

I murmur, "So we're okay?"

He squeezes my hand. "Of course we are. It's not you I'm mad at—it's him. I hate that guy."

Right. I should've known it wasn't anger Jordan was directing my way: it was concern. Fear. Any fury boiling in Jordan's veins is directed at Miles.

"So what was with the SOS?" Liv asks me.

I glance over at Jordan. I really don't want to do this in front of him. "Maybe you can order a dessert? This is just going to be boring girl-talk."

Jordan settles back into his chair. "Doesn't bother me. As

long as I get to be with my girlfriend." He smiles and kisses me again. I love kissing him, but not so much after he's been drinking. His breath turns sour and his tongue sloppy.

"Ugh," Liv says. "You two are nauseating."

"They're *adorable*," Natalie argues.

A server carrying a tray of milkshakes catches his toe on a chair leg and tumbles, the drinks crashing to the floor. Amid the clatter, smashing glass, and gasps, Jordan rushes over to help. He's such a great guy.

I lean closer to Natalie and Liv. "Can I ask you guys about something?"

"Sure." Natalie dips a spoon into her chocolate mousse.

"Do you actually think Sophie ran away?"

Both of their heads jerk up. Natalie opens her mouth, but Liv cuts her off. "Why?" she demands.

"Because," I whisper. "I think the same person who's stalking me was stalking her."

Natalie's eyes widen, but Liv scoffs and stabs at her cake. "Sophie didn't have a stalker."

"She did. She just didn't tell you about it."

Liv drops her fork with a clatter. "So how the hell would *you* know about it?"

"Miles told me."

Natalie covers her mouth and whispers, "Oh my god."

But Liv rolls her eyes. "Like I'd believe anything that asshole says."

"You don't have to believe him—he has proof. I've seen it."

"Don't you think it's pretty convenient that he's the only person who knows anything about Sophie being stalked? Who has any proof?" Liv raises an eyebrow. "Doesn't seem like much of a coincidence to me."

I want to scream at her that it's not Miles, but Liv made up her mind about him a long time ago. "Did you notice her acting differently before she disappeared?"

Liv freezes, and Natalie reaches out to hold her hand. "Yeah," my best friend whispers. "She was. For weeks."

I nod. Sophie was scared, trying to figure out who the hell her stalker could be, and keeping it all a secret.

But look where keeping a secret like that got her.

"Did either of you see Sophie at Jordan's party?" I ask.

They both nod. "The last time I saw her, she told me she was going upstairs to get a drink. I was already tipsy and distracted." Liv squeezes Natalie's hand. Right. I remember the two of them on the couch together looking very cozy. "So I didn't think about it in the moment, but Jordan's parents keep all the alcohol at the bar downstairs. She had no reason to leave the basement. I spent the rest of the night with Natalie, so I didn't see her again after that."

"That was the last time I saw her too." Natalie sighs solemnly.

"So you think she was lying about where she was headed?"

Liv shrugs. "I've been over that night in my head so many times, I honestly don't know what to think anymore. She used to tell me everything, but by that night . . . it was like there was a whole ocean of things she was keeping from me."

"Do you think that's when she ran away?"

Liv bites her lip, then leans toward me. "I don't think she ran away."

"You think something happened to her?"

"I . . ." She glances over at Natalie, whose eyes have gone glassy. "I don't know what to think. But I do think, if something happened to her, Miles is behind it."

"He definitely is." Natalie wipes at her eyes with her napkin. "He hurt her. I know he did."

"But *why*? What could he have to gain from making his sister disappear?" No one seems to be able to answer that question.

"All I know is they never got along," Liv says. "I'd go to her mom's house or her dad's house in Hartford, and whenever Miles was there, they'd argue the whole time. Sophie blamed him for their parents splitting up. He was a slacker and didn't want to listen to anybody, and their parents couldn't agree on what to do about it. Then he punched her and they wanted to keep the two of them apart, for Sophie's protection."

His parents wanted to keep him and Sophie apart to protect her. But the whole reason Miles punched Sophie was to protect me.

Sophie is a shitty sister for blaming her brother for her parents' divorce. If she was here now, I'd give her an earful.

Jordan stands, shaking hands with tiny, frail Mrs. Wallis, who thanks him for helping her employee with the mess.

"Siblings fight," I say. "That doesn't mean Miles hurt her."

"You don't know how many death threats I heard him make. He told her to get hit by a truck, go jump off a cliff, go lay in traffic." Liv glances around to make sure no one else is listening. "He told her he was going to kill her."

CHAPTER TWELVE

EVEN WHEN I'M brushing my teeth, I feel eyes on me.

I keep glancing in the mirror to make sure I'm alone. At the door to make sure I locked it.

I have. I'm alone.

But I don't feel alone.

Right as I splash my face with cold water, my phone pings.

you wanted to be her didnt you

this is what happens to girls like sophie mariano

How can someone make my heart hammer with just a few words?

They haven't hurt me. Yet. But I have no idea what the person on the other side of these messages is capable of.

This sounds like something Ash would say. *Why are you trying so hard to be like her?*

If anyone in Beaumont is convinced I wanted to not just replace Sophie but *be* her, it's Ash. Or Miles's mom. But she wouldn't be the one stalking me, and she definitely wouldn't stalk her own daughter.

Luckily, if Ash is my stalker, I can probably get her to crack.

She's never been a good liar. The tricky part is getting her to talk to me.

A split second after I set my phone back down, a loud *bang* reverberates in the house.

I jump and a scream rips out of my throat.

Was that the front door? Did someone break in?

I sprint for my bedroom, still in my towel, and slam the door shut behind me. *Shit.* I forgot my phone. How am I supposed to call the police about my stalker breaking into my house when my phone is in another room? I don't know if I should risk sneaking back across the hall. My stalker could be heading up the stairs right now—

Someone pounds on my door to Mabel's side of the duplex. "Madalyn?" Miles calls. "You good?"

My heart is in my throat, preventing any words from forming.

He barges in without waiting for an answer. And his gaze lands directly on the tiny white towel barely covering my naked body.

"I heard a thud," I breathe. "I . . . I thought . . ."

"Shit. That was probably the bookshelf I'm putting up. It fell over." For once, he actually has the decency to look sheepish.

I press a hand to my chest, willing my heart to slow. *Thank god.* No one broke into my house. "Okay, well, thanks for scaring the shit out of me. You can go now."

He told her he was going to kill her. I shake Liv's words out of my mind.

Miles stretches and places his hands on his head, flashing the flat plane of his abdomen. My breath catches at the hint of abs, at the *V* that disappears into his jeans. "I'm not in a hurry."

I clear my throat. "You need to be. I have to get dressed."

His smirk tells me I said the wrong thing. "I'm not stopping you."

I roll my eyes, even as his gaze travels from my neck to my legs and sets every inch of me on fire. He's imagining what lies beneath the towel, and he'll have to keep imagining because he's never going to find out. "Get out of my room."

Miles surveys my wall art of landmarks from New York—the Statue of Liberty, the Empire State Building, the skyline at night.

There's something mesmerizing about the features of his face in the dim light. The line of his lips, the sharp edge to his jaw, the way his eyes dance. All of it beckoning you to stare, daring you to look away if you can.

"Somebody loves the city," Miles says.

"Quit stalling."

"You wanna live there?"

He's not going anywhere. Maybe if I indulge him, he'll get bored and leave. "Yeah. I've wanted to live there since I was, like, ten."

"That where you're going to college?"

"No, Jordan got recruited by a college in California."

His eyebrows scrunch together. "Okay . . . that doesn't tell me where you're going."

"The same place, obviously." My towel is growing loose. I clutch it to my chest.

"Nothing obvious about it. Why not live in the place you've been dreaming about since you were ten?"

"Do you know how expensive New York is?"

He gives a short laugh. "Do you know how expensive California is?"

I roll my eyes. "I don't need you to explain cost-of-living to me." I already have Mom chastising me for my choice of college—I don't need to hear it from Miles too. Besides, Jordan's parents are paying for our apartment. My cost of living will be lower in California with Jordan than in New York alone.

"You should go to a cheap college here and then go live in New York. Do your book stuff there."

"How do you know about that?" The hair along the back of my neck stands up. I've only told Mom about the plans I once had to work in publishing.

"Sixth grade. We had to put our dream job up on some board. Yours was 'book publisher in New York.'"

Something in my chest flutters. He remembers that. Sixth-grade me never felt anything other than forgettable, invisible.

To everyone except Miles Mariano.

I shrug like it doesn't matter. "Not anymore."

In a few quick steps, he closes the space between us, his chest nearly pressing against mine. Not a single muscle in my body moves. "You know what I don't get?" His voice is low, dangerous. "Why you hide who you really are. Why you pretend to be someone you're not."

I swallow the lump in my throat. "I'm not pretending. This is me." But the words don't sound convincing, even to my ears.

He shakes his head. "No, it isn't."

His fingers brush against my bare shoulder . . . before drifting lazily to my collarbone. The nerve endings there spring to life, and all I can hear is my pulse thrumming in my ears and my ragged breaths. I can't help the shudder that rattles my bones. The goosebumps that prick up along my skin.

I should stop him. Push him away from me. But I don't want to.

"The Madalyn I know?" His quiet voice sends liquid heat pooling between my legs. He trails a finger leisurely from my collarbone up to my neck, turning my knees to jelly. "Wants to live in New York. Wants to add new books to the world." He leans so close, his breath caresses my ear. "Wants me."

I force myself to shove his chest, propelling us apart. "I've never wanted you."

He snorts. "You're even pretending with yourself."

"No. You're just an arrogant asshole."

He bends at the knees until we're eye level. "An arrogant asshole you want touching you," he says. "All. Over."

God, yes.

No. Wait. Hell *no.*

"No, I don't."

He steps closer, forcing me to back up. When he leans in, I brace myself. He's about to kiss me—

But he bends around me and snatches the book off my bedside table. "So do you and Jordan act out your favorite books?"

"What? Don't be gross." I try to snatch the book back from him. On a spice scale, this one is scorching, and I don't want Miles to know what I use to take my mind off life at the end of each night.

He chuckles. "Oh, so sex with Jordan is gross. Poor guy."

"You know that's not what I meant. You just don't need to know about my sex life with Jordan. It's none of your business."

"That's why you read these books, though, right? For ideas?" His fingers drift down the spine, and I can still feel the ghost of his touch on my shoulder. On my collarbone. On my neck.

"Is that why you watch porn? For ideas? Because let me tell you, that's probably the last place you should be getting your material."

"Nah, I actually ask a girl what she likes." He waves the book in the air. "Or I read what's on her bedside table."

I grab for the book again, but in the scuffle, my towel starts to drop. I clutch it before it can fall to the floor.

Miles tosses the clothes from the top of my dresser onto my bed. "Get dressed." He holds up the book. "I'll start reading."

I stomp out, slamming my bedroom door and then the bathroom door to make it clear how much he pisses me off. Once I'm in my denim shorts and crop top, I head back for my room, where Miles is on the floor with his back pressed against the wall, already on the fifth page. The first sex scene is on page ten.

I grab my brush and start yanking at my hair and don't even care when the pain makes me teary.

His dark, beautiful eyes flick up to me and he shuts the book with a quiet *fwap* before standing. He sets the book back on my bedside table and holds his hand out.

"What?" I ask.

"The brush."

I hand it to him slowly, totally confused. He sits on my bed and pats the space between his legs.

"Um. No."

"Trust me, I'm a pro. Mom and Soph made me brush their hair all the time when I was a kid."

"I'm not getting on my bed with you."

He smirks. "Afraid of what you'll do?"

"Yeah. I might punch you or knee you in the groin."

"I'll be brushing your hair. Totally innocent. I won't touch you anywhere else until you ask me."

Until. Cocky son of a bitch.

I huff. "You better not pull it," I warn him, and sit between his legs.

His knees are spread far enough apart that we don't touch. Just his hand on my head, holding me surprisingly tenderly as he runs the brush gently through my hair. Tingles race down from my scalp to my toes. I can't remember the last time someone brushed my hair. A guy definitely never has.

I swallow hard and keep talking because if I don't, I might lean back against him. "Why does everyone say you and Sophie didn't get along?"

Instead of getting defensive like I expect, he snorts. "Because we were brother and sister, born less than a year apart. No one knows how to push your buttons better. She got under my skin; I got under hers. Didn't help that we were so different. We couldn't agree on shit. Not even what kind of pizza to order."

"Please tell me you're not a pineapple-on-pizza person."

"Hell no. I'm not a psycho."

That brings a smile to my face. Until I remember what Liv said about him. "Liv seemed to think your arguments were more serious than pizza toppings."

"Liv doesn't know shit. And she's loyal to a fault. She always took Soph's side, even if she was the one starting shit half the time. I know Liv buys into all the media and internet bullshit that I'm involved. But I don't need to waste my time proving myself to her. Or anybody. Just need to find my sister and the scumbag who was following her."

"So what changed? Why did Sophie want you to go with her to Jordan's party if you two didn't get along?"

He shrugs. "She changed. She realized she shouldn't have been blaming me for our parents' split, and then the stalking started. She needed me. Shitty it took something like that to get us on the same team." His mouth twists with regret.

He finally started to get his sister back. And then she was yanked away from him again.

"I'm going to try to talk to Ash," I tell him. "I really think she's the stalker, and if she is, maybe I can get her to crack and tell me what she knows about Sophie."

Miles lifts my hair off my neck, skimming my skin, and I can't help it—I shiver. I can practically hear him holding back a satisfied chuckle. He finishes brushing my hair and I quickly slide off the bed and grab my book before he can start reading it again.

"Come on," he fake-whines. "I need a new book. I've read all of mine five times."

Reluctantly, I head for my bookshelf and skim the spines. I pluck out *Pride and Prejudice* and hand it over. A book written in

1800s English should keep him busy and out of my hair for a while.

Before he can take it, I press the paperback to my chest. "This is my favorite book," I tell him. "So if you even dog-ear a page, I'll burn every book in your room."

He gives an exaggerated gasp. "You *wouldn't*."

"Fuck around and find out."

He lets out a surprised, genuine laugh and I hate the way it curls my toes. "You're kidding me, right? This thing is falling apart."

The spine has several long, white cracks, and the pages may have turned brittle, but none of them have fallen out yet. "She's well-loved," I correct.

When his hand touches the knob, I almost ask him to stay.

But then the front door opens and Mom calls out, "Hey, kid! Your wonderful mother is home!"

Miles flashes me a smile. "Thanks for the book."

Once he's gone, I can breathe again. I run my fingers through my hair. Not a single knot or tangle.

The Miles I know and the one everyone else sees are starting to seem like two totally different people.

I ask Ash to meet me at Mariano's after my shift. I nearly fall off my stool behind the register when she texts back two hours later: *k.*

When she drops into the chair across from me, she pulls her vape out. After our friendship ended, she added vaping to her personality. Polluting the girls' bathroom with the sweet, citrusy scent. Glowering at me and whichever friend I brought with me as we made our way from the stalls to the sinks.

Before she can puff on it, I hold up my hand. "Um. You're not allowed to use that in here."

She rolls her eyes, as if I'm the one who made the rule. "Fine. Then you can buy me a coffee. So what do you want?"

"I want to ask you something, and I want you to be honest."

She snorts. "And you couldn't have texted me?"

No, because then I couldn't tell if you're lying.

Miles saunters over to us. "You ordering?"

Ash doesn't even glance up from her phone at him. "Coffee."

"I'm good, thanks."

He raises an eyebrow at me, points to her, and mouths: *Ash?*

When I nod, she glances back and forth between us. "Why are you still here?"

"Right. Tea coming right up."

"Coffee!" she shouts after him, drawing a few stares from a weary old couple and the stay-at-home mom club with the strollers and screeching toddlers.

I lean closer to Ash and lower my voice. "Have you been stalking me?"

Ash cackles. "*Stalking* you? Don't worry. I have much better things to do with my time."

I track all the subtle movements of her face, but she actually seems genuine. "So you didn't send me any DMs from a burner account? Or take pictures of me?"

Ash hunches over the table, dark-rimmed eyes narrowed. "Listen. I know you think everyone's obsessed with you, but let me tell you something. No one in this town could give less of a shit about you. Especially me. So no. I'm not *stalking* you."

God, she's awful. I don't know how I forced myself to be friends with her for so many years. "Fine. Good."

She flops back in her seat. "Besides, it's obvious who it is."

"Who?"

She searches the diner until she finds Miles, cleaning the counter by the coffee maker with a rag. "Your new neighbor."

I roll my eyes because I'm sick of people accusing Miles with no proof and even sicker of repeating myself.

"He's into you." She admits it begrudgingly.

I open my mouth to protest, but that's when Miles brings her coffee over. She immediately dumps three packets of sugar into her mug.

He plants both hands on the table and leans down toward me. "Ten minutes before tutoring time. I'm *so* excited to learn."

When he heads back to the counter, Ash raises a pierced eyebrow as if to say, *See?* But she doesn't comment.

"Have you heard anything about Sophie's disappearance?" I ask her.

"Plenty. Drug overdose, suicide, runaway—"

"But what do you actually believe?"

"I thought you were glad she was gone." Her brown eyes are cool. "Or have you changed your mind because you're fucking her brother?"

My spine goes rigid, but I try to keep my voice even. "Of course not. I'm trying to figure out what happened because I'm pretty sure whoever is stalking me was stalking her too."

She laughs again, but when I keep glaring at her, she rolls her eyes. "All right. Say you actually are being stalked." A few choice names I could call her pop into my head, but I bite my tongue. "If you're looking for someone who was obsessed with Sophie, look at her best friend. Everyone knows Liv was in love with her and tried to split Jordan and Sophie up."

I stiffen, but doubt quickly seeps in. "But then why would she make Sophie disappear if she wanted to be with her?"

"Maybe Sophie rejected her, and Liv couldn't handle it."

Ash could be onto something. If Liv had feelings for Sophie, maybe she admitted to them and their friendship changed after Sophie rejected her.

I need to talk to someone who was closer to Sophie and Liv to figure out what actually happened between them.

A black backpack thunks onto our table. Miles starts pulling out his books. A small part of me is relieved to see him, that his presence gives Ash a reason to leave.

"Question," she says. "What's it like to kill someone?"

Miles stops moving. My breath catches in my throat. "Ash—"

"I'm just curious," she tells me. All fake-innocence.

A second ago she was accusing Liv. Now she's back to Miles.

His movements stiffen, but he keeps his mouth clamped shut. The silence between us grows tangible, a weight pressing down on me.

This is why so many people think he was involved in Sophie's disappearance. Not just because of his reputation—because he never defends himself. Not to the media, not to the press, not on social media, and not now.

Because he still feels guilty for not being there when she needed him.

"Hey, Ash?" I match her high, singsong voice. "You don't know what the hell you're talking about, so why don't you shut the fuck up."

Ash drains the rest of her coffee, smacks her mug back down on the table, and stands. "I'm leaving. She's paying for my coffee."

For a few seconds, the only sounds are dishes clattering in the kitchen, diners chattering, and Miles flipping pages in his study guide.

I lean closer to him and stop just before our arms touch. "Why don't you ever defend yourself?"

He doesn't lift his gaze from his book. "What's it matter when no one's listening?"

"Because at least you give them the option of believing the truth instead of just . . . letting them continue believing a lie."

Finally, his eyes meet mine. Dark and piercing, yet

somehow still warm. Eyes I'll see in my dreams. "You believe me, right?"

I nod. He wouldn't be helping me if he was behind this.

"That's all I care about." The intensity in his gaze, in his voice, sends goosebumps down my arms. I rub them away before he can notice, and he returns his attention to his book.

I'm the one he wants to believe him. Not the media, not his neighbors, not his mom.

Me.

CHAPTER THIRTEEN

I PULL open the fourth drawer on my dresser for my favorite pair of silk pajama shorts. When I can't find them, I search in my hamper. Then in my other drawers, even though I always put them in the fourth drawer. I check Mom's dresser because she has a bad habit of grabbing all the clothes from the dryer and tossing them in her dresser. But they aren't in her room either.

They're gone.

Maybe my thong wasn't eaten by the dryer at all. Someone has been in my room. Touching my stuff and taking it.

And Miles is the one with the best opportunity to sneak into my room. He's been in here before. Maybe he pocketed my shorts when I was changing in the bathroom the other day.

Jordan would say this is proof Miles is my stalker, but even if he did take my thong and shorts, it doesn't necessarily mean he's stalking me. He could just be a perv. Or trying to piss me off.

Screw him. I'm marching in there, getting my clothes back, and putting a chain lock on my door.

I sneak through to the landing that separates my room from

Miles's and leads up to the attic. Chaotic drums and guitars coming from his phone remind me of those old punk rock bands from the 2000s that Mom still likes to blast on Sunday mornings when she makes pancakes. The sound isn't coming from his room, though.

When I knock, there's no answer. I try the knob, and somehow, my heart pounds even harder when it turns.

Miles isn't in his room. His bedroom door is open, and when I step around the end of his bed, I spot the bathroom door across the hall cracked open. Mixed with his music is the spray of the shower.

Perfect.

Miles's room is spare, almost as if he doesn't live here at all. His bed is a tangled mess of black sheets, a blanket kicked off onto the floor. A few socks, shirts, and a pair of jeans are scattered across the pale carpet. One of the drawers on his dresser hangs out, and his closet door is open, the inside bare. Not even a single hanger in sight. His laptop sits near his pillow, the charger plugged in by the nightstand that holds nothing but a lamp and my copy of *Pride and Prejudice*. A wooden bookshelf shoved against the wall is stuffed with paperbacks and hardcovers. Stephen King, Shirley Jackson, Gillian Flynn. My favorite book sticks out like a sore thumb among his collection.

I check under the bed for my clothes. Nothing. Not even a forgotten shoe or a dust bunny. Mabel must've deep-cleaned before he moved in. Quietly, I open his dressers and dig through them. His shirts, pants, socks, boxers. So he's a boxers guy.

I yank my hand out. Gross. I don't need to know that.

Except I can't stop picturing it. Miles, in nothing but these black boxers, sprawled across his bed with that smirk on his face. Inviting me to join him.

I give his room one last sweep, but it's clear he hasn't taken my clothes.

Relief races through me until I realize what this means. If Miles hasn't taken my clothes, someone else has.

Someone else has been in my room.

I sneak back toward the door. And that's when I notice the shower isn't running.

Shit.

His music is still playing. Something angry but morose. Mournful. Evanescence, maybe? As long as his music is playing, he should be—

Something slams into me from behind, shoving me toward the wall so fast, I'm afraid I'm going to collide with it face first until I'm spun around and my back thuds against the plaster instead.

Miles braces his arms on either side of my head, leaning so close, the sandalwood scent of his shampoo floods my nose. A drop of water hits my cheek from the dark, dripping hair that nearly falls into his eyes.

He's in nothing but a pair of thin pajama pants that sit low on his hips. His biceps, his shoulders, his abs are still damp. I ache to touch every single inch. Starting at the soft skin on his neck and working my way down. Slowly.

He isn't touching me, but his entire body might as well be crushing mine because I can't breathe. Can't move. Can hardly remember my name.

Madalyn. No, Maddie.

"So I can't go in your room, but you can come in mine?" The rumble of his voice reverberates all the way down to my toes.

I swallow once, twice, but the lump in my throat isn't going away. "I thought you took my clothes. They're missing."

His mouth twists up. "I don't steal clothes." He drops his hand from beside my head and plays with the hem of my shirt. "I peel them off and leave them on the floor."

"I thought you . . . um." God, I can't think with him this

close to me. With his taut, toned body looming over me. "Haven't been with a girl before."

Maybe that's changed since our conversation. Maybe he found someone to bring to his bed. If so, I'm glad I wasn't around to hear it.

"I've never fucked a girl," he clarifies. A wicked smile blooms across his face. "Wanna show me how it's done?"

More than anything. But I force myself to say, "Actually, I think I'll let you die a virgin."

Somehow, he gets even closer without touching me. I don't know how that's possible. There can't be more than a centimeter of space between our chests now. "Tell me you actually love that asshole. Try to convince me."

"Jordan—" But my voice quavers when I say his name. I clear my throat. "Jordan isn't an asshole. And I do. Love him."

Of course I love Jordan. He's the perfect boyfriend. I've planned my whole life around him.

But I can't deny it anymore—I want Miles Mariano. I want to travel to an alternate dimension where Jordan doesn't exist and ride Miles all night until I'm screaming just so I can get it out of my system.

He smirks at me. "That wasn't convincing. If I had to guess, I'd say you didn't come in here looking for missing clothes." His mouth is so close to mine now, his cool breath hits my skin. "You came in here looking for me. So you could beg me to make you come."

I flatten my hands against the wall in a desperate attempt to stay upright. My knees are jelly. About to give out any second. "I have a boyfriend and a vibrator for that. I don't need anything from you. Certainly not . . . *that.*"

"But you want it. Don't you, Madalyn?" He brushes my hair behind my ear, sending an electric current down my spine. His palm rests against my neck, and some wild part of me wants his hand to move to my throat and squeeze. "You want someone who will make you scream. That's why you're still here. That's why every time I touch you, you wish I was using my mouth."

I can't take it anymore. I'm either going to jump on him or have an orgasm right here in front of him, and he hasn't even kissed me yet.

No. He can't kiss me. I have a boyfriend. Jordan is perfect. He deserves a loyal girlfriend. He told me he's been cheated on before—I won't do that to him.

I consider shoving Miles away, but touching his bare chest will unravel me. Instead, I hip-check him and head for the door. Somehow, walking away from him is one of the hardest things I've ever done.

"This?" I wave a finger back and forth between us. "Isn't happening. Got it?"

His arrogant smile tells me he doesn't believe me for a second. "Sure, Madalyn. You let me know when you're done pretending. When you want something real, you know where to find me."

I wake to my phone blowing up. Dreams of Miles kissing his way down my body and making me scream with pleasure quickly fade when I notice each notification is a DM from madyoungfan.

All images. No words.

In one picture, I'm opening the door to Mariano's, my copper brown hair in a braid so I don't get it in a patron's food.

In another, Mom and I are leaving the grocery store, cloth bags dangling from our arms. The next is us leaving Sweet Tooth with a box of freshly made donuts.

Then I'm alone again. My back to the camera, cutting through the town square to get home.

Sitting at an umbrella table outside of Mariano's.

The last one is blurrier, but my heart stops when I recognize my house.

My stalker zoomed in. Their camera aimed at the window.

Through the glass, I'm sitting on the couch in the living room. Alone.

My phone screen blurs. How did I not know they were out there? Why didn't I feel their eyes on me?

Tears slip down my cheeks.

There's no way my stalker can see me ten feet away from my second-story window, but I still duck beneath my bedsheet, searching for the privacy I can no longer seem to find.

When my phone rings, my heart leaps into my throat.

An unknown number.

I stare at the screen, letting the phone ring twice, three times, four times. Then it stops.

How would my stalker get my number? No, it's probably just a spam caller.

But my relief is cut short when the screen lights up again with another call.

I let out a slow breath. Then swipe my thumb across the screen.

Neither of us says a word.

I don't even hear anyone breathing, no matter how close I press the phone to my ear.

"Hello?"

Still nothing.

"Answer me." The voice that comes out of me is loud but shaky. "At least have the guts to say something."

More silence. Shortly followed by the beep of the call ending.

"Hey, hon?" Mom's strained voice calls up the stairs. "Can you come down here?"

I slip downstairs like a ghost. All I wanted was to not be an invisible girl, lingering in the shadows. Now I've gotten what I wanted, and all I want is to be invisible again. Be someone no one cares about enough to follow, to torment, to obsess over.

Mom is standing in the driveway, clutching both arms to her chest. Standing in front of a police cruiser.

Across the garage door, someone spray-painted *DIE SLUT* in big block letters.

Each letter is a stab to the gut. I wrap my arms around my stomach, like if I make myself small enough, I'll disappear.

How many people have driven past and seen this? When did *Mom* see this?

I text Jordan.

> My stalker vandalized our garage...

His response is immediate.

> Wtfffff

> I'm coming over. Be there soon.

I almost want to tell him not to come. I don't want him to see those words, obviously left for me. But I also want him to hold me and tell me everything's going to be okay.

Mom gestures me over, and I head toward her and the police officer even though all I want to do is crawl back into bed and bury my face in my pillow. Some days aren't worth waking up to.

The officer holds out his hand to me. He looks like Dr. Avery from Grey's Anatomy, and despite the situation, Mom is clearly appreciative.

"Hey there. Officer Jackson." When I don't respond, he adds, "Maddie, right?"

"Right."

"Your mom called us about some vandalism." He nods to

the garage. Like I could've missed that. "You have any idea who would've done something like this?"

"I know exactly who did this."

They're both surprised at that. "Who?" Mom asks.

"Well. I don't know their name," I admit. "But there's someone online who's been stalking me."

Mom spins to face me, eyes wide. "Stalking you?"

I should've told her about this a while ago. Before it got this bad. I was stupid to think whoever's doing this would get bored and stop on their own.

"They've been following me around for a while. Taking really creepy pictures of me, sending me these threatening messages, emails, stealing my clothes."

"What pictures?" Mom asks. "What *clothes*? What's going on?"

I look Officer Jackson right in the eye. "They were stalking Sophie Mariano too."

He holds up his hands. "Okay, okay. Let's back up. When did this start?"

"Um. A few weeks ago."

Mom's lips compress. "Why am I just now hearing about this?"

"I didn't think it was that big of a deal. I thought they'd go away." I turn back to Officer Jackson. "But then I found out Sophie and I have the same stalker. I think maybe whatever they did to her . . ." I can't bring myself to finish the thought out loud.

Officer Jackson's eyebrows fold together. "How do you know they're the same person?"

"Miles showed me the screenshots."

"Miles Mariano?"

"Yes. Sophie's brother."

Officer Jackson and Mom exchange a look. "I'll be honest

with you, Miss Young. I wouldn't take Miles Mariano at his word."

"I'm not." I can't help the frustration that leaks into my voice. "He showed me the screenshots. I saw proof."

Mom pinches the bridge of her nose. "Let me see this."

I pull out my phone to show her the messages. She frowns at the screen for a few seconds, then holds up my phone to Officer Jackson. "What are you going to do about this?"

Relief floods through me. Mom's on my side. She believes me. Sees how scary this is. She's going to put a stop to it.

"There's not a whole lot we can do with what you've got here," he admits.

"There's nothing you can do?" I will my voice to come out forceful, angry, but instead, I sound like a small, terrified child.

Mom wraps an arm around me.

"We need proof of an identity," he says.

As if I'm supposed to find that out myself. They're the police —it's their job to do the investigating. Why is the entire burden of tracking down my stalker falling onto my shoulders?

"Isn't it obvious? It's that Mariano boy."

I stiffen beneath Mom's arm. "No, it isn't."

"Hon. You just said your clothes have gone missing. There's only one person who could've gotten in your room without us noticing."

"I know it isn't him."

"How?"

I can't tell her I snuck into Miles's room. Definitely not in front of Officer Jackson. "Um. He invited me over. And he went to the bathroom, and I kind of scoped things out. None of my stuff was in his room."

Mom's voice goes up an octave. "You're hanging out with him?"

Officer Jackson steps forward to interject. "Do you have a security system?"

"No, but what does that matter when this boy is sneaking in through my daughter's bedroom door? What we need is a deadbolt."

"That's a good first step. The next thing I'd do is get a security camera." He turns to me. "And keep the evidence. That'll help build your case—give us something to work with."

Officer Jackson leaves us his card and tells us to give him a call if we need anything. In silence, Mom and I find brushes and vinegar to scrub the spray paint off the garage.

"You've gotta tell me these things, kid. No more secrets, okay?"

I nod, even though Mom's already dealing with the stress of her promotion and saving up for all my college expenses. The last thing I want to do is add another burden.

"What clothes are you missing?"

"A pair of pajama shorts and underwear." My face warms at the thought of someone digging into my drawers and taking my thong. At having to admit that out loud to my mom.

"I'll look in my room just to make sure I didn't take them by accident." Mom scrubs at the black *S*. "I wish you hadn't kept this from me. We could've gone to the police sooner."

"I did go to the police. They wouldn't do anything."

Mom pauses her scrubbing. "When did you go to the police?"

"A couple weeks ago. Miles took me."

"Miles?"

A screen door smacks shut. *Speak of the devil.*

Miles leans against the porch railing. "What happened over there?"

My face warms, thinking of the dreams I had about him last night. About our encounter in his room.

Mom scowls at him and turns back to the garage door.

"Graffiti," I manage.

Instead of taking the stairs, he hops over the railing in an effortless arc and saunters up to us.

"Here." He holds out his hand and I give him the brush. He scrubs hard and loud, and I'm grateful for a break.

But Mom looks like she smells something sour. "I need some water," she tells me before dropping her brush and disappearing inside.

"Sorry you had to see this," Miles says.

"What are you talking about?"

"Someone is tired of me sleeping around, I guess. They must've left this as a message for me."

A short laugh bursts free from my chest. I pick up the brush Mom discarded on the pavement. "Slut-shaming. Not a fan."

"Me neither. So thanks for helping me get rid of this."

A small flicker of light ignites in my chest. Somehow, Miles managed to make me laugh about this awful situation. Managed to make me feel better, even for just a few seconds.

Behind us, a car rumbles into the driveway. Jordan's BMW. I forgot I texted him.

He slams the door a bit harder than necessary. "Hey." His voice is tight. The way it always is whenever Miles is around.

After the argument outside of Mariano's, the last thing I want is for Jordan and Miles to be anywhere near each other.

I sweep my hair up in a ponytail and fan my face. Where's Mom with the water?

"Go," Jordan tells Miles. "I've got this."

Jordan rips the brush out of his hand and dips it back in our bucket of vinegar and water.

Miles shrugs and takes an easygoing step back. "Be my guest."

Then he wraps an arm around my waist.

Jordan's eyes bug out of his head.

I freeze, but Jordan leaps into action. With a huge, meaty palm, he shoves Miles away from me.

"Jordan!"

Miles barely stumbles back a step. "Relax. She likes it."

Oh my *god*. "No, I don't!"

"Buddy, you better fuck off," Jordan growls.

Miles shrugs, hands in his pockets, and flashes me a half-smile before disappearing inside.

Jordan hisses, "He needs to stay the hell away from you." He scrubs vigorously at the graffiti. "Why don't you ever tell him to leave you alone?"

I don't get why Jordan's anger is directed at me now. I don't control what Miles does.

Before I can defend myself, Jordan gestures to the spray paint. "He's obviously the one who did this."

"Miles?"

"Who else?"

Except it can't be Miles. He wouldn't call me a slut. He wouldn't spray paint his own garage door or help me scrub the word off if he put it there. I'm tired of everyone jumping to the same conclusion with no proof.

"Liv," I blurt.

Jordan frowns, his forehead sweaty. "Why her?"

If you're looking for someone who was obsessed with Sophie, look at her best friend. Maybe Liv can't stand that I took Sophie's place. Maybe I remind her too much of the girl she loved who would never love her back.

I take a step toward Jordan and catch a whiff of something. The piss-warm stink of beer? But no, he wouldn't drive if he'd been drinking. "I just have a bad feeling about her."

Jordan shakes his head, and a lump forms in my throat. "That doesn't make any sense. No offense, but Liv doesn't even want to be around you, let alone follow you." He points the brush at our house. "But that guy? He's always around. He lives with you. Works with you. *Touches* you. He's obviously obsessed with you. It makes me sick."

I know Jordan's wrong, and it sucks that we can't be on the same side about this. I'll just have to prove it's Liv.

"If you don't tell him to stay away from you," Jordan says, "I will."

I lure Brett away from his video games with the promise of free food. I drop the money for his fries and grilled ham and cheese into the register before I take the basket of food out to him on my break.

Across from me at the umbrella table, Brett scarfs down his sandwich. The sky is cloudy today, so we keep the umbrella shut.

I'm not actually sure how much valuable information Brett can give me. He's like an overgrown puppy— likable but dopey. But he's also the one person closest to Sophie and Liv who I can actually ask about what happened between them.

"So what's up?" Brett drowns his fries in a ketchup lake.

"I have a question for you. Before Sophie went missing, did anything happen between her and Liv?"

Bits of potato fly from his mouth when he speaks. "Like what?"

"Like maybe they got in a fight? Did things seem off between them?"

Brett nods slowly, waiting to swallow before opening his mouth this time. "I tried not to get involved in all that drama, but yeah. I guess things got so bad, Sophie told Liv she was done with her."

"What do you mean? Like she broke off their friendship?"

He nods.

"When did she do that?"

"Jordan's party." Liv definitely didn't mention *that*. She made it sound like she was wrapped up in Natalie all night.

Maybe that's because she has something to hide.

"But why? I thought they were best friends."

"They were until Liv started making things weird. I guess she was always blowing up Sophie's phone when she was hanging out with Jordan. Didn't like being apart from her."

I freeze. *Blowing up Sophie's phone.* Just like my stalker does to me.

If Sophie ended her friendship with Liv the night of Jordan's party and Sophie went missing that same night . . . that means Liv had a motive for getting rid of her.

If she couldn't have Sophie, no one could.

"Why would Natalie date her if she knows how toxic Liv was to Sophie, though?"

Brett shrugs, chomping on a fistful of fries. "Maybe she doesn't know. Sophie was really private those last few months or so. I only know because Jordan told me."

Natalie doesn't even know what her own girlfriend might be capable of.

I don't want to hear the answer, but I have to know. I need to get to the bottom of this. "Has Liv ever said anything about me?"

Brett finally glances up at me from his food. "You don't know?"

My heart beats harder. I shake my head.

"Yeah, I guess Jordan wouldn't want you to. Protective boyfriend and all that." He gives a small smile before it drops and he returns his attention back to his food. "But yeah. Apparently, she hates your guts."

CHAPTER FOURTEEN

NEW GIRL PLAYS on the TV in the living room, and Natalie watches the show in her bedroom while FaceTiming me. She shoves a handful of pecans in her mouth, her TV snack of choice.

"Aww, I love how Nick will literally trespass on someone's property to keep Jess safe," Natalie gushes.

I want to ask her about Liv. If she heard about Sophie and Liv's fight the night of Jordan's party. What Liv has said about me behind my back.

Except I know Natalie. She's book smart but gullible. She's the bubbly, sweet girl who would never think the girl she loves is dangerous.

My phone buzzes.

i know you are on your phone

I swallow. Easy guess.

"Who's texting you?" Natalie asks.

Your psycho girlfriend. "My stalker."

answer me

or im coming inside

Natalie's eyes widen. "Oh my god. What are they saying?"

My phone buzzes again.

dont believe me?

you are wearing shorts

a pink shirt

I jump off my couch and fumble with my pocketknife before clutching it in my fist. That's exactly what I'm wearing.

I don't want to look, don't want to see the face on the other side of the window, but if it's Liv, I need proof it's her. Need Natalie to see that we need to get the *hell* away from this crazy girl.

But when I wrench the curtain back, there's no one there. No one in my front yard, no one across the street.

How does she know where I am? I've gone silent on social media. Does she just wander around town looking for me?

Leave me alone.

Or I'll call the cops.

My stalker messages back immediately: *do that and you will regret it*

"Maddie, what's going on?" Natalie's voice is urgent now.

I run to the window that overlooks our tiny backyard. Nothing. "My stalker is outside watching me."

"Oh my god. They're outside your *house*?"

"Yes. And they've been in my house before. They stole my clothes." My voice trembles.

"Maybe you should call the police."

"I'm going to call Jordan first. He can get here faster."

"Okay. Text me as soon as he gets there."

Heart thudding in my head, my ears, I sneak slowly toward the door. My legs tremble and threaten to give out beneath me. If someone is standing on the other side of the door, my heart might actually burst.

I peer through the window . . . and there's no one waiting

for me. I scan our porch, our yard, our empty driveway. No one's out there.

Not that I can see, anyway.

Jordan answers on the second ring. "Hey, baby. Miss me?" I can practically hear his grin through the phone.

"I need you," I whisper.

"What's going on? Are you okay?" His voice is lower now, concerned, and it makes me want to cry.

"I think my stalker is outside my house." My voice cracks on the last word. "Can you come over?"

"I'm leaving now. Don't hang up."

I race upstairs and curl into a ball on my bed, the blade of my pocketknife out. Too terrified to move while Jordan narrates *I'm getting in my car, I'm almost there,* until he announces, "I'm here."

I sheathe the knife and leap down the stairs. When I throw my arms around him, he squeezes me tight and I wonder if he can feel the hard, erratic beating of my heart.

A wave of guilt crashes over me. I've been fantasizing about Miles, but it's Jordan here protecting me now. It's Jordan who comes when I call. It's Jordan who loves me. I hate that Miles living in my house has made me lose sight of that. I won't make that mistake again.

Jordan checks every window. Peers through the glass on the front and back doors. "I don't see anyone."

No one is out there.

But of course they are. Or at least, they were.

They know what I'm wearing. They know what I'm doing. They're just faster than I am. They got away before they could be spotted.

"I'm really scared," I admit. "I know they haven't done anything, but . . ."

"But *will* he?" Jordan grasps my shoulders. "Trust me, baby.

I get it. I can't imagine being a tiny girl like you. That's why you have me."

He wraps me in a bear hug, and I wish I could stay in this safe place forever. Not need to worry about being a tiny, vulnerable girl.

"Whenever you need me, you tell me and I'll be here. I don't care if it's the middle of the night. I'm your boyfriend. Protecting you is my job."

All I can manage is a hoarse "Thank you." I take a few long, deep breaths.

Jordan leads me to a chair. "Sit. You're shaking."

"Can you make me some tea?" I clasp my trembling hands together on the table. "That should help."

Jordan kisses my forehead before digging in the cupboard.

I click on my phone. No new messages from my stalker.

Is it really Liv?

Apparently she hates your guts. This is exactly what someone who hates me would do. She probably did exactly the same thing to Sophie.

Even though it's seeming less and less likely every day, I have to hold onto hope that Sophie somehow really did run away. That she managed to escape. Because she knew it was safer to disappear.

While Jordan makes tea, I deactivate all my social media accounts and delete the apps from my phone.

Maybe I'll be safer if I disappear too.

At Mariano's for dinner, Mom sniffs loudly. "Those fries smell *good*."

An "Mhmm" is all I can manage.

I'm too busy staring at the text from my stalker.

enjoy your dinner

Every text from them makes nausea ripple through my stomach. Deleting my social media hasn't done anything to stop them from contacting me. I'm starting to wonder if anything I do will.

In her signature whisper-shout, Tess gossips to Mrs. Wallis a few tables away. "There's a maniac terrorizin' our town!"

"I bet it's that Mariano boy," Mrs. Wallis tells her.

"Mom!" I whisper. "Did you tell Tess?"

"I . . ." Mom gives me a sheepish look. "She asked why the police were at our house."

"*Mom*. Tess? Really? Of all people."

"I didn't think she'd tell the whole town about it!"

"Have you *met* Tess?"

A middle-aged man leans back from his own table toward the women. "How do we even know the girl's telling the truth? Kids these days are all about attention. Could be making it up."

I move to stride over there and tell him off, show him the proof, but Mom places a hand on my shoulder.

"He vandalized their garage!" Tess tells him. "I'm tellin' ya. It's that new kid—Mabel's grandson. Ever since he showed up, he's brought this town nothin' but trouble."

Mrs. Wallis sips at her cup of tea. "We've got to get that boy out of here."

To Mom, I hiss, "They have no idea what they're talking about. It's not Miles."

But Mom doesn't give any indication that she agrees with me. Instead, she casts a wary look in my direction.

The same look Officer Callahan gave me. Liv. Ash. Even Jordan.

Like she doesn't believe me. They've already chosen their culprit.

Mabel sets our order down in front of us. Mom's enormous

ribeye and my chicken salad. I'm not sure I'll even be able to stomach the lettuce.

My phone vibrates in my lap.

When I see it's another image from my stalker, my heart sinks.

In the first photo, I'm sitting in front of my laptop, looking down at my phone on my desk. The angle is so close, one thing is startlingly, horrifyingly clear.

This picture was taken from my room. From my webcam.

And in the next picture . . .

My stomach does a violent flip.

In this one, I'm facing my bed, taking my shirt off. A glimpse of my purple bra showing.

Nausea and fear and rage claw at my insides.

How is this even possible? Did they hack my computer somehow?

I'm sick of this. If this is Liv, I need proof it's her. And when I have it, I'm going to do whatever it takes to stop her.

I text Miles.

> Did Sophie ever get pictures from her stalker that were taken from her own webcam?

I manage to swallow a few bites of salad before he responds.

> Not sure. We can check her computer at my mom's.

> Now?

> Miss me that bad huh?

> No. I need evidence for the police.

> Meet you there in 15.

I'm going to get the proof I need. And then I'm going to put an end to this.

I tell Mom I'm heading to Natalie's and she makes me promise to call as soon as I get there. I take a shortcut to Miles's mom's house. For the first time in months, I pass Ash's rundown two-story with the crumbling siding and vines crawling up the porch.

Someone is knocking on the front door. A giant with bulky muscles and a red number fourteen on his letterman jacket. I can't see his face, but I'd recognize him anywhere.

Jordan.

What the hell is Jordan doing here?

I consider calling out to him, but then the door swings open. Ash twirls her blue hair with a finger and smiles at him.

They haven't seen me yet, so I duck behind a tree before they do.

This doesn't make any sense. When Jordan found out about those TikToks Ash posted, he called her *some random girl*. I didn't think he even knew her name. Is he buying weed from her? He doesn't smoke, but maybe he's buying it for Brett or one of his other buddies. She doesn't deal, but she's known for selling some of her own stash to friends for the right price.

That must be it. Nothing more than a transaction.

When the door shuts, they're gone. Until they appear again in Ash's kitchen, the window wide open for anyone to see.

Ash jumps onto the kitchen table, wraps her legs around Jordan's hips, and pulls him in by his jacket.

No. *No, no, no.* He wouldn't—

He won't—

Jordan grabs the back of her head and smashes his mouth against hers. He grips her thigh, digging his fingers into her flesh like he can't get enough of her. Then he slips his hand up her shirt.

He's stuffing his hands up my former friend's shirt while I'm being stalked.

Every heartbeat echoes in my ears like a ticking bomb. *Five, four, three, two—*

In one swift movement, Jordan lifts Ash up by her ass and carries her away. Out of view and into the darkness.

My heart hits the ground in front of me and shatters completely.

CHAPTER FIFTEEN

DESPITE THE SEVENTY-DEGREE WEATHER, I'm shaking when I reach Miles's mom's house. Her car isn't in the driveway and neither is Miles's Mustang, but when I knock, he swings the door open.

He looks somehow normal despite my world turning upside down. Black shirt, black hoodie, dark jeans, hands in his pockets, hair nearly falling into his eyes.

"God, do you wear anything other than black?"

His lips twist up into an amused smirk. "Glad to see you're in a great mood."

"Let's just get this over with."

He ushers me in and I slip my shoes off. Then he hands me a book. My copy of *Pride and Prejudice*, the pages barely still glued to the spine. I clutch the book to my chest—the exact piece of comfort I need right now. Mr. Darcy never did anything like this to Elizabeth.

"You didn't tell me it was written in gibberish," Miles says.

"It's one of the greatest romance novels of all time."

He leads the way down the narrow hall. "You said boring

books don't have any smut. So I expect the next one to be loaded with it."

When we reach the end of the hall, he pushes a door open.

Sophie's room still smells faintly of sweet, flowery perfume. I expected awards and pictures with her friends across her walls, a huge vanity in the corner, and pink everything. Instead, her room is mostly soft blue. The walls, her sheets, her pillowcases. Her bed is unmade, and her walls are lined with art from romance movies. *Pride and Prejudice, Twilight, Mamma Mia, Beauty and the Beast.*

She loves love. Just like me.

Did Jordan cheat on her too? Or did he love her enough to stay faithful?

A weight crushes my chest so hard, I want to be sick. Purge the heartbreak from my body. I pin my hands under my arms so Miles doesn't see them shake.

How could Jordan cheat on me? How could he cheat on me with *Ash*? I never, ever saw this coming. I thought he was as head over heels for me as I am for him.

My gaze drops to the promise ring on my hand. Once a symbol of the life we planned together. Now a symbol of the promise he broke.

We're going to college together in a couple of months. Sharing an apartment. We planned our whole lives around each other. Now that entire future has disappeared like a puff of smoke.

"What'd your stalker send you this time?" Miles asks.

He thinks I'm shaken because of my stalker. Good. I hand over my phone. While he examines the photos taken from my webcam, I turn my attention back to Sophie's room. On her desk are her laptop and phone.

"Do you know her laptop password?" I ask.

"Nope."

I open it and luck out. There's no password required. Maybe the police disabled the passwords on her devices.

Miles hands my phone back. "This guy has worse."

"What do you mean?"

"These photos he sent you? They're the tame ones. He's keeping the other ones for himself."

My stomach churns at the thought of some old man jerking off to screenshots he took from my webcam.

When I search for the Photos app on Sophie's laptop, Miles heads for the door and leans against it, scrolling through his phone. "You've gotta be the one to look."

He doesn't want to see the photos. His sister, possibly exposed. Her privacy invaded.

I open the Photos app, and I'm inundated with picture after picture of Sophie's smiling face, usually accompanied by a friend or Jordan. Seeing his face—always laughing or smiling—brings tears to my eyes, but I blink them away. I can cry as much as I want when I'm alone in my bed later. I'm not crying in front of Miles.

I click on the album called *Stalker*.

The images that fill the screen make my gut wrench. I'm glad Miles doesn't have to see them.

I recognize a few of the ones Miles showed me and Officer Callahan in the screenshots. But there are so many more. All of them eerily familiar—a zoomed-in, blurry shot of Sophie through her bedroom window, in her sports bra after a workout, walking toward her car in a parking lot with eyes wide. She knew she was being watched, but she couldn't find them either.

There. A close-up shot of Sophie's delicate face, elbows propped up on the desk I'm sitting at now, phone in her hands. Another of her bent down in the middle of her room, shorts halfway to her ankles.

This is the tip of the iceberg. Miles is right. Our stalker sent us each just a few of the screenshots they took of us in our bedrooms, doing homework, sleeping, undressing. Everything we thought we could do in the privacy of our own rooms without eyes on us.

I close the app and turn away, disgusted.

"Find anything?" Miles asks.

"Yes."

There's no way it could be Miles now. He'd never spy on his sister like this, take these kinds of screenshots of her. That'd be sick on a whole other level.

"But how are they accessing our webcams?"

Miles looms beside me. I just stare for a second, admiring the sparse constellation of freckles on his face, until he says, "Move so I can take over or sit on my lap. Either way, I need to get into her computer."

I roll my eyes and vacate the seat. "Do you have to make everything sexual?"

"With you? I don't have a choice."

My face burns at the thought of sitting on his lap, even though it shouldn't at this point. Jordan is cheating on me, so I don't need to be loyal to him anymore. Yet I still can't bring myself to betray him.

Miles opens up Chrome, already logged into Sophie's account. A quick search of her Gmail inbox pulls up a single email from our stalker, sophiemarianofan@gmail.com. I only got one email too.

"Is it the emails? Are they able to hack our webcams that way?"

He frowns. "Maybe. I'm thinking it's a RAT."

"A RAT? Like . . . the rodent?"

"A Remote Access Trojan. Pretty easy to put a RAT on someone's computer. Then you have access to all their files and their screen. And their webcam. That's how they got those pictures of you and Soph. You opened that email from them?"

"Yeah, only the one. But I didn't download anything."

Miles shrugs. "Doesn't matter. They could've attached it, and you wouldn't have even noticed because it doesn't slow your computer down."

"So what do I do?"

"Get an anti-malware tool. You should be okay after that. But don't open any more emails from them."

Has my stalker been tracking my movements from my webcam? Spying on me so they know exactly when I come and go? My phone grows heavy in my back pocket. "Do you think they could put a RAT on my phone too?"

Miles presses his lips together. "Not likely. Unless maybe they somehow got access to your phone."

I shake my head. "No. I'm never without my phone."

My phone is both the source of my nightmare and my lifeline. I could chuck it into the sea, but how would I call for help if my stalker shows up at my house? No. My phone isn't the problem. It's the person on the other end.

My ringtone pierces the quiet, as if my stalker can sense me thinking about them.

Except it's not my stalker calling me this time. It's a FaceTime request from Jordan.

My stomach drops.

There's no way I can answer. He's probably still in Ash's bed. And she'll be silently cackling in the background while he lies to me about where he is and what he's up to.

How can he want to video chat with me right now? Pretend like everything's normal after what he's just done.

I hit Decline.

Before I can slip my phone into my pocket, it vibrates again. Texts this time.

> You're done with work, right?

> Want to hang out?

I turn my screen off. The thought of confronting him about cheating on me, breaking up with him, nauseates me. Who will I be without Jordan?

"Your stalker?" Miles asks.

I shake my head. "Jordan."

He tilts his head. "Trouble in paradise?"

Tears sting my eyes. "Um, yeah." I try to clear my throat, blink the tears away, but the sob just keeps welling up in my chest. *Shit.* "He's cheating on me."

The words land in the silence between us like an anchor. I can't believe I just said that out loud. The reality hasn't even fully sunk in yet. Jordan kissed Ash. Jordan. Kissed. Ash. And probably did a lot more with her after they left her kitchen.

Maybe she lied to me at Mariano's. She was so convincing, but . . . she could still be my stalker. She obviously wants me out of the way so she can date Jordan.

She got rid of one of his girlfriends. Time to get rid of another.

Miles stands. I expect him to roll his eyes. Tell me I should've seen this coming. That of course Jordan doesn't want me because I'm *one of those girls*. Nothing special. Replaceable.

But he doesn't say any of that. He closes the space between us, stopping when our toes are nearly touching. "So dump him. You deserve better." He says it like it's that simple.

"I don't," I breathe.

Miles's brows fold down low over his eyes. "Why not?"

"Jordan is the best thing that ever happened to me. Without him, I'm nothing." The first tear slips down my cheek, followed quickly by another. When my lip starts to tremble, I clamp my hand over my mouth before the cry can escape.

Jordan is my everything. My whole life. I gave up my college plans to follow him to California. I gave up my dream to move to New York and work in book publishing for him. For a future in Beaumont together. With the ring on my finger, he promised me that future.

Now everything I've planned, everything I've ever dreamed of, has been ripped away from me.

He's the one who nicknamed me Maddie. Now who will I be?

Miles hooks a gentle finger under my chin and tilts my face up to his. So I can't hide my tears from him. "The only way you're nothing is if you stay with him."

"He made me who I am," I whisper.

Miles shakes his head. "No, he didn't. He changed you." He sweeps a lock of hair over my shoulder, trailing his fingertips along my skin. "But you didn't need to change. You were already perfect. You get that, don't you?"

My heart squeezes. I'm almost starting to think Miles cares about me more than Jordan does.

When I can't answer, he gives me a sad smile. "You don't." He wipes a tear off my cheek with his thumb. "Someday you will."

When we get back to the duplex, Jordan is sitting on the front steps.

My heart nearly explodes. A bottle of Jack Daniels rests between his knees, a deep scowl on his face.

I knew I'd have to confront him, but I didn't think it'd be as soon as I got home. I haven't even had time to process what he did, let alone figure out what I'm going to say.

With each step toward him, my heart hammers harder. The closer I get, the clearer the fury contorting his features becomes. A twist to his lips, a steely clench to his jaw, a blaze in his eyes.

What the hell does he have to be angry about? I'm the one who should be pissed. I'm the one who was betrayed.

He tips the bottle up, swallowing, and stands before Miles can get too close. Towering over him.

"You know," Miles calls. "Sitting on a girl's steps waiting for her to come home kinda makes you look like a stalker."

Jordan snatches the collar of Miles's shirt and yanks him close, a snarl across his face.

"*Jordan*. Stop!"

Miles doesn't let an ounce of fear flash across his face. He just gives Jordan a smirk. "Guess I hit a sore spot."

Jordan shoves him away. "Get the hell out of here." He spins to face me. "Inside."

I balk. Since when does Jordan give me orders?

When he starts to stomp away, Miles grazes his fingers down my arm. "You okay?" he murmurs.

The touch is nearly imperceptible, but nothing gets past Jordan. He whirls on Miles, closing the distance between them.

Miles pulls back just as Jordan swings, but the punch still manages to connect with his nose hard enough to make him stagger back.

"Miles!"

It's the wrong name leaving my lips. Jordan's eyes flash in my direction, and Miles takes advantage of his distraction, sweeping Jordan's feet out from under him.

Jordan goes down, and Miles moves so fast, my breath catches. He's on my boyfriend and landing punch after punch against the arms Jordan has braced in front of his face, but it won't last long. The second Jordan gets Miles off him, he'll be dead—

I rush forward. "Stop!"

One of Miles's frantic elbows barrels toward me, and before I can react, collides with my nose.

Tears spring to my eyes. My vision blurs for just a second before everything goes dark.

And I hit the ground.

CHAPTER SIXTEEN

"GET AWAY FROM HER!" Jordan shouts.

Miles is at my side before Jordan shoves him away. Jordan is unscathed, but blood is smeared beneath Miles's nose. Still, his concern is for me, not himself.

Jordan helps me to my feet. My nose throbs, but it isn't bleeding. "Stay the hell away from her," he warns Miles.

He leads me into the house, a steely grip on my arm. Miles stands alone in the yard, one hand in his pocket, the other swiping at the blood on his face.

Jordan slams the door behind us. My eyes are watery, and I want to hold a cold compress against my nose.

"Explain it to me, Maddie." He paces the middle of the kitchen. "Because I'm obviously an idiot. I've told you how many times I don't want you around that guy. I call you, I ask you to hang out and you ignore me, and meanwhile, you're with *him*?"

"And who were you with?" I spit.

Jordan freezes. I've never fired back at him. Ever. "What are you talking about? I was trying to hang out with you, but I guess you don't even want to be with me anymore." The Jack

Daniels sloshes in the bottle when he throws his arms up. "I send you flowers, bring you chocolates, make you dinner, buy you a phone, take you on dates, give you a ring. I treat you like a queen. I protect you. So please explain to me why you'd rather be around that loser."

"We went to his mom's house to look through Sophie's laptop," I snap. "There. Is that what you wanted to hear? My stalker took photos of me from my webcam, and guess what? They did the same thing to Sophie. If I get enough evidence, I can figure out who's stalking us and what happened to her. But you don't even care about that, do you?"

Jordan collapses against the wall and rubs a hand down his face. "She's been missing for almost a *year*, Maddie." He isn't infuriated anymore. He's . . . defeated. "You know how unlikely it is that she'll ever come back? You know how unlikely it is that she's even still *alive*? If the detectives couldn't find answers, what makes you think you can?"

I want to tell him that he's wrong, that I'm capable of so much more than he believes, but . . . he's right. I definitely don't know more than the detectives. I'm not more capable of doing their job than they are. I'm an eighteen-year-old who knows a lot about romance novels and cheerleading routines, but I don't know anything about investigating a disappearance. I don't know how to track down a stalker. I don't know how to stop them.

Sophie didn't either. And look how it ended for her.

"If I don't try, they'll kill me." My voice wavers.

"No, they won't," Jordan insists. "You have me to protect you, remember? You know you can call me whenever you need me. But you have to choose. It's him or me, Maddie." Jordan pushes off the wall, like I've exhausted him. "You can be with the guy who loves the hell out of you, who protects you, who's going to college with you, who wants to be with you forever—" He gestures to the other side of the duplex. "—or you can be with the creep in the room next door who probably killed his goddamn sister. Your choice."

He turns to leave, but when his hand reaches the knob, I blurt, "I choose Miles."

He stops. "What?"

I swallow the rock in my throat. "I saw you," I tell him. "With her. With . . . Ash."

His face gives nothing away. Still playing innocent.

"I saw you at her house. Kissing her."

His thick brows draw together. "What are you talking about? Who's Ash?"

I roll my eyes. "Don't play dumb."

"I'm not playing anything," he snaps. "I don't know what you think you saw, Maddie, but it wasn't me with some other girl. I've been at the country club all day. I got off my shift and texted you to hang out. Why the hell would I be kissing someone else?"

"I . . ." I don't know what to say. Could I have imagined it? His hands up her shirt, her legs pinning his hips between her knees.

I was pretty far away. Maybe I didn't actually see the number fourteen on that guy's jacket. Maybe it was another football player. It's not like Jordan is the only tall, muscular guy on the team.

And I didn't actually see his face.

I've been spiraling for the past hour, and I didn't even see what I thought I saw.

Jordan would never cheat on me. He loves me. I can't believe I doubted him.

My face crumbles. "I'm so sorry. I thought I saw you with her. I thought . . ."

He closes the space between us and wraps me in a hug. I let myself cry in his arms.

Thank god. Thank god that wasn't him. I don't know what I would've done. I'd be lost without Jordan.

He waits for me to compose myself. "Miles is trying to get in your head. This is why you need to stay away from him." He grabs my hand and holds it up. The amethyst on my ring, while still beautiful, doesn't glisten like it used to. "Remember who gave you this. I'm the one who wants you. Forever. Don't forget that."

After Jordan leaves in his BMW, I get two minutes to rest in peace with an ice pack against my nose before there's a knock on the front door.

The blood under Miles's nose is starting to dry. Small, dark stains splatter his shirt. He nods to the ice pack. "You okay?"

He's the one bleeding and he's asking if I'm okay.

"A lot better than you."

Miles takes a seat at the table without waiting for an invitation.

I pass him the cold compress. "You need this more than I do." While he holds it against his face, I dampen a paper towel and dab at the dried blood above his mouth.

"Aww." He smirks. "You know, a lot of porn starts this way. Nurse-patient. One of my favorites."

"I'm only cleaning up the blood so you don't get it all over my house."

"Have any nurse-patient books? I'll also take doctor-patient. Or maybe one about a reader and the hot neighbor." Judging by the sly grin across his face, he's talking about us.

"Which one of us is the reader and which one is the hot neighbor?"

"Exactly." Miles stands and presses the ice pack to my nose. "So how'd Jordan take the breakup?"

"I was wrong, actually. He didn't cheat on me."

Miles sets the compress on the table with a thud. I throw the paper towel away, his face free of dried blood, but his nose is still swollen. He'll probably have a black eye tomorrow. "So you just imagined he cheated on you?"

"I thought he was the guy at Ash's house, but I was wrong. I must've been seeing things." I can't believe my brain convinced my eyes they were seeing Jordan with Ash when it was clearly someone else.

Miles drops back into his chair. "He's messing with your head."

I stiffen. He has no idea what he's talking about. "That's what he said about you."

Suddenly, Miles grips my hips and pulls me onto his lap. I'm straddling him, trapped here. He smells of sandalwood and mint and it's so intoxicating, I want to lose myself in it. In him.

"You don't have to buy his bullshit. You know you can get dick a lot closer to home, right? Just one knock away."

I wriggle, trying to get away, but that just makes him hiss at the feel of me grinding against the hardness in his pants. *Oh god.* That. I didn't expect . . . *that.* My whole body is hot, heart pounding. I've fantasized about being in this position with him so many times. Except in my fantasies, there weren't any layers between us.

All it would take is me yanking down his zipper and him pushing my panties to the side—

"Jordan isn't just a quick fuck," I breathe. "He's my boyfriend. I love him."

Miles leans in close, hot breath whispering across my neck. "I'm not a quick fuck either."

The pulsing between my legs makes me try to push off him again, but his arms tighten around me. He knows I want this. Want him. He's so warm and inviting and the adrenaline coursing hot in my veins makes me want to beg him to bend me over the table.

But I can't do this to Jordan. Seeing Jordan—who I thought was Jordan, anyway—with Ash was enough to break me. I can't inflict that kind of pain.

So I say the words I know will get Miles to release me. "The night Sophie disappeared? I'm the reason she left."

The night of Jordan's big house party, Ash spent three hours begging me to go with her. She insisted there would be great weed, booze, and guys. None of which particularly interested me. I tried weed once—nearly hacked up a lung. Booze? Tasted so bad, I shoved three sticks of gum in my mouth after a single gulp. And there was only one guy I wanted to **see** at that party, and I knew he wouldn't be there.

Finally, Ash threatened to make me sit alone at lunch when school started again if I didn't go with her. I didn't know who she'd sit with instead, but I knew she'd follow through on her threat if I didn't do what she wanted, and I couldn't imagine anything worse than being the one person in the cafeteria without a single friend to sit with.

So I snuck out to meet Ash at the end of our street. She wore ripped black jeans with so many holes, she might as well have been wearing shorts, and her top was basically a glorified bra. When she saw me, she snorted. "Haven't you worn that outfit to school?"

I glanced down at the jeans, t-shirt, and sandals. "Yeah. So?"

She shook her head and led the way to Jordan's house.

When we got there, I was surprised to find . . . no one. No one in the living room, in the kitchen. But I could hear muffled laughter, feel the vibrations of a bass.

Ash pulled open a door that led to the basement. Talking, shouting, laughter, and rap floated up.

Jordan kept his parties relegated to the basement—his domain. He was allowed to furbish the space exactly as he wanted. A massive stereo, a huge TV on the wall, a sectional sofa, a pool table, even a pinball machine in the corner. I assumed the bar against the back wall was intended for the nights his parents had their own guests to entertain, but no one seemed to consider it off-limits.

Natalie Shin was curled up on the couch with Liv Hernandez, leaning in close and fiddling with the ends of her dark hair. Jordan sat on one of the barstools, his usual grin spread across his face, his cheeks flushed from the alcohol. Sophie in his lap.

"I'm going to smoke." Ash nodded to some guys passing a bong around in the corner. "You coming?"

"Nah, I'm good."

She rolled her eyes at me like she always did. "Fine. Bye, loser."

I leaned against the wall, sipping from a red cup filled with piss-warm beer and reading on my phone, feeling just as invisible as I did every day in school. I never should've agreed to come. I should've known Ash would ditch me the second we got here. She just didn't want to go alone. I was only ever good enough when she wanted to use me for something.

I found myself Googling *Miles Mariano*, hoping he'd miraculously show up and whisk me away. Be the hero I needed to save me from this terrible night. Finally, I couldn't take it anymore and hurried up the stairs.

And ran right into Brett Rayburn.

"Whoa!" He held a beer in each hand, arms up while he stepped out of my way. "Easy, killer."

I mumbled an apology, hurried through the kitchen, and threw open the sliding glass door. I needed air.

The only light in Jordan's backyard emitted from the depths of the heated pool. His family didn't just have a pool—they had a heated pool. In Connecticut. He was that kind of rich.

I took my sandals off and slipped my feet into the water.

I didn't know how long it was before the door slid open again. I assumed it was Ash, coming to berate me for ditching her even though she was the one who ditched me.

But it wasn't Ash who sat beside me.

Sophie's dark hair cascaded down her back in gentle waves, a sharp contrast to her white tank top. Her legs were long and slender beneath her tiny denim shorts. A girl with effortless grace and beauty to hide her thorns and claws.

She smiled at me and dipped her toes in the pool too. A wolf in sheep's clothing.

We sat in silence for so long, I almost worked up the courage to tell her off for bullying me all those years ago. She'd made my life hell in elementary and middle school. Even after she and her lackeys finally backed off and ignored me, the damage had already been done.

Finally, she broke the silence. "You're friends with that Ash girl, right?"

I was surprised she knew Ash's name. Surprised she even knew either of us existed. "Yeah. Why?"

Her pretty face contorted in disgust. "I don't know how you can hang out with a girl like that."

Even though I didn't even like Ash all that much, I felt an overwhelming urge to defend her. Maybe because she was my only friend, the only person who liked me enough to spend time with me.

"I don't know how anyone can hang out with a girl like you," I snapped.

Sophie's eyes widened. But before she could say another word, I shoved her into the pool.

She came up sputtering and I couldn't help the smile that

spread across my face, seeing her perfect hair and makeup ruined. She swiped at her eyes, spreading mascara and liner across her skin. "What the hell was that for?"

"Remember pushing me off the swing when I was reading my book at recess? It was for that," I told her. "Or the time you made fun of my sneakers and mocked me with all your friends? It was for that too. And the time you coordinated with all the girls in P.E. to target me—just me—during dodgeball. You know what? Now that I think about it, you deserve a lot worse than being shoved into a pool."

She actually had the audacity to look shocked. She sloshed through the water slowly, arms wrapped tight around her torso while she shivered.

I rolled my eyes. "It's a heated pool."

"I honestly don't remember any of that," she admitted. "But I'm sorry."

"Is that supposed to make me feel better? You bully me and conveniently forget what a bitch you were, so I should forgive you? Kiss your ass like everyone else at this school?"

Sophie shook her head. She looked terrible with raccoon eyes and it helped, just a little, to know she wasn't perfect all the time. "No, I know I was a bitch." She gave a mirthless laugh. "I was mean to everyone back then. My parents were fighting all the time, and I was just . . . angry at the whole world. But that's no excuse."

She was a great actress. I'd give her that. "No, it's not."

I knew Sophie was only saying what I wanted to hear because she needed everyone to like her. But I wouldn't give her the satisfaction.

She used the ladder to climb out of the pool, water raining off her hair and clothes. Her white tank now sheer and clinging to her skin, showing off the pink bra underneath. Then she pulled a wad of wet cash out of her pocket. Ruined. Her face fell, and for a second, I worried she might cry. "This was my ticket out," she whispered, more to herself than to me.

I shouldn't have cared, but I took the bait. "Out of where?"

"Beaumont."

"Why would you want to leave? Everyone here likes you."

She was the cheer captain. Prom queen. Girlfriend of the hottest, richest guy in school. She had all the friends and beauty and brains a girl could want.

Who would want to leave behind the perfect life?

"Not everyone," she said.

"I would trade places with you in a heartbeat." For a second, I froze. I couldn't believe I'd actually admitted that out loud.

She shook her head. "No, you wouldn't. Trust me."

I stood, pulled out the tip money I forgot to deposit at the bank, and handed it to her. She just stared at it. "Take it," I told her.

"What? No. I can't take your money."

"You can if I'm giving it to you." I shake it in the air between us. "Come on. I'm the one who ruined your cash. This should at least be enough for a tank of gas and a motel."

"You sure?" she asked, delicate eyebrows raised.

"Yes. Now take it."

Hesitantly, she reached out and grabbed the money. She gazed past Jordan's massive house, past the road, to whatever lay beyond. "You can't tell anyone about this, okay?"

I smiled. "I won't."

———

Miles leans against the front door with his arms crossed, a frown etched deep into his face. "Why the hell didn't you tell me about that?"

"She told me not to."

He rolls his eyes. "Like you give a shit about what my sister wanted."

I swallow. "I knew you'd be angry that I didn't say something sooner. That I didn't go to the police after she went missing."

"Well, giving my sister money to skip town is kind of an important thing to mention, so yeah." His lip curls. "I'm pretty fucking angry."

"But aren't you glad she ran away? She got away from her stalker. She's okay. She's still out there somewhere."

He's in front of me in seconds, peering down at me like I'm the scum of the earth. "You better hope she is. Because if she's not?" He pokes me in the chest. "I'm holding you responsible."

When he turns for the door, I know I'll regret the words that tumble out of my mouth: "I thought I was helping out a classmate. You let your sister go to a party alone, knowing someone there wanted to kill her."

Miles doesn't glance back before slamming the door shut behind him.

CHAPTER SEVENTEEN

JORDAN IS DRIVING me to a party at Natalie's tonight and I plan on getting shitfaced. For the past two days, Miles has been giving me the silent treatment, skipping his shifts at the diner just to avoid me, and I've been mainly spending my time with Jordan. In his pool, playing video games with him and the guys, turning up the volume on his TV to drown out our moans. My stalker hasn't stopped their onslaught of texts and calls, but I feel safer with Jordan around.

I text him a mirror selfie in my short, tight skirt and pink crop top. One of the outfits he bought for me on our first shopping trip. The only downside is the lack of pockets, which means I can't bring the knife Miles gave me.

I expect Jordan's usual row of heart-eye or drooling emojis, but I get neither.

Hope that's not what you're wearing tonight.

What's wrong with it?

You've got a stalker right?

Maybe you should try blending in more

You can wear that just for me later…

I hate that I'm expected to change because someone decided to stalk me. *Get off social media. Wear different clothes.* Like I brought this upon myself. Like the clothes I choose to wear draw the wrong kind of attention. Like I can somehow control someone else's actions.

The only blame should be reserved for my stalker.

When Jordan beeps from my driveway, I slip on black heels that go perfectly with my skirt and top. He frowns at my outfit when I slide in beside him. "I thought I told you to change."

"I didn't want to."

After a short sigh, he smiles. "I guess I can't complain about my girl looking hot. You'll just have to stick by my side tonight."

Sometime between leaving the house and getting in Jordan's car, I got another text from my stalker.

see you soon

My stomach lurches.

Miles was afraid Sophie's stalker would be at Jordan's house party the night she disappeared. Now they're going to be at Natalie's tonight.

Waiting for me.

Before we've even shut the car doors behind us, Brett hands us each a cup full of beer. Jordan downs his drink in two gulps, and even though I vowed to get drunk tonight and forget, I can't bring myself to take more than a few sips.

I follow Jordan around the party, making small talk and watching him laugh and challenge his buddies to drinking contests. Even though I'm sure everyone must know by now that someone's stalking me, no one asks about it. No one really asks about me at all. It's all about Jordan, and I just happen to be the girl standing next to him. I should be used to this. This is what I wanted. Up until a few months ago, this is what made me happy. But for some reason, it feels empty now.

I know I'm safe at Jordan's side, but I keep glancing over my shoulder. At the faces around us. At the ones lurking in the shadows. Fear digs its claws into me and doesn't let go.

An hour later, I spot Natalie heading into her house alone. Now's my chance.

Jordan is at least six drinks in, face flushed and beads of sweat on his forehead. I shake his arm to get his attention over the deep, pulsing boom of the bass. "I'm going to find Natalie!" I yell.

He nods. "Don't be gone long."

"I won't."

Inside, the laughter and music are only slightly muffled. The house is mostly dark, off-limits except for the bathroom. I head for the kitchen, the only room with a light on, but it's empty.

I'm about to call out to Natalie when two hands cover my eyes.

I let out a scream and try to rip the hands off me, but they won't budge.

Oh my god. They've found me. They've found me alone and I don't have the knife Miles gave me. I have no way to defend myself, and now they're going to—

Natalie doubles over laughing, finally dropping her hands from my eyes.

"Jesus, Natalie," I hiss. My heart still pounds in my ears, and I drink a glass of tap water to calm my nerves. I should be used to her pranks after months of friendship, but she should understand why sneaking up on me and covering my eyes would be crossing the line.

"I couldn't resist. I'm so glad you're here! It's been too long since we've hung out." Natalie holds her phone up. "Selfie time!"

She snaps a photo of us. I manage a hideous forced smile, and Natalie either ignores it or doesn't care that I look terrible because she looks flawless. Her thumbs fly over the screen.

"What are you doing?" I ask.

"Posting this to my Snapchat story."

I snatch her phone away. "No! You can't post that."

"What? Maddie, what's wrong with you?" She reaches for her phone, but I turn away from her and delete the photo before handing it back. "Why did you do that?"

"You can't be posting pictures with me. You have your Snapchat location on. I don't want my stalker to know where I am."

Her face falls, turning sheepish. "Oh my gosh, Maddie. I'm so sorry. I didn't even think about that."

"I know. It's okay." She doesn't have to think about it all day, every day like I do because it's not happening to her. "Anyway, I have a favor to ask. Can you get into Liv's phone?"

Her dark eyebrows crinkle with uncertainty. "What? Why?"

"I know you're not going to want to hear this, but . . . Liv might be the one who was stalking Sophie. And now me."

The confusion in Natalie's eyes swiftly turns to outrage. "You've got to be kidding me. You think between working at the country club, taking care of her abuela, and being with me, Liv really has the time to follow you all over town?" She shakes her head. "I get that someone's following you and you're scared, I do. But now you think my *girlfriend* is stalking you? That's insane, Maddie."

"No, you have to listen to me. I know Liv was obsessed with Sophie before she disappeared. I know Sophie told Liv that night that they couldn't be friends anymore. And I know she's been telling people she hates me." I take a step toward Natalie, reach out for her. "You have to believe me. Please, if we can get in Liv's phone, I can see if she's the one who sent those messages and photos—"

A couple girls stumble into the kitchen. Juniors. "Where's the bathroom?" one half-shouts.

Natalie points them down the hall before stepping out of my reach and lowering her voice. "When's the last time you asked me how I'm doing? How I'm balancing a chaotic schedule with a girlfriend? How I'm feeling about going to college in the fall and being apart from Liv? How I'm dealing with basically living alone because my mom is always traveling for work and my dad isn't even in the country? I thought you were my friend, but maybe Liv was right."

"Right about what?"

"Maybe you don't actually care about me. About any of us. You just wanted to know what it was like to be Sophie."

My heart hammers. That's why Liv hates me. And now I'm losing Natalie too. Like sand through my fingers, she's slipping away from me. "That's not true. You're my best friend."

"If this is how you treat your best friend, I'd hate to see how you treat an enemy." She backs up to her spot by the island and picks up her drink. "I think you should leave. I don't even know who you are anymore."

I'm torn between wanting to cry and wanting to shake sense into her. She's so in love, she's lost her ability to see clearly. To see that the girl she loves could be the most dangerous person we know.

"I'm sorry I've been so wrapped up in all of this. But this is my life on the line. I need your help, Natalie. Just give me her passcode, that's all I—"

"*No*, Maddie. You need to leave. Now."

My vision blurs, and I spin on my heel. Liv walks into the room, glancing between the two of us. "What's up with you two?"

"Nothing. Maddie's not feeling well." Natalie's voice is icy.

Liv's chin juts out, dark eyes nearly black, her skin void of makeup and face pretty in a sharp, angular way.

Is it really her? Am I looking my stalker in the eye right now?

She could be the one making my life a living nightmare. The one who hates me. Who wants to kill me. Who may have killed already.

"Let me see your phone." I try to keep the quaver of fear out of my voice.

She jerks back. "What? No." The guarded, defiant expression in her eyes tells me all I need to know. She's hiding something.

I grab for her back pocket, but she twists away. "Get the hell away from me!"

"I need to see your phone!"

Natalie smacks her glass down with a crack. "Stop it, Maddie!"

Liv pins my arms to my sides. Her iron grip freezes me. She has the kind of strength that could kill a girl.

"Calm down." Her voice is surprisingly steady. Low and chilling. "You're acting insane."

If she tried to hurt me, would Natalie even stop her? Maybe Natalie already knows Liv did something to Sophie.

I shake off Liv's grip and get the hell away from them both.

Before I can reach the front door, it swings open. Ash gives me a sickly sweet smile.

I groan. I don't want to deal with her tonight too.

"Where's your boyfriend?" she asks in her most annoying singsong voice.

"Going to find him right now." I brush past her. I'll find Jordan and then I can get the hell away from this party.

"I know you saw us," she tells me. "Just like Sophie did."

I freeze with my hand on the doorknob. The hairs on the

back of my neck stand up. I know exactly what she's talking about, but I play dumb. "Saw who?"

"Where do you think your boyfriend is right now?"

She's baiting me and I'm not in the mood for her mind games. "Outside. Goodbye, Ash."

She shakes her head and points upstairs. Then she takes a single step toward me, the devilish little smile never leaving her lips. "If it was me up there with him, you'd already know exactly where he is. He can be loud if you give it to him right. But I guess you wouldn't know that, huh, Maddie?"

Ash grabs the bottle of vodka she must've been looking for and disappears back out the door. She's lying. But . . . I have to know for sure.

I head up the carpeted stairs, moving as fast as I can without making any noise. Each of the doors is closed to Natalie's room, the guest room, her mom's room, the office, the bathroom, and their home gym. I start at the closest room—the guest room—and press my ear to the door. No sounds on the other side. I listen at each of the bedrooms, but they're all silent.

I knew it. Ash was lying. Of course she was. Just trying to get under my skin, like usual.

But then a soft thud comes from the room at the end of the hall—the office.

I pad quietly down the hallway, heart beating wildly when I turn the knob, centimeter by careful centimeter.

Illuminated by nothing more than the lights outside shining in through the enormous window are two people—one of them bent over the desk, and the other thrusting into her from behind. Her moans are high and whiny and she screeches, "*Yes, yes, yes!*" He gives a low, guttural groan every time his hips smack against her ass.

Chelsea is naked, but the only clothing Jordan bothered to discard is his letterman jacket.

Do I scream at him? Throw something? I'm frozen with indecision. I want to hurt him as badly as he's hurting me, but to do that, I'd have to kill him.

Chelsea moans. "Yes! Harder, Jordan!" Then she turns to look back at him and spots me. "*Shit!*"

She pushes him off her and scrambles to cover herself up. He whirls around, and when he finds me, his eyes widen.

I slam the door and take off back down the stairs.

He's right on my heels. "Maddie! Stop!" I'm back outside before he manages to catch up with me and yank me to a halt. "Let me explain."

"What the fuck is there to explain, Jordan?" I snap. "I saw you!"

We're catching our friends'—no, *his* friends'—attention, but for the first time, I couldn't give less of a shit about what anyone thinks.

There's no way he's talking his way out of this one. He cheated on me with Chelsea. With Ash too. And god knows how many other girls. He's probably been doing it all summer. Maybe even longer.

"I'm drunk!" he says, his ice-blue eyes wild. "She was all over me. She—"

I hold up a hand. "*She's* not dating me. *You* are. You knew exactly what you were doing."

Everyone is watching us now.

"I thought she was you! I'm messed up. You know how I get when I'm drunk." His cheeks are still flushed, from the alcohol and the fucking.

"I'm going home." I turn my back on him, the first of many tears spilling out.

"Come on, Sophie—"

I whirl on him. "What did you call me?"

His eyes are flat, lips pressed in a line. "What do you mean? I called you Maddie."

"No. You called me Sophie." Ice floods my veins. He called me *Sophie*.

He called me his ex-girlfriend's name.

Jordan stares at me through red, hooded eyes. "No, I didn't."

For the first time, the sight of him doesn't make me melt. The cold blue irises, the slight cleft to his chin, the thin lips, the white scar on his cheek, the thick, caterpillar eyebrows. None of it stirs an aching want low in my belly anymore. He's nowhere near the perfect guy I thought he was.

He's a cheater. He's a liar. He's everything Miles said he was —a future frat boy with a drinking problem, banging every sorority girl who will have him.

Yet as furious as I am with Jordan, my heart still breaks when I tell him, "We're done."

CHAPTER EIGHTEEN

EVEN THOUGH HE must hate me for what I said to him, Miles shows up when I text asking for a ride home.

His Mustang rumbles up beside me and all he says is, "Get in."

I hop in the passenger seat and manage a grateful smile despite my eyes and nose already swollen from crying. "Thanks for picking me up."

The side of his nose and the skin around his eye have turned a deep purple. I wince. Jordan did that to him. And for what? He's acted jealous of Miles from day one, even though he's the one who's been cheating on me. Miles has tempted me many times since he moved into my duplex, but I've never acted on it. Never even kissed him, let alone fucked him.

But now? All bets are off.

Except now that I actually want him in my bed, I'm the last person he wants to share one with.

"Makes killing you a lot easier when you get in my car willingly." His voice is flat.

"I shouldn't have said that about you letting Sophie go to

the party alone," I sputter. "You're not responsible for anything that happened that night."

I can't believe I said that to him, knowing how deep those words would cut.

He shrugs, jaw set. He doesn't say anything, and I can't blame him.

"And I'm sorry I didn't tell you sooner about helping Sophie run away. I didn't want to upset you, but . . . you deserved to know. That was selfish of me."

"Keeping that from me was fucked up," he agrees. He grinds his teeth together, and a tendon in his neck twitches as he wars with himself. "But for some reason . . . I can't stop thinking about you."

A hopeful little bird flutters in my chest. I've been waiting my whole life to hear him say that.

"You're in my fucking head. Day and night. And I keep thinking, what if you gave my sister that cash and saved her life?"

"I hope I did." And I mean it. For the first time, I hope Sophie returns to Beaumont. I hope she's alive and well and Miles can stop living with his guilt.

But she can't come back yet. It's not safe. Our stalker is still out there.

"You're in my head too," I whisper.

"Bet your boyfriend loves that."

I pull off the promise ring Jordan gave me. "I don't have a boyfriend."

Miles arches a brow and finally takes his eyes off the road to glance at me. "Yeah?"

"Yeah. Turns out, he really was cheating on me. A different girl this time." I give a humorless laugh. "I'm an idiot."

"Glad you're finally catching on." But a hint of a smile pulls at the corner of his mouth. "He never deserved you. Even when your personality sucked."

"My personality never *sucked*."

"When it wasn't your personality, yeah, it did." He twists his hand around the steering wheel. "Why did you change for *him*? That's what I don't get. Is it his money? The meathead, frat boy look?"

"I . . . changed to be the girl I knew he wanted. He's more than just money and good looks. He treated me like a queen." An image of him fucking Chelsea and the sounds of him panting and groaning pop into my head. "At least, I thought he did. He bought me clothes, flowers, chocolates, my prom dress, my phone."

"So . . . his money."

"No." My hands curl into fists, and I hate that Miles is making me defend my relationship with Jordan when that's the last thing I want to do right now. "That was his way of showing he cared about me. That's what I loved—he cared about me so much. He wanted to be with me forever."

Cared. Wanted. We're already past tense.

Miles is silent for a few seconds before he says, "Those flowers he gave you? Those are my sister's favorites."

"The white roses?"

He nods.

My heartbeat echoes in my head like a train picking up speed.

"And let me guess? Those chocolates he got you—they were dark chocolate."

"How did you . . ." Slowly, the pieces are starting to click into place. The white roses, the dark chocolate I didn't even like—

"That red dress you wore to prom. Bet he picked that out too."

My red prom dress. Just like the one Sophie wore. "He did," I whisper.

"And the whole pom-pom thing?" Miles lifts an eyebrow at me. "Your idea? Or his?"

His.

Miles doesn't need to hear my answer. "He bought you clothes like she used to wear. He called her baby; he calls you baby. Hell, he even nicknamed you *Maddie. Sophie? Maddie?* Not much of a coincidence, is it?"

Sophie.

Maddie.

Sophie, Maddie, Sophie, Maddie—

"He called me her tonight," I mutter into the tangible silence. "He called me Sophie."

I was never special to Jordan. I was always just the replacement.

Miles was right. This whole time, he told me I was just another one of those girls. That's how Jordan saw me. How everyone saw me.

If I disappear, Jordan will just find another girl to replace me with. Ash or Chelsea or some other girl, and he'll dress her up and dye her hair brown so she'll be another version of Sophie. The girl he's never gotten over. The girl he really wants. And if he can't have her, he'll take everybody else and pretend the girl he's inside is the one he lost months ago.

A tear falls down my cheek. This whole time, I've been worrying about what it would mean if I'm not with Jordan, if I'm not Maddie.

Now, I don't want to be her anymore.

"You're definitely broken up?" Miles asks.

I nod, tucking the promise ring in my pocket. "We're definitely broken up."

I'm not sure how I'm going to break the news to Mom. She'll have a thousand questions—*What happened? Are you still going to USC? Are you going to pursue book publishing now?*—and I won't have any answers for her.

I want to cry on Natalie's shoulder, but I know she won't answer if I call. I'm not sure she even wants to be my friend anymore. And after she hears about the breakup, maybe she'll choose Jordan over me. They were friends first, after all.

"So is this just a ride home?" Miles asks. "Or rebound sex?"

I know he's trying to lighten the mood, but I don't feel like joking around. "A ride home. You're not a rebound."

His deep brown eyes find mine in the dark. "Good. I don't want to be your rebound."

What does that mean? He wants more than sex?

I click on my phone for a distraction, but it's a mistake. Countless texts are waiting for me from my stalker. The latest:

> roses are red

> violets are blue

> that girl is dead

> and you will be too

Miles's voice eventually breaks through the buzzing in my head. "Madalyn?" This isn't the first time he's called my name.

I want to cry, throw up, scream—

They're saying Sophie is dead. That I'm next.

They could be lying. They could be . . . but I know they're not. Sophie didn't make it out of Beaumont alive. I sent her off with the cash she needed, but before she could escape, our stalker found her.

They killed her.

And they want to kill me too.

I throw my phone onto the floor. "I'm sick of this! The texts, the calls, the threats. I delete my social media, so they text and call me instead. I'd block their number, but I know they'll just find another way to get to me."

"Don't block them," Miles warns. "You don't want to engage

in any way. Don't let them know they're getting to you. Probably shouldn't have deleted your social media, actually."

"That's what the police told me to do."

"Yeah, well, look how good they are at their jobs. My sister's still missing." Miles sighs through his nose like a bull. "Towns like Creekview and Beaumont don't see a lot of serious cases. They deal with petty theft and speeding. Not stalking or abduction or murder. So they don't know how to handle them. That's why me and Soph did so much research. Stalkers want to get your attention, get a reaction out of you. They want to know they're scaring you. Best thing you can do is not give this lowlife what they want."

We pull into our driveway. Miles flicks the headlights off, but neither of us moves.

"Thanks for the ride." My voice comes out watery, weak.

He nods to my phone, still on the floor at my feet. "What did your stalker send you?"

But I can't tell Miles that. I can't confirm his worst fear: that he's not going to find his sister alive. That he'll never talk to her again, never see her smile, never hear her laugh. That he let her go to that party on her own—the last place she would be seen alive—and he'll never get to tell her he's sorry.

CHAPTER NINETEEN

THE NEXT DAY, I ask Miles to do something illegal with me. For a good cause.

When we reach Liv's house, we get lucky—her family keeps a spare key under a potted plant, and no one is home.

Nausea churns in my gut when we cross the threshold. This is wrong. This is what someone has been doing to me, and now I'm doing it to someone else.

But I'm only breaking in to get proof, not to scare the shit out of her and everyone she lives with. I definitely don't want to scare her poor grandmother.

"We need to be quick," I whisper.

Miles snorts. "That's what she—"

"No." I press my finger to my lips, and Miles feigns zipping his shut.

Downstairs is a messy kitchen with ingredients everywhere. Nothing is cooking on the stove or in the oven, but something smells delicious. The bathroom door is open and there's a chair in the shower.

How much care does her abuela need? Liv never talks about it. She never talks about anything personal, really. At least not when I'm around. I've never asked either, and I feel a pang in my chest. Natalie was right about one thing—I've been a shitty friend.

Every step up the narrow staircase creaks. I cringe every time, waiting for someone to burst out of a room and attack us. But no one does.

Upstairs are two bedrooms and an open area that's been converted to a tiny office space with an old, chipped wooden desk and a monstrous laptop.

Liv's room is a mess. Clothes are scattered across the floor, and the overflowing hamper reeks of sweat. The room is only big enough to fit her twin bed and a dresser. Her walls are bare except for a bulletin board.

"Here we go," Miles murmurs.

The board is covered with pushpins and sticky notes.

August 5 - Sophie last seen at Jordan's party

Last saw her going upstairs to "get a drink"

Left her phone at Jordan's. Why leave it if she was running away?

Hiding something?

Every note is about Sophie. But not in a creepy stalker way like I expected. Liv is trying to figure out what happened to her best friend too.

Even though it should bring me relief, my gut only twists. Another dead end.

At the bottom of Liv's bulletin board are four sticky notes, each with a single name scrawled across.

Miles?

Jordan?

Ash?

Maddie?

Are we her suspects?

A door bangs downstairs.

Miles and I glance at each other, eyes wide. He leaps into

action first, scrambling for a closet door and pulling me in. My heartbeat thunders in my ears.

Shit, shit, shit. We're about to get caught. Liv might not be a stalker or a murderer, but she will fuck us up if she finds us in here.

Miles eases the door shut as quietly as possible behind him and wedges in across from me. The closet is tiny and narrow, barely big enough for the two of us.

My breasts are pressed fully against his hard chest. His intoxicating scent fills my nose, and god, my self-control is waning. I don't know how I'm supposed to share a space this small with him and not touch him. I try to give him room, flattening against the wall, but there's no escaping the alluring warmth of his body.

His breath is minty sweet and curls around my cheeks and neck every time he lets out a ragged breath. He presses into me, nearly every inch of my body touching his, and now I have nowhere to go.

"God, you're soft." His whisper is low and sultry in my ear. My knees wobble.

I hold my breath. So whoever is in this house with us doesn't hear. And so Miles doesn't find out that just three words from him can undo me.

Downstairs, a woman speaks slowly in Spanish. That must be Liv's abuela. The walls are so thin I can make out every word, but four years of Spanish class have done little for my comprehension.

When Liv's husky voice responds, a chill runs down my spine. What if she comes upstairs and finds us in here?

"My heart's going to explode," I whisper.

Miles's fingertips brush the outside of my bare thigh, and I hiss. "Then let's distract you," he murmurs.

"That won't—" I'm about to tell him, *That won't help*, but the first brush of his lips against my shoulder stops me. Maybe this is the distraction I need because suddenly, I don't care if Liv swings the closet door open and finds us here. All I care about is feeling Miles on every inch of me.

His lips are featherlight on my skin, drifting from my shoulder . . . to the hollow behind my collarbone . . . to the curve of my neck. I shudder.

I feel him smile against my skin. The whisper of his lips up my neck is echoed by the trail of his fingers skimming my thigh. Slow inch by slow inch, higher and higher until he reaches the hem of my shorts. I almost whisper a grateful prayer that I didn't wear a skirt. Otherwise, I'd be unzipping his jeans and easing him inside me right here in Liv's closet.

We're in her *closet*.

Feet bound up the stairs and Miles feels me tense up again. His fingers skim the hem of my shorts until he reaches the space where my thighs meet. Wetness pools there, eager for his touch.

But his hand keeps moving, trailing along the bottom of my shorts and down my other thigh. Every muscle in my body has turned to jelly. My brain only able to focus on every brush of his skin against mine.

Liv digs through her dresser. What if she opens her closet to grab a pair of shoes?

Miles's tongue flicks out, licking up my neck to my ear. Setting me on fire. My legs nearly give out and I moan.

He quickly covers my mouth with his hand, both of us freezing.

The drawer clatters shut and the room falls silent. My lungs burn. I need air, but I don't dare breathe.

From downstairs, Liv's abuela calls for her in a thin, frail voice. And, after a few moments' hesitation, Liv bounds back down the stairs.

I suck in a deep breath, but Miles doesn't drop his hand from my mouth. Instead, he presses harder when his lips return to my neck. Kissing first. Then tasting me with a soft sweep of his tongue. And finally sucking my skin into his mouth. Hard.

My knees do give out this time, but Miles shoves me deeper into the wall, keeping me upright. The solid length of him digs into my shorts, the sweet friction making me melt.

I want him to pick me up and fuck me against this wall. But not here. We can't do this in Liv's closet. We need to get the hell out of this house.

Beneath his hand, I whisper his name.

"Say it again." His command reverberates across my skin, down my spine.

"Miles," I tell him. "We have to go."

He grinds against me and I moan again.

"Shh," he whispers in my ear with a chuckle. "You'll get us caught."

Downstairs, Liv asks about where something is. Beef maybe? Her abuela murmurs and Liv sighs. There's shuffling. Then the door creaks open and shuts again, their voices fading.

All the muscles in my body relax.

"Guess they forgot something at the store," Miles murmurs. He drops his hand from my mouth, and I miss his touch the second it's gone.

I want that hand back on my mouth. Muffling my noises while he makes me scream.

"Thank god," I whisper, even though we're alone. "That was way too close."

Miles turns the knob and cracks the closet door open. A sliver of light casts across his face, illuminating the discolored skin around his eye. The bruise he got for me. I suppress the urge to reach out and skim a finger along the hard edges of his face.

"You sure you want to leave? I kind of like it in here with you." His voice is like gooey chocolate.

"I'm sure. I don't want to be arrested for breaking and entering." I take his hand, and every nerve in my palm sings like I'm holding a sparkler. I lean toward him, the one whispering in his ear this time. "But guess what? We have plenty of closets at home to choose from."

Miles doesn't pull me in a closet again when we get home. Not when he sees Mom's car in the driveway. Disappointment sits heavy in my stomach.

The smell of chicken lo mein hits me as soon as I'm through the front door.

"Guess who got Chinese food?" Mom calls from the counter where she's heaping noodles and rice on plates.

"The best mom in the world?"

"Ding ding! You win a plate!" She holds one out to me. "What's Jordan doing tonight? You can invite him over if you want. Chinese and movie night."

Reflexively, I open Instagram for something to look at other than Mom's face when I tell her the news.

Of course, Jordan's flushed, beaming face pops up first. His arm slung over Brett's. Having plenty of fun without me.

When I click on his profile, my heart sinks. He's already removed me from his bio. It shouldn't hurt as much as it does—I broke up with him, he cheated on me—but this confirms it's real. The party wasn't just a nightmare. I'm not Jordan Goldman's girlfriend anymore.

I have a text from Natalie.

> I'm still mad at you so don't respond but I'm sorry about Jordan

My thumbs fly across the screen.

I wait for the three dots that indicate she's typing, but they don't come. She's not ready to forgive me yet.

"Hon?" Mom asks. "Are you texting Jordan?" She takes a seat at the table and I follow suit.

"Um. Jordan's busy tonight," I tell her.

Mom scoffs. "Tell him he's lame and we will *not* miss him."

"He's actually . . . not going to be coming over anymore."

She pauses with her fork hovering over her plate, her typical chipper demeanor slipping away. "Oh no. Did something happen?"

I nod, biting my lip hard to stop it from quivering. "We broke up."

"Oh, hon." Her face falls. "I'm sorry. Nothing you two could work out?"

I manage a small "no." I can't tell my mom that my boyfriend—*ex*-boyfriend—cheated on me. It's too humiliating.

"This is tough, I know," Mom says. "First breakups are usually the hardest ones. Especially when you had a boyfriend as great as Jordan. But you know what? I'm glad you had such a great first boyfriend. That means you'll have high standards for the next guy who comes along."

I know she's trying to help, but listening to her talk about how great Jordan is isn't helping at all. He was the best first boyfriend I could've asked for. I thought he would be my husband someday. I didn't think I'd ever date anyone else.

Now he's deleted me from his bio, probably already hooked up with two more girls, and I was just pressed up against Miles Mariano in a closet.

"What are your college plans now?" Mom asks. "Are you still going to USC?"

"No idea." I poke at my chicken lo mein. "Honestly? College is kind of the last thing on my mind right now."

Between Jordan and Miles and my stalker, I haven't thought about college in weeks.

"What about the community college like we talked about? There's still time to enroll. Then you can get your basic courses out of the way and transfer to a four-year school when you've decided your major."

"Actually, I'm not undecided. I want to be an English major." I'm not sure where the certainty comes from, but I've never been more sure about anything.

I've always loved books. I want to read them, edit them, sell them, market them, any of it. All of it. As long as I'm working with books, I know I'll be happy.

Mom beams. "That's great, hon." She takes my hand across the table and squeezes. "You can major in English and take that publishing course. Work in New York like you've always wanted. You only get one lifetime to follow your dream. Now's your chance."

"I still want to move out, though," I blurt. When Mom's face turns wounded, I add, "To get away from my stalker. I want an apartment."

Hopefully, they won't be able to follow me there. Maybe all my stalker wants is to get me out of Beaumont.

"We'll make sure that's all over before then." I don't know how she can sound so sure. "But we can look for an apartment near the college for you. How about we go visit the campus this weekend and do some shopping? I'll pick you up after work tomorrow."

"That sounds great." I can't help the smile that spreads across my face.

Even though I'm still hurt by what Jordan did and I wish things could've worked out between us, this new future in which I go to college to study English and work in book publishing sounds almost as good.

And for some reason, the first person I want to tell is Miles.

I decide to read on the roof in the waning sunlight, even though it's possible my stalker might be out there watching me right now. Let them. Let them try to come for me so I can finally figure out who the hell they are and end this. I'm done changing who I am and how I live my life because someone wants to scare me. I'm going to reactivate my social media accounts, I'm going to wear the clothes I want, and I'm going to sit on my roof and read like I've been doing for years.

A screen door whines and smacks shut. A dark figure hurries out into the yard and peers up.

Shit. They've found me—

"Hey, hon? I've gotta head to the inn!" Mom calls. "The chef started a fire in the kitchen again!"

The frantic pounding of my heart slows. "Sounds like you need a new chef!" I yell.

"She's a great chef! I just wish she wasn't an arsonist! I'll be back as soon as I can!"

Once Mom's car backs out of the driveway, I return my focus to my book, but my mind keeps drifting, and not just because of the stalker out there somewhere. Even the wild threesome on a secluded ranch isn't enough to distract me from the boy in the room next door. God, the heroine in this book is so lucky. I want to ride his face and have hot, sweaty sex all night and then again when we wake up three hours later, still exhausted but hungry for each other.

I shouldn't rush into anything, though. Not that I even know if there's anything Miles would want to rush into with me. He's made it clear he wants my body. But whether he wants me is another question entirely.

Jordan and I just broke up. I told Miles he isn't a rebound, and he said he doesn't want to be one. Plus, the sting of Jordan's betrayal is still sharp. He cheated on me, right under my nose. Who knows what Miles gets up to when he's not with me.

He said he's never had sex. But if there's anything I've learned in the past few weeks, it's that anyone can lie easily, right to your face.

Still, I don't think Miles is lying. I actually think he's the most honest person I've ever met. Somehow, I know I can trust him.

The squeak of plastic makes me jump. Miles climbs out of his window.

He doesn't say a word. Just smirks and swaggers my way before plopping onto the roof beside me. The bruise around his eye has turned an even deeper purple.

"I have news," I announce.

"Yeah?"

"I'm majoring in English. At the community college. Mom and I are going to visit this weekend."

He grins. "So you finally decided to listen to me."

"No, you had nothing to do with it."

He stretches his arms over his head, smiling like the Cheshire cat. "And then you're going to New York and doing your book stuff. Just like I told you."

I roll my eyes, but I'm grinning like an idiot. I never realized how sad it made me to let go of that dream to be with Jordan until now. Imagining a future with Jordan made me happy, but not like this.

The night is growing darker as lights flicker out, as the town hunkers down to sleep. We'll see more stars peeking out soon until they're all the light we have.

I love this spot on the roof. I love the peace and quiet of our small town, the way the mountains become a darker and darker blue the farther out you look.

"Are you commuting?" Miles asks.

"I'll probably get an apartment close to school."

"Maybe I can visit." He lowers his voice. "You know, check out the shower. The table. The bed. Make sure everything's working right."

A small lump forms in my throat. "Maybe. It's an hour away, though."

"Great. Gives me at least two hours to listen to an audiobook and two hours away from Gran."

I don't want to admit to him how great that sounds. How I want him there every night, doing things to me I've been daydreaming about for years. But Jordan just ripped out my heart and stomped on it—I'm not ready to give it away to someone else yet.

Miles leans closer to me and points, his arm reaching over my legs. "Look." I turn to where his finger points. A constellation of stars. "Orion."

"How can you tell?"

"Can't. Just making shit up."

For the first time in I-don't-know-how-long, I laugh.

Miles is still leaning close to me. I can feel his nearness without looking at him, smell the Old Spice cologne that brings back the feel of his body pressed against mine in that closet. My heart stutters.

He slides his hand up my arm, the nerves under every inch of skin bursting like fireworks. His hand stops at my cheek. Caressing me more tenderly than anyone ever has. With the slightest pressure, he turns my face toward him.

We're so close now, mere inches apart. His warm chocolate eyes search mine for an answer. "Do you need another distraction?" he murmurs.

A distraction sounds lovely. Something to draw my thoughts away from my stalker, from Jordan's betrayal, from my fight with Natalie, but I already know whatever happens with Miles won't be just a distraction. He's always been more.

I shake my head. His seductive smile flickers until I whisper, "I don't want a distraction from this."

His fingers thread through my hair, but I'm the one who closes the space between us. At the first brush of my lips against his, my stomach somersaults violently, my breath catching in my throat.

I've imagined this—our first kiss—so many times, I can't count them all. But this is better—this is real. I'm actually kissing Miles Mariano. And his lips are softer than I ever imagined.

Our lips part, fitting perfectly together. Somehow, even though just hours earlier he was sucking on my neck and the hard length of him was grinding against me, this kiss feels like the most intimate touch so far.

He leans back a fraction of an inch, a cool breeze whispering between our mouths, before kissing me again. His hand fists my hair, and he pulls me into him, opening my mouth wider and slipping his tongue in. I moan into him.

Way better than I imagined.

When he pulls away, he keeps his eyes closed for a few more seconds. A shit-eating grin across his face. My heart thuds like I just finished a five-mile run.

The world is not always a dark and scary place. Sometimes you get moments on the roof with a boy who kisses you for the first time and already knows exactly how to kiss you.

"You have no idea how long I've been wanting to do that," he says.

"Before or after you saw me again at Natalie's party?"

He tips his forehead against mine. "Always."

"Then you should do it again."

But instead of leaning in, Miles grabs my hand and kisses my fingertips. It almost feels more intimate than sharing a kiss.

I watch him. Mesmerized.

Wherever he touches me, my skin buzzes. Like my body has been hibernating until now. Until him. "God," I whisper.

With a wicked grin, he says, "It's Miles."

He leans toward me, but I retreat. "We shouldn't." I shake my head, trying to pull myself out of this Miles-induced haze. "I've been single for, like, two days. We should . . . slow down." The words are nearly impossible to get out. That's the last thing I want to do.

Miles doesn't let me go. "Stop worrying about what other people think you should or shouldn't do, and do what you want. What do you want?"

"You," I whisper.

His eyes turn ravenous. "Then lay down."

So I do. Another cool breeze glides along the exposed skin on my face and neck and legs, making me shiver, even though every other part of me is on fire.

His jeans scrape across the roof as he inches closer. He keeps himself propped up on his elbow and threads his hand into my hair again, running his fingertips back and forth. I wish he would do that all night.

The first kiss starts slow. A gentle press of lips against lips before his tongue brushes against mine. I open for him, and his tongue sweeps in. So expertly I wonder what else he can do with that tongue.

We kiss for so long, I have to turn my head away to suck in a breath. His face is getting harder to see in the darkness. Even though I can only make out the outline of him, I know exactly how he's looking at me—like a predator, starved after months in hibernation.

He doesn't let me catch my breath for long. He turns my head back to him and kisses me hungrily, groaning into my mouth. I've never heard him make that sound before, and my god, I want to make him do it again.

Then he pulls my bottom lip in his mouth and sucks. I'm about to combust. I'm already soaked and aching for him.

When he releases my lip from between his teeth, I stand and he follows. I grab his hand and climb back in through my window. All sense and logic are gone—I don't care about anything except getting Miles's mouth on me. All over me.

"Told you." He smirks.

"Told me what?"

"That you'd invite me into your room."

I roll my eyes but can't help the laugh that escapes my chest. He was right.

I keep the light off, and before we've even made it halfway across the room, he sweeps me into his arms. I wrap my legs around his hips and he crushes my lips against his.

Finally.

For a brief flicker of a moment, I wonder if he's not going to know what to do with me. He's never had sex, and I still don't know how far he's gone. Virgins don't usually know what they're doing, do they?

But then I think of what he said to me. *Wanna show me how it's done?* And suddenly I don't care about the experience he does or doesn't have—I want to show him exactly how it's done with me.

When I started having sex with Jordan, he'd already been with Sophie. Probably pictured her every time he was with me, compared in his head all the ways she was better. Closed his eyes and imagined she was the one he was thrusting inside. With Miles, I don't have to worry about that, even though I know there have been other girls. I know he has eyes only for me. He has from day one.

He sets me on the edge of the bed, kissing me so hard, my neck tips back. But he keeps me upright with a firm hand on the back of my head.

His mouth moves down my neck, sucking and licking and

nibbling. A shiver races down my spine. He repeats the movement on the other side, and I can already feel the hickeys blooming there. "I've been wanting to do this a long, long time," he murmurs against my skin. "So we're going to be here a while."

"Good. I'm not going anywhere."

He doesn't rip my tank top and bra off. Instead, he peels my top over my head slowly, dropping it on the floor. His fiery gaze falls to my breasts, heaving under my bra.

When he leans in to brush a kiss against my lips, his face is almost pained. "Can I touch you?" he whispers, a beg underlying his words. I want to hear him beg for me all night.

"Now you ask?" I laugh.

But he doesn't crack a smile. "I want you. Every inch." He brushes my hair behind my ear and my heart stutters. "But I only want what you want to give me."

"And what if I only wanted you to go down on me?" I tease.

Miles plants his hands on either side of me, boxing me in. "Then that's all we'd do, and I'd make sure at the end of it, you're soaked and trembling and can't take anymore."

My breath catches in my chest and I don't know when—if— I'll ever breathe normally again.

"And if I want to give you everything?" I whisper.

"I don't think you're ready for that yet."

"How would you know?"

"Because I know you just broke up with your asshole ex. Even if he was a dick who didn't deserve you, part of you still loves him."

Sometimes, it unnerves me how well he can read my thoughts without being inside my head. "But this isn't about love."

His eyes turn stormy and I wonder if that was the wrong thing to say. "You said everything." He presses a hand over my heart. "That's everything."

I want to give him that, I do. He's the first boy I ever loved, and I don't think I ever completely fell out of love with him. But he's right. Part of me still loves Jordan. I need more time before I can give my whole heart to someone else.

"That might take a while," I tell him.

He slips a bra strap off my shoulder. "I've got time."

Miles kneels on the floor between my legs, and the sight of him on his knees before me is nearly enough to undo me. His hand slips around my back and deftly releases the clasp on my bra. His throat bobs as he slides it off me.

His eyes eat me up. I'm on a stage with only him in the audience. "*Fuck*." He whispers the word like a prayer.

His hands slide up my ribcage until his knuckles skim the undersides of my breasts. Then he reaches up to cover them, massaging gently. I gasp at the touch. His palms scrape over my nipples, making them peak, and a groan escapes his lips.

"Jesus Christ, you're perfect." The words are barely out of his mouth before he wraps his lips around my nipple and sucks.

A sharp intake of breath hisses through my teeth, hands flying to his hair and he doesn't shake me off or pin my hands down. He pushes his head into my palm, giving me permission to do whatever I want.

Warmth pools between my legs when he releases my nipple with a soft *pop* and latches onto the other. A sharp, electric shock strikes down my body. *This*. It's never been like this. Even in the beginning with Jordan, it's never been—

Miles swirls his tongue around my nipple, then sucks the skin around it into his mouth. He sucks so hard, I whimper. I've never had hickeys on my breasts, but I have a feeling I will tomorrow.

He keeps going back and forth, sucking, nibbling, licking until I can't take it anymore and push his head down, whimpering. He replaces his mouth with his hands, squeezing while he sucks at the skin along my ribcage. A gasp escapes my throat. No one's ever done that before, and holy shit. I never thought I could get so turned on by someone's mouth on my stomach.

Miles Mariano's mouth on my stomach. When he said every inch, he meant it.

His head dips lower until he's trailing kisses just above the waistband of my shorts. The further south he goes, the more sensitive my skin gets. I'm boiling, a tea kettle on the verge of screaming.

Suddenly, his mouth latches onto my inner thigh and he sucks so hard, my eyes nearly cross. I claw at his hair, but he's not budging.

"Miles!" I gasp.

A tiny, arrogant smile flickers across his lips. "That's my girl."

Then his mouth is on me again, sucking like I'm the most delicious candy. He switches to my other thigh, pulling hard at my skin. When he nibbles, I cry out.

He hasn't even reached the place I'm aching for him most, and I'm already putty in his hands. He's Mozart and he plays my body like his favorite grand piano.

He kisses down my thigh all the way to my ankle and does the same to my other leg. The ache for him is turning to agony. I need him. Now.

As if sensing my growing need, he unbuttons my shorts and yanks them off me, tearing a hole in the fraying hem. Neither of us cares. He kisses at the peak of my thighs. Then across my panties.

I jerk involuntarily and he clamps my thighs down. "You're not going anywhere," he growls.

"Wasn't planning on it," I breathe.

This is happening. This is really happening. With Miles Mariano.

He doesn't lift me up so he can take my panties off. Instead, he hooks a finger in them and pushes them to the side, baring me.

We both suck in a breath. "*Fuck*, Madalyn," he groans.

My legs and heart tremble in unison. I love hearing him say my name like that. Like he's on the verge of breaking.

He leans in, the warmth of his breath heating the pool of wetness waiting for him. He plants a tender kiss against me and I whimper. "Please."

He smirks. "Only because you asked nicely."

His tongue glides up me in one long, luxurious stroke. Swirling once, twice at the peak.

I stop breathing. I can't believe I was worried he might not know what he's doing. He knows *exactly* what he's doing.

Then he stops. So suddenly I worry something's wrong. He's changed his mind. He doesn't want to do this. Not with me. I freeze and open my mouth to ask—

But then his lips wrap around my clit and he sucks. *Hard.*

My back arches and a moan escapes. I'm worried I'm going to fall back, but he keeps me upright with unrelenting hands clamped on my hips. He was right—I'm not going anywhere.

"Is this what you like?" he murmurs.

"Love," I gasp.

His tongue flicks out to lick in circles before stroking again and again between my folds. Alternating between sucking and tasting me.

Every movement, every sound that passes my lips is involuntary, uncontrollable. With Jordan, every moan was projected for his benefit. Because I knew my sounds got him off faster. But with Miles, I don't want this to go fast.

I want him to take his time with me. I want the delicious torture. Want him to wring every ounce of pleasure out of me until I'm immobile, so drained I can't even think. And I know that's what he wants too.

When he sucks my clit again, my thighs tremble. He gives a low chuckle. "So that's how I make your thighs shake."

He leans up so he can suck harder. *Oh, fuck.* My heart hammers wildly, my skin on fire. Pleasure is building up, up, from my toes to my temples.

"Don't stop," I beg him.

In answer, he sucks harder and slowly slips a finger inside me. I cry out.

He hisses. "You're so fucking tight."

He waits until his finger stretches me before slipping it out and sliding it slowly back in. After the third slow thrust, I move into his hand, and he doesn't hold back anymore.

I feel his groan through my clit and gasp. He keeps sucking while thrusting his finger in and out, curling it to hit that sweet spot. I'm so full, burning, soaked. My thighs shake uncontrollably now, clamped tight over his ears.

He's not letting up. He sucks me harder, finger fucking me faster.

That familiar buildup of pleasure mounts. Holy shit. This is really happening. The inevitable explosion coming to a crest—

Stars explode across my vision as my orgasm barrels through me. A loud, uncontrollable moan bursts out of my chest. Miles keeps sucking and pumping his finger inside me, the squelching nearly drowning out my cry.

He doesn't stop until I'm almost in tears, shaking and whimpering from the overwhelming pleasure.

I fall back on the bed, and the strokes of his tongue grow softer, slower. Following me as I come back down.

Then his lips wrap around my clit and suck hard one more time. Making me cry out again and arch my back off the bed.

Exactly as he wanted me. Soaked, trembling, and unable to take anymore.

No one's ever made me come before. All the times I had sex with Jordan, it didn't happen once. I just figured it was something only I could make happen with my hand or a vibrator. But Miles . . .

Miles.

I expect him to stand and unzip his jeans. I'm drained, limp, but he could still fuck me if he wanted. I'd wrap my legs around him tight and ask him to rub my clit until he makes me come again.

But when I find enough strength to sit back up, he's still kneeling in front of me with a smirk across his face. "Let me know when you're ready for another."

CHAPTER TWENTY

THE FIRST TIME I had sex with Jordan, I expected to feel changed. A different girl. Everyone makes such a big deal about your first time, but it's like a birthday. I woke up the next day and felt exactly the same.

But one night with Miles and I'm changed forever.

Even my stalker can't bring me down from my high, despite how hard they try. All throughout my shift at Mariano's, my phone keeps flashing. DMs, texts, calls. I reactivated my social media—a clear message to my stalker: *You will not make me disappear.* A message they didn't like, apparently.

Even if I someday get an answer from my stalker about why they've done all this, it'll never be explanation enough for this level of obsession.

During the lulls, I draft an evidence email in my Gmail account. Officer Jackson told me to keep all the evidence, so that's what I'm doing.

This morning, Mabel finally approved Miles to sign up for his GED tests and let him cook on the grill. Under her supervision. I'm secretly glad he's spent most of the day back in the kitchen because every second I'm around him, the air is charged. I can feel the electricity pulsing through me and all I can picture is him shoving me up against a wall, bending my knee to the side, and fucking me right here in the diner.

When Miles finally emerges from the kitchen with George's to-go order before closing, he's got a smear of flour across his forehead and a dusting of sugar at the corner of his mouth. I want to lick it off.

"Is hell worth minimum wage?" he asks me.

I laugh, and when I can't take my eyes off his mouth, return my focus to the register. No one can know about us, and I don't want George picking up on anything.

He opens the bag Miles hands him with a loud crinkle. "I ordered six. There's only five in here."

"Guess you're not very good at counting."

"You ate my sixth donut!"

The evidence *is* all over Miles's face. But he shrugs. "I don't know what you're talking about, man. You can pay for your donuts or you can leave empty-handed. Your choice."

George shakes his head and hands the money to me. "Whatever you did to get that shiner," he tells Miles, "I bet you earned it."

"You should see the other guy."

It isn't true—the blows Miles landed on Jordan didn't leave a mark where anyone could see—but his comment is enough to send George skittering out the door.

Miles locks it behind him. "Thank god that nightmare's over."

"You were back in the kitchen most of the day. You didn't experience half the nightmare out here."

"That was more than enough." He comes around the counter and brushes a hand against my hip. "Did you miss me?"

After last night, I've been missing him every single second.

"You two are closing up tonight!" Mabel shouts, striding out of the kitchen.

We leap apart. Luckily, she doesn't notice. Too busy hurrying to the door and fishing her keys from her pocket.

"Thought you didn't trust me to close up," Miles says.

"I don't, but I trust her." She points at me. "I pulled a muscle in my back, so you get to do all the heavy lifting tonight. Have fun."

With that, she's out the door.

Miles turns to me with a wicked grin and flicks off the lights so the only illumination comes from the street lamps outside. "Oh. I intend to have fun."

"What about the—"

But before I can ask about all the work we still have left to do—wiping down the tables, mopping the floor—Miles shoves me up against the wall, every inch of him pressed against every inch of me. He can read my mind.

"Be gentle," I whisper, even though I don't completely mean it. "I'm still recovering from yesterday. My boobs look like they were in a fight."

He chuckles and pushes his hand up my shirt, caressing my breast over my bra. "I'll be gentle until you don't want me to be."

His words melt me. "Perfect."

Miles scoops me up in his arms and carries me into the kitchen, where we're guaranteed privacy from prying eyes. He sets me down on the counter, on the only spot not covered in dishes and food, and spreads my legs. He fits between them and crushes my mouth to his.

I'm still so hungry for him. Last night was the appetizer. Tonight, I want the full course. "Can we pick up where we left off?" I murmur.

He shakes his head, and disappointment makes my stomach dip. "We're starting from the beginning."

This time, he shoves my shirt above my breasts with zero patience and pulls my bra down. He keeps his kisses and licks gentle until I dig my hands in his hair and whisper, "More."

His mouth turns ravenous, sucking at the still-tender skin and making me want to burst. If any human could be classified as a drug, it would be him.

He moves his mouth up to my neck, pawing at my breasts before sliding his hands up my skirt and gripping my ass. I'm already aching for him, squeezing my thighs for some relief even though he's between them. I won't get the relief I want until he uses his tongue.

Miles pulls away, both of us already breathing heavily, and grabs a condom from his pocket. "You want to use this?"

I nod. "*Yes.*"

Instead of unzipping his jeans and slipping it on, he drops it on the counter beside us and moves in for a hungry kiss. His tongue sweeps in my mouth and it's the worst kind of teasing. I love his tongue in my mouth, but right now, I want it somewhere else.

I tug his shirt over his head, desperate to see him. We don't have as much light as we did that day I snuck into his room, when he was shirtless and wet from his shower, bracing himself over me, but I can still make out the curves of hard muscle on his arms and shoulders, the divots of his abs, the dark ink below his shoulder.

But before I let my palms touch him the way I ache to, I brush my fingers as gently as I can against the purple skin around his eye. "I'm sorry he did that to you."

Miles's jaw sets. "I don't want to talk about him right now. Or ever again."

I trail my palms over his shoulders, down his arms, across his abs. When I brush against the skin just above his waistband, he growls. I love every inch of him.

"Me neither." And I mean it. I want to move on. I want to

forget about Jordan and who I was with him. I want to forget about the future we planned. I want to forget about Chelsea and Ash and my stalker and pretend none of this ever happened. Start over, start fresh, with Miles.

He likes my answer. He skips working his way down my body and goes straight for my panties, tugging them off and unleashing himself on me.

I cry out as his tongue sweeps across me, flicking at the apex and sending tingles from my head to my toes. The strokes of his tongue turn obscene as I grow wetter for him. He groans and slips a finger into me.

I don't know how much longer I can take it. My heart thunders in my chest, and I want him inside me. But I also can't bear the thought of him stopping.

"Keep going," I whisper.

"You think I'm stopping anytime soon?" he asks. "Not until you come for me. I'll be here all night if I have to."

If last night is any indication, it won't take nearly that long.

His mouth is back on me, sucking my clit this time, and I hiss. I clutch at his hair so hard I worry I'm hurting him, but I have to pull on something.

When my thighs start trembling, he sucks harder, licks faster, pumps his finger inside me. The growing pleasure mounts and I wonder how I went so long not having orgasms with Jordan when I could've been coming undone every night with Miles.

He thrusts his finger inside me so hard, over and over, I'm worried I might have to beg him to stop until I start to clench around him and overwhelming pleasure barrels through me. I lose myself, lose all sense of everything except the feeling of Miles's mouth on me, still working me through the throes of my orgasm and not relenting until I'm a whimpering mess in his hands.

He's got the condom on and probing at my entrance before

I've even opened my eyes. He rolls his hips back and forth, rubbing against my clit and sending shockwaves of pleasure through me.

I clutch at his arms. "Now. Please."

"Your wish—" I stop breathing when he nudges the tip in— "is my command."

Oh my god, this is happening. This is really—

In one slow, luxuriating stroke, Miles buries himself inside me.

I cry out at the same time he emits a low groan. "*Fuck* me," he mutters. "You're so fucking perfect."

My nails dig into his biceps as he stretches me. *Finally.* "I've been wanting to do this a long, long time," I whisper, echoing his words from last night.

He grins against my lips. "Is this what you pictured for our first time?"

"More like missionary in my bed." He freezes until I add, "But this is better."

His hand wraps around the back of my head, fisting in my hair at the same time he thrusts slowly into me and I gasp. "We can do every position you want. I will do whatever you want me to do to you." Another long, slow thrust. "And I will love every second of it."

When I pull his hips into me, he picks up speed just slightly. He wants to take his time. He doesn't want this to be over too fast. Neither do I.

His hand drifts between my legs and rubs my clit, gently at first. When I thrust my hips forward to meet his, his thumb starts to rub harder and harder as he moves faster. My heart is a train picking up speed, but there's no way I can come again.

"How does this compare to your books?" A smirk across his delicious lips.

"So much better."

His mouth latches onto my neck and I'm about to combust

from the pleasure. Him thrusting between my legs, rubbing me, sucking me. This amount of pleasure isn't survivable. I'm going to die like this and I'll die happy.

"Yes," I breathe. "Don't stop."

He pounds harder, the slap of skin against skin filling the room. "I love fucking you," he growls.

My breasts bounce, and when he catches sight of them, he latches on to my nipple. I gasp and claw at him harder. My clit throbs beneath his hand.

"I love"—I stop myself before I can say what I really want. What I've been thinking for years—"fucking you too."

He picks up speed, hitting deeper. Making my head spin. It's never been this deep, this . . . mind-blowing before. Every cell in my body is singing.

My blood rushes through my veins and that familiar pleasure builds again. No, it can't happen again. It won't—

Miles thrusts inside me harder. His breaths come fast in my ear. "Come for me," he murmurs.

My heart explodes as the pleasure charges through me. My eyes cross and I let out a scream. Clenching around him and pulsing. He keeps fucking me through it, as fast as he can.

"That's it," he gasps. "Scream for me."

I couldn't stop even if he told me to. I scream so loud and so long, my throat goes hoarse, and still, he doesn't stop.

He groans, and it's the sexiest sound I've ever heard. He pulls me against him hard so I can't go anywhere and thrusts inside me one last time, throbbing over and over. "Jesus," he hisses.

I can't speak. Can't even move. I just sit limply in his arms, waiting for the erratic slamming of my heart against my ribcage to slow. Gulping down air.

When I can finally form words, I whisper, "We need to do that again."

He laughs, the sweetest music, and pulls my head toward

him for a kiss. The frenzy is over now. This time, his kiss is tender and . . . loving. It makes my heart squeeze.

"How was your first time?" I ask.

"Better than I ever imagined." His voice is so full of sincerity, butterflies burst free of their cocoons in my chest. "But I think next time will be even better."

"Wow. Already thinking about the next girl before you're even out of me," I tease.

He gives a slow, hard thrust inside me, making me gasp. A warning. A promise. "Next time with *you*."

The bell hanging on the diner door clangs, announcing someone's arrival.

Shit. We both freeze, eyes wide. Did we forget to lock the door?

"Hey, hon?" Mom calls. "You still here?"

I shove Miles off me, scramble to adjust my clothes, and comb my fingers through my hair so it doesn't look like I was just fucking Miles Mariano in the kitchen.

I completely forgot Mom said she'd pick me up after work tonight so we could visit the college campus this weekend.

Miles smirks at my frenzy, slipping his shirt on casually like we're not about to get caught post-fucking. I try to tame his hair, but it's no use.

"Yeah!" I bustle out of the kitchen, heart in my throat, and grab my phone from under the register. "Sorry, we were in the middle of closing up."

Mom takes in the rest of the diner that we haven't even touched yet.

"I'll take care of it," Miles offers, stacking a chair on a table. I don't know how he can sound so calm and casual when I'm completely breathless.

"Excellent." Mom grins at me. She has no idea what Miles and I were really doing in that kitchen. Thank god. That was way too close. "Let's go."

As we head out the door, Miles winks at me, and I'm actually disappointed that I'll be going a whole forty-eight hours without seeing him. I went six years without him, and now I can't last five minutes.

I'm officially addicted to him, and I already can't wait to find out where I get him alone next.

———

Mabel's truck bumps into our driveway. Mom's car had a flat tire this morning in the hotel parking lot, so Mabel picked us up after we called the tow truck. The whole trip home, I've been jostled between her shoulder and Mom's.

My first thought was that my stalker followed us to the hotel and punctured the tire. But no, I'm leaving Beaumont to get away from them. They can't follow me to college too. There has to be an escape.

Mom and I spent the entire weekend touring the Tunxis campus and exploring the rest of Farmington. We ordered from every food delivery service so I'd know which ones to keep patronizing when I'm in school, I put in an application for a cute apartment, and we shopped for school and apartment supplies. And none of it was enough to take my mind off Miles, who spent most of the weekend texting me all the things he wanted to do to me when I got home.

"My boss wants to buy horses for the inn," Mom is saying now. "*Horses!* Don't get me wrong, I love a cute pony as much as the next girl, but does she realize how expensive horses are? Food, water, shelter, vet, someone to clean up after them. I'll brush a horse, but I'm not shoveling what comes out of it."

"Don't know why she doesn't just give you the reins to the place," Mabel says. "You already run it, anyway."

I follow Mom out of the truck and up the driveway. "Har-har, good pun," Mom says.

Mabel raises an eyebrow at her. "What pun?"

"'Give you the reins?' We were just talking about horses?"

Mabel rolls her eyes so hard, her head must hurt. "I've never made a pun on purpose."

"Oh, I love a good pun," Mom says. "What about you, hon? Are you pro- or anti-pun?"

I stop dead in my tracks. Our window is open. The curtains dance gently in the breeze.

We never leave the windows open. Mom keeps the AC unit running upstairs to cool the house in the summer, so the windows stay sealed during the day.

They both follow my gaze. Mom whispers, "Oh my god. We need to get back in the truck."

She takes my shoulders and hurries me down the driveway. Mabel is already on the phone with the police when she climbs in the driver's seat.

"Is your grandson in the house?" Mom asks.

Mabel shakes her head. "Shouldn't be."

The police tell her to stay on the line, so I call Miles.

He picks up on the third ring. "Hey, beautiful."

His voice makes warmth flood my chest. I press the phone closer to my ear and hope Mom didn't hear him. "Hey, are you home?"

"Nope. Just mowed the lawn at my mom's. Miss me?"

"Um." I glance at Mom, but she's not listening, her eyes fixated on our open window. "I just wanted to let you know someone broke into our house."

"Holy shit." His voice drops. "Are you good? Is Gran good?"

"Yeah, everyone's okay. The police are on their way."

"So am I."

Before I can tell him not to come home yet, he hangs up.

Mom tries to distract us with chatter, but even she runs out of things to say.

Miles shows up before the police, and he climbs into the

bed of the truck. I slide open the window behind me. "Good?" he asks me.

I nod and tuck my hand in my pocket, where my knife sits.

It takes forty minutes for Officer Jackson and Callahan to show up, so it's a good thing my stalker didn't come out wielding an ax.

"Great." Miles groans. "That the same cop who told us to get lost?"

"Yep," I mumble.

Officer Jackson taps on Mabel's window and instructs us to stay in the car while they secure the property. They go through our side of the duplex first, then Mabel's. Then all around the backyard and in the garage.

Neither of them looks particularly concerned when they mosey back to us. "Property's secure," Officer Jackson announces. "Let's have you all take a look around. See if anything's been taken."

Even though I know the police have searched the entire property, sweat pools under my arms when we step inside. Someone was in here, and I can feel the ghost of their presence like a blanket.

Besides the window, there aren't any other signs of forced entry. Officer Callahan tells us we need to start locking our doors and windows, and Mom snaps that we never leave anything unlocked.

Mabel's half of the duplex is untouched, and ours is far from ransacked. In fact, all of our valuables are exactly where we left them—our TV, our laptops, Mom's phone that she forgot on the counter.

"Some robber," Miles mumbles. Mabel elbows him.

My room is another story.

Every dresser drawer is open and all my clothes have been dumped on the floor. But I don't see any of my underwear. Not even the new ones I bought last week. My bed has been unmade, and I swallow down bile at the thought of someone touching it. Lying in it.

One glance at my bedside table tells me the promise ring from Jordan is gone too.

Mom wraps me in a hug. Over her shoulder, I spot Miles, his jaw clamped shut and hands in his pockets. Remembering this life. What his sister lived through.

We head back to the kitchen and Officer Jackson writes down the items that were taken, while Officer Callahan picks at her nails. They act like they're on their way out the door when she says, "Call us if you notice anything else is missing."

"Thanks, Officers," Mom starts, but I cut her off.

"That's it? You're not going to do anything?"

"What would you like us to do?" Callahan asks, monotone.

"You need to do *something*. My stalker broke into our *house*."

Mom places a reassuring hand on my shoulder and gives a gentle squeeze. "It's okay, honey," she murmurs.

Callahan narrows her eyes at me. "We've done everything we can. There's nothing more we can do for you at the moment."

"There *is* something you can do. Find them. Get them for gross use of technology. Do *something*."

They've underestimated me. I've done my research. I know they can do more, but they just don't care enough to. Exactly like Miles said.

Callahan examines her phone screen and I want to slap it out of her hand. "Have you thought about moving?"

"Moving?" I repeat.

"You said you have a stalker, right?" She says it like she still doesn't believe me. Even after this. "A lot of stalking victims move to another town or state."

I can't believe she's actually suggesting our best option is to move. To let my stalker drive us out of town. It's one thing for me to get an apartment while I'm in school—it's another for

Mom to buy a completely different house somewhere else. Away from the life we've built here, away from the memories we've made, away from our neighbors and her job and friends.

Away from Miles.

"So I have to uproot *my* life? Why can't you guys just catch this person and stop them?"

I'm tired of being the one who has to accommodate the criminal. *Blend in, wear clothes that don't draw attention, change your routine, get off social media, move away and leave your whole life behind.*

They're the one who needs to change. Not me.

Miles leans against the wall in the corner. "My sister went through this same shit. If you don't do your jobs, you'll have another missing person on your hands."

Me. I could be the girl on the posters.

Mom reaches for my hand and squeezes.

"Is that a threat?" Callahan asks.

Miles rolls his eyes, but before he can say another word, Mabel steps in. "That's enough. My grandson wasn't involved in my granddaughter's disappearance, and he's not involved in whatever's going on now."

Officer Jackson holds up his hands, stepping between me and Callahan when she opens her mouth again. He crouches in front of me and takes the hand Mom isn't holding. A part of me wants to cry at the tenderness, at the way he makes himself smaller to make me feel safer.

"No matter what anyone else has to say, I believe you, Maddie. I'll do whatever I can to help." He sounds convincing, even if his actions up until now have indicated otherwise. Maybe this is what needed to happen for him to take me seriously. "I can't imagine how shaken up you must be. This isn't something anyone should have to deal with but especially not an eighteen-year-old. From now on, I want you to call me anytime something comes up, okay? No matter how small it may seem. We need to put a stop to this."

"Okay."

"Document everything—every form of contact—and how it made you feel. That's really important. Don't forget that part. And write down anything you've changed in your routine to make yourself feel safe. All of that will help build your case."

I try to swallow the lump in my throat to speak but can't. So Mom wraps an arm around my shoulders and answers for me. "Thank you, Officer."

"Andre." He holds his hand out to her.

She's back to looking at him like he's Dr. Avery. "Thank you so much, Andre. We really appreciate it."

He hands Mom his card and tells us to give him a call if we want a referral for a security company that can install cameras and an alarm system for us. I don't even want to think about how much that will cost.

Mabel insists on making us dinner and gives us tips on self-defense in her kitchen until I go outside for fresh air. From my spot on the porch, I pull out my phone. I should tell Natalie about the break-in, even if she's still pissed at me.

But all thoughts are wiped from my head when I notice the text from my stalker. A video.

Not of me this time—of my stalker walking through my empty house.

I hit Save and then turn the volume all the way up, but they turned the sound off. They're careful not to show their feet or their hands reaching for anything. Nothing that could be used to identify them.

They end the video on the promise ring from Jordan sitting on my bedside table.

A new promise: they'll be back.

For me.

CHAPTER TWENTY-ONE

ON THE WAY to Mariano's for dinner, Mom fans herself and groans. "I miss winter."

How anyone can miss winter in Connecticut is a mystery to me.

Pale gray clouds blot out the sun and the blue sky, but I keep my sunglasses on. Hoping that, somehow, the poor disguise will be enough to keep my stalker from noticing me.

"So," Mom says. "Jordan stopped by earlier."

I freeze in my tracks. "What? Why? What did he say?"

Mom scans the street, and I can't tell if she's making sure we're not being followed or if she just doesn't want to meet my gaze. "He stopped by to see me. He's really worried about you, kid."

"About my stalker?" If he was so worried about me, he shouldn't have screwed up our relationship. Then we could still be together and he could be protecting me.

But . . . I'm actually glad we're not together anymore. A few months ago, I thought Jordan and I would never break up. I thought if anything ever happened to him, to us, I'd never recover. But now I'm basically with Miles and Jordan has been far from my mind.

I thought losing Jordan was the worst thing that could ever happen to me, but I'm actually . . . okay. Better than okay.

"Since when did you start hanging out with Miles?" Mom asks, a clipped edge to her voice.

Her question throws me. Miles? What does Miles have to do with Jordan worrying about me? I thought this was about my stalker. "Um. Since he moved here," I admit.

"I thought I told you I wanted you to stay away from him." Her voice is tight now. But she's trying to restrain herself so we don't have a full-blown argument in the middle of the sidewalk. "I've known guys like him, kid. He could get you in trouble. He could *be* trouble."

He could be my stalker, is what she wants to say.

"What exactly did Jordan tell you?" And why was he running to my mother to talk about me behind my back? He and I aren't together anymore.

"He said you've been spending more time with Miles and that you pulled away from him before your breakup." We reach Mariano's, and Mom pulls me to the side, out of earshot. "Nothing's going on between you and Miles, right?"

I stiffen. Jordan actually blamed me for our breakup, and my mom believes him. "Why would it matter if there was?"

Mom's frown deepens. "Because he isn't good for you."

"You don't even know him. You're just buying into all those dumb rumors. If you actually got to know him, you'd be glad someone like Miles cares about me."

Miles has been by my side since the beginning. When my best friend told me the stalking was nothing to worry about, Miles took me to the police station. When his mother suggested I was making it all up, Miles helped me look for evidence. When the police called me a liar, Miles stood up for me.

He's made sure I haven't had to face a second of this alone.

"With everything that's been going on . . . I just don't know how clearly you're thinking right now," Mom says. "I don't want you to put your trust in the wrong people."

"I'm not."

"Hon, Miles lives in our house." Mom's voice is hard now. "And someone is breaking in. Only two people we know have access to our home."

"I'm not an idiot!" She jerks back. I never snap at her. Ever. "I know how it looks. But it isn't Miles. I *know* it isn't."

Before Mom can say another word, we both catch sight of someone approaching us. Tall, bulky, tanned, handsome.

Jordan.

My stomach twists into a tight knot.

"I'll go get us a table," Mom tells me, and disappears inside Mariano's.

He's wearing khakis and a polo shirt. "Hey, bab—Maddie."

I suppress a flinch. He almost called me *baby*. I guess being broken up for a week isn't long enough to shake our old habits. Even though I've been tangled up in Miles since our breakup, seeing Jordan in front of me now leaves my heart with a hollow ache.

I still don't get how he could cheat on me when we were so perfect together.

"Were you working today?" I manage to ask him.

His brows furrow, confused by my question. "Yeah? Just got done."

"So when did you stop by my house to talk to my mom about me? During your lunch break?"

His eyes grow cloudy. Impossible to read. What goes on inside Jordan's head has always been a mystery to me.

Miles is the opposite. I've never had a problem reading him.

"I'm worried about you." Jordan takes my hand. "I don't care how much you push me away—I'm going to keep you safe. I won't lose another girlfriend."

A few months ago—hell, a few weeks ago—those words would've made my knees weak, would've made me crumble. But this is over now.

I pull out of his grasp. "You already did. We broke up. Remember?"

His jaw twitches. "Of course I remember. I just meant I won't let Miles hurt you like Sophie. I still care about you."

"Why did you tell my mom I've been hanging out with him?"

"Because you are?" His face contorts in disgust. "I still don't get why you hang around that freak. Why do you think he moved in with his grandma instead of his mom? So he could be closer to you. It's so obvious he's your stalker, but you don't even see it."

I hesitate. Miles said his mom didn't ask him to stay with her when he decided to come back to Beaumont. But what if Jordan's right? What if Miles wanted to stay with Mabel so he could be closer to me?

No. I know Miles isn't my stalker. That's impossible. "That's not your concern anymore," I tell Jordan. "*I'm* not your concern anymore."

Jordan steps back and sighs. "He's got you completely brainwashed. But I'm not giving up on you."

When we finally get Mom's car back, the mechanic tells us he found a GPS tracker attached to the undercarriage. Mom reports it to the police, but I know they won't do anything. They'll give us the same bullshit excuse that they can't do anything because I don't know who's responsible.

No. I need to handle this myself.

I drive to Home Depot, and the cashier doesn't even raise an eyebrow at my selections: razor blades and glue.

The razors blend in nicely with the car's undercarriage.

Whoever reaches for the tracker won't get away unscathed. Their flesh will turn to ribbons, and I'll have my proof. I'll know exactly who they are once I see the evidence on their arm.

An image of Miles reaching for the tracker flashes in my mind. I shake my head. I don't care what Jordan says, I don't care how convinced he is, Miles isn't my stalker. He wouldn't do this to me. He wouldn't get this close to me, trick me into falling for him, and torment me when my back is turned. He wouldn't do this to Sophie either.

I want to take a shower to clear my head, but Mom's already in there, using up all the hot water for the next hour. I pace in my room instead.

Things are amazing with Miles. I shouldn't let Jordan get in my head. But I thought things were amazing with Jordan too, and he was cheating on me. Miles could be doing the same. We never said we were a couple, so he has every right to be with other girls, but I would be heartbroken all over again.

Even worse . . . what if Jordan is right about him? What if Miles moved back here, into this duplex, so he could stalk me? Maybe that's how he convinced me to fall for him. Because he knows me in a way no one else does.

I need to talk to him. To say what . . . I don't know.

I rush for the door to the attic and fling it open—

He's already standing there, fist poised to knock.

When he flashes his signature smirk, all the thoughts and worries leave my head and I pounce on him.

He catches my hips and stumbles backward. Surprised, but meeting my lips. He drops onto the narrow staircase that leads up to the attic and I straddle him.

I let Jordan get in my head. But he's wrong. I know Miles. I know the real Miles. I can trust him. With my body and my heart.

In the diner, we took our time. This time, I want the frenzy.

He threads his hands through my hair and I grind on his lap until he moans into my mouth. Every sound he makes sends a shiver down to my toes. I want to hear it again. Louder.

I'm the one to drop to my knees this time.

I unzip his jeans and he's already rock-hard. He hooks a finger under my chin and whispers a kiss across my lips.

"You don't have to," he murmurs.

"I know." I've never wanted to do this with Jordan, but with Miles, I want to give as much pleasure as I get.

I take him in my mouth, swirling my tongue around the tip. His head falls back, elbows dropping onto the wooden step behind him, and he makes a guttural noise deep in his throat.

I almost smile. And when I lick up the length of him and he shudders, I do.

He's in my mouth again, and I move up and down slowly, keeping my tongue out to stroke him while I suck. I must be doing something right, because his eyes stay closed and his hand drifts to the back of my head, guiding me up and down.

When I suck as hard as I can from the bottom to the top, straining my jaw, his hips jerk up. "Jesus!" he gasps.

"How am I doing?" I murmur. "Better than the other girls?"

He leans down, face serious, and lifts my chin. "There are no other girls."

Good. I take him in my mouth and he falls back again. I quickly learn he likes when I stroke and suck at the same time, swirling my tongue around the tip when I get to the top.

"You gotta stop," he groans, "or this is going to be over really soon."

Fuck that.

I climb on top of him and pull off his shirt, tossing it behind him. Then I reach into his pocket for a condom.

His hands grip my waist. "Wait," he pleads. "I want to taste you." His honey-warm eyes search my face like he's seeking permission.

"As if I would stop you."

He flashes a wicked grin. In one swift movement, he scoops me up and switches places with me. He doesn't give me time to even think about what could happen next before he's tasting me, licking up and down before his tongue dives in.

It's my turn to shudder.

He sucks on my clit the way he knows I like, and when my thighs start to tremble, he grips them hard and flattens them against his head. So I can't go anywhere. I'm at his mercy and nothing turns me on more.

But I don't want to come this way this time. I want him inside me. Now.

I pull back and tilt his face up. His chocolate brown eyes are imploring. The purple skin is starting to fade into yellow, and I count each of the freckles on his face. My own personal constellation. He's the most beautiful boy I've ever seen.

When I stand, he follows. Until I push him back toward the stairs. "I want to fuck you, Miles."

He lounges on the staircase with a cocky grin. "Be my guest."

I straddle him again and roll the condom down. His eyes don't move from my face, but the arrogant smile slips away. Replaced with lust. Desire. Need.

I press his hand between my legs while I slide him inside me. He rubs, helping me stretch around him and we both groan. The sound echoes up to the empty attic and he claps a hand over my mouth.

I rock my hips back and forth slowly at first. Tormenting him the way he did to me. "Rub me harder," I tell him.

When he does, I reward him. I tug his earlobe between my

teeth and fuck him faster, rising up and smacking my ass back down as hard as I can.

His breathing hitches and he has to drop the hand from my mouth to hang onto my hips. "Fuck," he breathes. "I had no idea you'd be like this."

I love that he's not the one in control this time. He's the one who's losing his mind, who's coming undone.

I yank my shirt up, bra already gone, and he groans before wrapping his lips around my nipple and sucking. I slow my movements, unable to fuck him as fast as I want when he's distracting me like this.

"Every inch of you is perfect," he murmurs. "You know that?"

I thrust my hips forward, burying him deeper inside me. "I do now."

To him, I am. And that's all that matters. What he thinks of me, and what I think of me. And for the first time in a long time, maybe ever, I like the person I am almost as much as he does.

Miles brings my hips up and back down. "Faster, Madalyn," he pleads.

All it takes is hearing him say my name. I'll do whatever he wants.

The stairs creak beneath us as I ride him faster, jerking my hips back and forth, my breasts swaying in his face. Every time one gets too close, he licks or drags his teeth along my sensitive skin. Somehow, he knows exactly what I want. He can read me like a book.

"You're so fucking sexy when you ride me hard." He sets the pace with me, hands on my hips, until my moans start to echo off the walls again.

He covers my mouth so I can moan into his palm as loud as I want. I pull his other hand to my throat.

"You want me to squeeze, gorgeous?" he asks.

My heart sings. *Gorgeous. Beautiful.* So much better than *baby*.

I nod, and when he squeezes the sides of my neck, a flood of wetness and warmth pools between my legs. A tingling sensation spreads down from my head, and it's almost like an out-of-body experience. I never thought sex could feel this good.

I hum against his hand, completely unable to control myself now.

"You're soaked," he murmurs, moving the hand from my mouth to between my legs.

"That's because you feel so fucking good," I gasp.

He rubs my clit faster, frantic. "You better slow down," he warns. "I'm gonna cum soon."

But I don't slow down. I'm too close to the edge. I rock against him harder, letting him fill me all the way up, my head buzzing. The pleasure mounts and mounts—

His hips suddenly jerk upward and he clenches his teeth together. "*Fuck.*"

I keep riding him through it, rougher, faster, chasing my own orgasm until it barrels through me and I cry out and collapse against him. He keeps fucking me from beneath as I pulse around him, holding me to him while the other hand keeps my hips steady. Driving as much pleasure through both of us as he can. Wringing every ounce of it from me.

I bite down on his shoulder to stifle my cries.

He pumps inside me once, twice, then collapses back on the staircase. Both of us sweaty and limp, chests heaving.

"That was a first," I breathe.

"What was?" He's breathless too. "Fucking on the stairs?"

I nod. "That, and being on top. I liked it."

He leans back to look at me. "You've never been on top before?"

"No, Jo—" I start to say *Jordan* but decide that's a bad idea while Miles is still inside me. "The . . . other person always liked to be on top. In control."

I never realized that wasn't a good thing until now. Until Miles. He's made me see everything differently.

He grips the back of my neck and pulls me into him for a rough kiss. "You can be on top whenever you want," he says. "Gives me a great view."

A ringing phone breaks through the silence. My phone.

Miles groans when I pull away.

"Give me five minutes and we can go for round two," I tell him. He beams. "You can just stay here. Unless you have somewhere else you'd like to try it. A closet, maybe?"

He stands and zips his jeans, brushing my hair over my shoulder. "Sounds fun, but I think maybe we should be a little crazy and try a bed for once."

"Why a bed? That's so boring."

"Not with you, it won't be." His eyes grow serious. Almost . . . nervous. "I don't want it to just be fucking. I want to show you . . ." He steps closer, and my heart leaps into my throat. ". . . how important you are to me. I want it to be . . ."

"Special?" I tease, even though that's exactly what I want.

He doesn't take the bait, his gaze intense. "Unforgettable."

My knees turn to jelly. I want that too. Every time with Miles has already been unforgettable, but I know what he means. More than fucking. *More.*

In my room, my phone rings again. I sigh and step toward the door, even though it's the last thing I want to do. "I'll be right back."

Miles snatches up his shirt and flicks my ass with it. I giggle and he tosses it through the door after me.

I expect the caller to be my stalker, but it's Mom. "Hello?"

"Hey, hon. Where are you?"

"In my room."

"Oh, good!" I hear the bathroom door open and the patter

of feet. She flings my bedroom door open. With the phone still pressed to her ear, she asks, "How do I look?"

She's in a form-fitting black dress. Her makeup is done, complete with gorgeous ruby lipstick, and she even curled her hair.

"Wow. Where are you going?"

She smiles. "On a date."

"*What*?" I finally end the call. This will be her first date in . . . ever, since I've been alive. "With who? *Please* don't say George."

She shrugs. "It's a secret. For now. If it turns into anything more serious, you'll be the first to know."

At the mention of a secret, my stomach twists. She has no idea the secret I'm keeping from her.

"I need you to look at the menu with me. I'm torn between a steak and—" Mom tilts her head before stepping into my room and grabbing something off the floor.

"Everything all ri—?" I start to ask. Then I see what she picked up.

Miles's shirt.

My stomach drops.

She dangles it in the air from her index finger and thumb like it's a soiled diaper. "What is this?"

"Um. Jordan must've left that here."

Her scowl deepens. Mom hates nothing more than being lied to. "*Jordan*? The size XL? No, he would never fit in this. This belongs to Miles, doesn't it? He's been in your room?"

I shrug because the truth is he's been in here a few times. "We're . . . friends."

"Seems like you're more than friends if he's walking around half-naked in your bedroom."

I open my mouth to protest, but she holds a hand up to stop me. "Is this why you and Jordan broke up?" She shakes the shirt. "This was really unfair to Jordan, kid. Not to mention I don't want you sneaking around with a boy under my roof."

"No, that's not why Jordan and I broke up! And Miles and I aren't sneaking around! *God.*"

Mom throws the shirt down on my bed. "I don't know what the hell is going on with you, kid. Jordan was the best first boyfriend you could've hoped for, and now, what? You're throwing that relationship away for a guy you've known for a couple of months? Is it the hair or some tattoos I don't know about? Or maybe it's the suspensions or the school expulsion."

"I'm *not*. And you don't know the first thing about Miles." She seriously has no idea what she's talking about. None.

"*You* don't know the first thing about Miles!" she shouts. "He just got here five seconds ago. How well do you really think you know him?"

I open my mouth to object, but . . . how can I? She's right. I barely knew him when we went to school together, and he's only been back a few months. Sure, we've spent a lot of time together since, but I also spent a lot of time with Jordan and he was having sex with other girls behind my back.

There was a lot I didn't know about Jordan. And there might be a lot I don't know about Miles.

"You and Jordan just broke up." Mom lowers her voice, trying to keep it even this time. "It's too early to be moving on. You need time to heal. After your first love—"

"Jordan isn't the perfect angel you think he is, Mom." I fold my arms. "I'm not the one who cheated. He did."

Her brows shoot up. "Jordan cheated on you?"

My eyes flood with tears. "Yes. That's why we're not together anymore."

"Oh, honey." Mom wraps me in a warm hug, and I didn't realize how badly I needed one until now. "I'm so sorry. Why didn't you tell me sooner?"

"Because it was humiliating." If Jordan wanted other girls, that means I wasn't enough. I've never been enough.

Mom steps back and holds onto my face. "Hey, you have nothing to be embarrassed about. He's the one who screwed up. He blew it with the best girl he ever met."

Despite the tears spilling down my cheeks, her words make me smile. "Thanks, Mom."

She hugs me again. "You're a wonderful girl with a huge heart. Any boy worth giving it to should treat you the way you deserve."

I sniffle into her shoulder. "Miles does. I know you haven't seen it, but you have to trust me. He understands me. He really cares about me."

He loves me, I want to tell her. But I don't know that for sure.

She sighs. "I still don't like him, but . . . if he means this much to you, then I hope that's true." She pulls back and fixes me with her usual grin. "Now. How about we change into our pajamas, watch crappy movies, eat way too much junk food, and complain about boys all night?"

I wipe the tears off my cheeks. "No way. You have a date! Go!"

"You sure?"

"Mom, I'll be fine. We can watch crappy movies in our pajamas tomorrow night."

She gives me another hug. "Okay, girls' night tomorrow. Mabel is here, so she'll keep an eye on things." She points to the attic door. "And I'm putting a lock on that door. I don't care if you're eighteen. You can sneak around in his car like every other teenager, not your bedroom."

"That was brutal." Miles slips into my room as soon as Mom's headlights retreat out of the driveway.

"Yeah." I don't want to talk about it right now. I want to lose myself in Miles like I have been for the past week. But then I remember Mom's not-at-all-subtle warning. "Mom said Mabel's keeping an eye on everything, so maybe you shouldn't be in here."

He chuckles. "She's already asleep. Heard her snores from downstairs. Even over your mom yelling."

I groan. "How much did you hear?"

He shrugs. "Only about the fan club she's starting for me. I like her suggestion to sneak around in my car, though."

That gets a smile spreading across my face. He can always get me to smile, even when I feel like I've forgotten how. "I like your bed idea better. And you can spend the night."

Sometimes, I daydreamed about that more than the sex. Miles curled up around me, holding me while we sleep. There when I wake up to kiss me and tell me I'm beautiful.

He snorts. "So your mom can find me in your bed and murder me in my sleep?"

"I can lock the door."

Miles closes the distance between us, looming over me and caressing my jaw to tilt my mouth up to his. "All right. As long as you promise to protect me from your mom."

As soon as his lips brush mine, I can already tell this time is going to be different. More.

We kiss so long, I get lost in him. He wraps an arm around me to hold me against him, keep me upright, while the other hand massages my scalp. I moan into his mouth.

He scoops me up and lays me with heartbreaking tenderness on the bed. I've actually never had sex in my bed before. Never even had Jordan in my room. I was always too ashamed. Ashamed of the books I used to get mocked for, ashamed of the dreams I abandoned for a boy, ashamed of the girl I used to be.

I'm glad I got to save this space, this moment, for Miles.

He climbs over me with this pure, happy smile on his face

that makes my chest squeeze. My heart aches to say those three words to him, but I bite my tongue. It's too soon, too fast. Like Mom said, I just broke up with Jordan.

But I know she's wrong. I've been falling for Miles a long time. It's not too soon or too fast. It's right.

Yet I still can't bring myself to say it.

Miles eases me up and gently slips my top over my head before turning me over onto my stomach. I assume he wants to take me from behind until he starts massaging my shoulders. I let out an involuntarily groan as he works out the knots. His expert fingers rub in circles down my back slowly, relaxing every muscle. I didn't realize how much I needed this, but he did.

"Sometimes I think you know me better than I know myself," I admit.

"Sometimes I think you do too." His hands don't stop working me over.

"Really?" I didn't expect him to feel the same way about me.

"Yeah. I didn't realize I was letting people blame me for Soph to make themselves feel better. Not until you said something."

Miles moves off me and the bed shifts under his movements. Then he picks up one of my feet and digs his thumbs in.

I sigh. "If you want to have sex, you better stop or you're going to put me to sleep."

"So sleep," he says simply. "I'll be here in the morning."

I'll be here in the morning. I grin into my pillow.

He rubs both my feet, then massages each of my legs. Taking his time over my calves and thighs. When he reaches my skirt, he pulls it off me gently before massaging my ass, which feels like a massage that's as much for him as it is for me. By the time he's done, I'm practically drooling and comatose.

He flips me on my back. "Front side now?"

I shake my head. Even though a front massage sounds great, I have other plans. "I want you to fuck me."

He smiles and brushes a kiss to my lips before pulling out a condom and setting it on the bedside table. Then he kisses up my neck before tugging my earlobe between his teeth and sucking—the sensation surprisingly erotic. I gasp, shocked by the wetness that pools between my legs.

He does the same to the other side before kissing down to my breasts and sucking my nipples gently. He tugs my breast out and releases it, then does the same to the other, making them jiggle before trailing kisses down my stomach. I writhe beneath him. I want him more than I ever have.

Miles sits up and pulls my panties off, admiring me. "I really, really like you, Madalyn," he murmurs. "The real you. I knew you were still in there somewhere."

Tears spring to my eyes, and he leans down to trail gentle kisses from my jaw to my shoulder. I wrap my arms around him and whisper, "I really like you too."

He kisses me again, and it doesn't feel like he likes me. It feels like much more.

His tongue sweeps into my mouth, giving me a preview of what's to come, before he moves down to my thighs. He plants kisses on them, moving back and forth from one to the other. Making his way up slowly.

Then he kisses between my thighs the way he kisses my mouth. Closed lips first, then he opens, caressing me with his cool breath until I shudder. His tongue sweeps out, tentative at first. Before stroking and making me jerk. "Agh!"

He doesn't smirk at my sounds this time—he just keeps going. Licking like I'm ice cream until I'm wriggling beneath him. Until finally, *finally*, he reaches the apex and darts the tip of his tongue out.

I arch off the bed, gasping. He's going to make this the most excruciating, tortuous pleasure yet.

I dig my fingers into his hair and tug him toward me. He does exactly what he knows I want him to: he wraps his lips around my clit and sucks.

I whimper, melting beneath him. He sucks softly at first, massaging the outside of my thighs at the same time. *Holy fuck.* Then his sucking gets gradually harder and harder as the pleasure inside me climbs. His hands on my thighs grip tighter, pressing them against his head when they start shaking.

When he senses me getting close, he stops sucking and I nearly cry. "Please," I beg.

But he replaces his mouth with his thumb, rubbing me in circles, and penetrates me with his tongue instead. I groan, loving his tongue thrusting inside me, but I want his mouth on my clit.

"No," I plead. "I want to come."

"You will," he promises. "But I'm making this one unforgettable."

Fuck.

He rubs softly, keeping me going but no closer to the edge. I rock my hips back and forth, riding his tongue. Every time I get close to the edge, he lessens the pressure on my clit. Making me whimper and grind into his hand, desperate for the release.

"*Miles,*" I whine.

He chuckles. "You want me to make you come, beautiful?"

"Yes."

He doesn't give me the frenzy I want. Instead, his tongue glides up me in one long, slow ascent. He laps at me, making me whimper uncontrollably again.

Until he plants a kiss where I want him. I jerk. Another kiss. I tug his hair, pull him into me. But he only "mmm"s and kisses me again, with tongue this time.

Horrible, perfect torment.

I nearly growl with frustration, but that's when his mouth latches onto my clit and pulls it between his teeth.

I cry out, hips bucking off the bed. He flattens a hand between my hips to keep me in place. His mouth makes a small slurping sound when he sucks me into his mouth. I'm soaked, the mattress beneath me already damp. And he's just getting started.

He takes his sweet time, tender at first. But thank god, he doesn't stop sucking. He moans against me and it reverberates through all my nerve endings that are already on fire.

I start pulsing beneath him, the muscles inside me contracting. My heartbeat echoes in my ears, my head. All the way down to where his mouth devours me. He sucks and slurps and licks like he's starved. Like he's waited his whole life for this and he's finally got it.

"Come on, Madalyn," he whispers. "Let me see you come."

His head pushes into me so hard, my breasts sway gently with his movements. When he suddenly slides a finger inside me, I can't help but yell out. "*Fuck!*"

"That's right," he murmurs, rocking his finger back and forth inside me. "I love when I make you lose your mind."

I gasp out the words: "You can . . . do it . . . anytime."

He curls his finger and sucks harder and I can't take another second of it. My heart is on the verge of exploding in my chest when I finally go over the edge, arching up and grasping at his hair while I cry out. The pleasure so overwhelming, my eyes water. He keeps sucking and pumping his finger inside me while I pulse around him. My body writhes, but he keeps me in place with the hand firmly across my hips.

My legs collapse onto the mattress when I start to come back down, completely limp now. He doesn't stop sucking, even when I whimper and try pushing his head away. I can't take any more. But he's not done.

"Please," I beg.

He gives a microscopic shake of his head. "I want another."

God, he's so fucking sexy when he says stuff like that. "So give me another. While you're inside me."

Finally, he looks up at me. "You don't want another like this?"

"There will be plenty of days to do that," I tell him. "I want you before I pass out."

He slips off his jeans and boxers before leaning over me and I manage to lift my exhausted arms long enough to caress the smooth skin along his arms and chest and stomach. Over the hard ridges and taut muscles. Across the letters delicately inked below his shoulder. Every inch of him is perfect.

"Then I'll oblige you," he says.

"Oblige? Big word."

He gives me his cocky little grin. "I read too, remember?"

Hell yes, I do. How could I forget? That's one of the sexiest things about him. Somewhere on the long, long list between his abs and his hair and his voice and his laugh and his smile and his freckles and his tattoo and his tongue—

Without his gaze leaving my face, he rubs his hard length between my thighs. I whimper. He's going to have to do all the work this time. His mouth made me useless. "Condom," I gasp.

His eyes are intense, pleading. "Can I feel you bare? Just for a second."

"Once you start," I warn, "you won't want to stop."

"If you want me to stop, then I will." He bends down, breath caressing my ear. Sending a shiver down my spine. "I'm at your mercy."

He always knows exactly what to say. Goosebumps race down my arms. "For a second."

He presses open-mouthed kisses against my neck, thanking me. Then he leans up on an elbow so he can watch my face while he eases himself inside me raw.

He slides in so easily, I gasp when he unexpectedly buries himself to the hilt. He lets out a sharp rasp I've never heard from him before. That sound alone makes me want to ride him until he cums harder than he ever has.

"Fuck, Madalyn." He's the one who can't take it this time, eyes squeezed shut. "You feel . . . so . . . fucking—" I clench around him and he hisses through his teeth, nearly collapsing on top of me. "*Shit.*"

"Fuck me, Miles."

He moves back until he's nearly out of me and then slowly stretches me as he eases back in. Then he stops again, the arm keeping him upright starting to shake. I love the effect I have on him.

I don't wait for him to move again. I wrap my legs around his and thrust my hips down.

He jerks and presses a heavy hand against my chest to stop me. "*Shit.* Wait. Let me put the condom on."

He pulls out of me, glistening with my wetness, and rolls the condom down.

"Maybe we can try that again sometime," I tell him. "When you've worked on your pull-out game."

He freezes and raises an eyebrow at me. "I hope you're fucking serious."

"I am."

"Ugh." He groans and crushes me with his body, devouring my mouth with his. "You're incredible."

I smile. "I know."

But he's not joking. "I hope you see how fucking hard I'm falling for you."

That stops my heart. The breath catches in my lungs. Miles is falling for me.

I'm pretty sure I've already fallen.

"Does that mean you'll fuck me now?"

He smirks, grabbing my ass and lifting me just off the bed before he swiftly buries himself inside me again. I gasp.

He keeps his pace slow, but every thrust is hard. Ramming

into me as deep as he can go. His eyes don't move from my face. Making sure I'm loving every second.

My eyes fall closed and mouth open as I moan, breasts bouncing with every slow, hard pump inside me. He doesn't cover my mouth with his hand or try to swallow my moans. He lets me be as loud as I want.

One hand squeezes my breast, and the other, my neck. He uses just the right amount of pressure to make the blood in my veins sing. "Is this what you pictured for our first time?" he whispers in my ear.

"Yes." The word comes out in a gasp. "But a thousand times better."

"Really?" I can hear his smile without opening my eyes. "Better than your imagination?"

"Way better."

He drops his hand from my breast and dips down to suck on my nipple. I whimper, legs wrapping halfheartedly around him. Then his hand drifts between my legs and presses. Hard.

My eyes spring open.

"I need you to come again," he pleads.

"I don't know if I can," I admit. This is the first time I've ever come twice. I don't know if a third is even possible. My body is so ragged, I doubt it.

"Fuck. Then I'm going to be inside you all night."

I clench around him. *Oh god.*

His eyes flash up to me. "Stop that. I lose my fucking mind when you do that."

"What?" I ask innocently. "This?" I clench around him again.

He hisses and closes his eyes. He thrusts inside me so violently, I cry out. If this is how I get him to keep doing *that*—

"I want you to come while I'm inside you, but if you keep doing that, I'll finish first."

I shrug. "I don't mind. I'm used to not finishing before it's over. I never did, actually. Before you."

His eyes turn stormy. "Well, get used to finishing every time. I'm not stopping until you do."

"And what if I can't?" I challenge.

"You can." His eyes rake down my naked body that jerks with every hard thrust of his hips. "I know you've got one more in there for me."

He stares right into my eyes when his thumb lands on my clit and presses down. I moan, clinging to the solid muscle on his arms. He increases the pressure every time he slams into me, and I cry out, over and over and over.

I'm torn between screaming in pleasure and weeping in exhaustion. I want another, but I don't know if my body can take much more.

As if he can read my mind, Miles picks up speed. His hips thrust faster, his thumb turns more frantic between my thighs, and the warm sensation spreads down my legs to my toes.

"Come on, Madalyn," he begs over the slap of skin against skin. "I need you to come for me. I need to see it."

I can only whimper in response. I'm like a ragdoll beneath him, limbs limp and lifeless. Completely his.

My pulse picks up speed, the pleasure mounting like the steady climb of a rollercoaster to the crest before the fall.

"You're so fucking beautiful when you come," he tells me. "I want to make you scream for me every night."

God, I want that too. More than anything.

"Don't. Stop," I command, my heart slamming against my ribcage in time with his thrusts.

"Don't hold back." He leans down to my ear, burying himself to the hilt at the same time his thumb makes wild circles over my clit. Making me see stars. "Give me everything."

Release shoots through me as a scream of pleasure rips out of my throat. The rollercoaster cresting. The bomb exploding.

Every cell in my body screams along with me.

"*Fuck, yes,*" he hisses and pumps inside me as fast as he can, skin smacking against skin. Tears leak from my eyes while I scream myself hoarse. He rubs me through wave after wave of my orgasm, my legs shaking so hard, I don't know when I'll be able to walk again. He keeps fucking me, long after I can't take it anymore. Until he slams in one last time and I feel the length of him throbbing as he spills inside me.

We breathe hard, chest to chest. I'm amazed my heart hasn't given out on me yet, when the rest of my body has.

Before I've caught my breath, Miles catches my mouth with his. "I love fucking you," he murmurs.

"I love fucking you too."

And that feels like the closest I can get to the truth right now. Because I don't just love fucking Miles Mariano.

I love everything about him.

I love him.

CHAPTER TWENTY-TWO

MILES IS STILL BREATHING SOFTLY beside me in the dark when the memories surface. Of everyone's warnings about him.

He watches you all night and the next day you have a stalker.

It's so obvious he's your stalker, but you don't even see it.

Don't trust him, Maddie.

Don't you think it's pretty convenient that he's the only person who knows anything about Sophie being stalked?

He told her he was going to kill her.

It's obvious who it is. Your new neighbor.

He could get you in trouble. He could be *trouble.*

No. I know he's not my stalker. I know that. But . . . Mom's right. There's still a lot I don't know about him. There was a lot I didn't know about Jordan, and we'd been together for months.

I find Miles's phone next to mine on the bedside table. He has a passcode, which makes the knot in my stomach coil tighter, even if it shouldn't. Everyone locks their phone. That doesn't mean they have something to hide.

I lean over and touch his hand. He doesn't stir. I press his thumb to the screen, and it unlocks.

His phone is minimalist with few apps. Kindle, Netflix,

YouTube. No social media, of course. The only recent texts are between him and his mom, dad, Mabel, and me. Then there are a few unread texts—from State Farm for his car insurance, an offer for a new phone from AT&T, a Paypal security code, an appointment reminder from the dentist. Texts to Sophie that haven't gotten a reply in months.

No texts to random girls. No Chelsea. No Ash.

Thank god. A relieved breath rushes from my chest.

But it's instantly swept under a wave of guilt. I should've known he's nothing like Jordan.

I spot my name in the most recent text to his dad. I don't want to invade his privacy further, but I'm too curious not to click.

> Can't wait for you to meet Madalyn.

I grin. He's texted his dad a few times, giving him updates on his life while his dad's in jail.

The day after Miles moved into the duplex, he texted:

> Made it to Gran's. Beautiful girl in the other unit.

> I used to have the biggest crush on her.

> Wish me luck, old man.

Something swells in my chest. Even though I knew he had a crush on me too, there's something special about seeing the words written out. Admitted out loud.

I'm about to put the phone back when I notice an unsaved number. I scroll up to the first message. Sent to Miles last August—a week after Sophie went missing.

> I'm okay

Oh my god. My mouth goes dry.

Is this her?

Is Sophie still alive?

But no. My stalker—*our* stalker—sent me a message that she was dead. Did they track her down after she disappeared? After she sent this message?

Miles responded to the text immediately.

Soph?

Is this you?

Where are you?

Can I come get you?

Don't care where you are. Give me an address and I'll be there.

All to no response. He kept texting at least once a day for two weeks after that.

Soph?

Please answer.

Need to know you're okay.

He never got another text from that number.

I AirDrop the messages to my phone.

When I glance over my shoulder to make sure Miles is still asleep, his eyes are wide open.

Staring right at me. Going through his phone.

In the silence, we can both hear my heart pounding.

Before he can go on the offense, I do. I hold up his phone. "Were you texting Sophie? After she disappeared?"

I didn't get a chance to look through his call log. Maybe he called her and was able to talk to her. He's been hiding this from me the entire time.

"I thought it was Soph." He sits up. His voice is low, gravelly with sleep. "Figured she texted from a burner phone since I never heard from her again."

"Why didn't you tell me this?" I hiss. "This is kind of a big thing not to share when I'm helping you figure out where she is."

He shrugs, eyes narrowed. "Cops said it was somebody messing with me. They got a lot of false sightings and tips."

All those posts on Reddit. All those people who claimed to see Sophie, alive and well, living her life. How many tips did the police follow up on before they realized people were either calling because they saw a girl who sorta-kinda resembled Sophie if you squint or because they wanted the attention? Wanted to insert themselves in a case that had nothing to do with them so they could play hero.

Miles climbs over me, off the bed, and snatches his phone back. "Here's a better question: why the fuck were you going through my phone?"

"I just . . ." I scramble for the right words, but none of them will be enough. "I wanted to make sure you weren't lying to me."

"Lying about what?" he spits.

"The other girls." My voice quavers because I know. I know I'm ruining this, and it's the best thing that ever happened to me.

"Are you serious, Madalyn?" he shouts. I glance at the door, hoping Mom is sleeping deeply enough that she doesn't hear. "I'm nothing like him. Stop comparing me to that asshole."

"How am I supposed to trust you? I barely know you!"

In a flash, his fists are braced on the bed and he's inches from my face. "You barely know me? I was just inside you, like, two hours ago."

I try to form words, but none come to mind.

"I want you. Only you." He straightens and shakes his head.

"But maybe your mom was right. Maybe you need more time before we can . . . be more."

My heart drops. I rise up on my knees. "No—"

He holds his hand up, stopping me. "When you're ready, we'll have our chance. But I'm not ruining us with bad timing. You're too important for that."

My vision blurs. I'm losing the first boy I ever loved all over again. "Miles—"

But he's already heading for the door. When he turns the knob, he doesn't slam it behind him. He eases the door shut with a final, deafening click.

I want to puke. Scream. Sob. I've fucked it up. I ruined this before it had barely begun.

Losing Jordan hurt. But losing Miles is agony. When I've finally, *finally* gotten him. When the boy of my dreams finally became my reality.

I race for his door and knock over and over, calling to him. But he doesn't answer. "Miles! *Miles!*"

He ignores me until I give up, defeated and exhausted, and collapse back into bed.

With shaking hands, I grab my phone and text the number that may or may not belong to Miles's missing sister.

> Is this Sophie?

Silence.

> If this is you, I need to know. This is Madalyn Young. Your stalker is after me now. Please.

No response.

Mom is inside making lunch while Officer Jackson—*Andre*—installs our new security cameras. Turns out Andre was Mom's date the other night. Now he's basically her boyfriend, jumping at any excuse to stop by and see her, like a burnt-out lightbulb or a wobbly table leg in need of fixing.

I haven't talked to Miles since that night, and I've been left with a hollow ache in my chest for days. This morning, I finally texted him. A shot in the dark. *I'm sorry.*

He hasn't responded. He has every right to give me the silent treatment.

I can't believe I thought he would betray me too. He's not Jordan. But the breakup, the cheating, it's too fresh. All of it's made things blurry. Even though it guts me not to be with Miles . . . I know he's right. I need time before I'm ready for more.

I still haven't gotten a reply from that number either. Another dead end.

Rain clouds are moving in. Droplets hit my bare legs hanging over the railing on the porch, but I don't care. It's nice to feel something.

When Andre holds his palm out, I hand him another screw.

Yards away, someone calls out to us. "Hey! Need some help?"

Jordan doesn't wait for an answer. He jogs up from the sidewalk in basketball shorts and sneakers, sweat soaked through his white shirt.

I suppress my groan. At least in a couple weeks, he'll be heading off to California and I won't have to worry about running into him until winter break.

For the first time since we broke up, my heart doesn't ache at the sight of him. I don't long for the days we were still together and everything seemed perfect. All I want now is time and space away from him so I can heal and move on.

Jordan stops abruptly halfway through our yard, squinting up at something above my head.

And then he's sprinting for me.

"He's up there!" he shouts.

"What are you talking about?" I call.

On the porch, he swings the door open. Andre glances between us, eyebrows furrowed.

"*Miles*," Jordan says. "He's in your room."

Shit. Of course Miles is in my room. He probably came in to find me, to talk, but I can't tell them that. I can't let Jordan know how quickly I moved on and I can't let Mom know that she was right, I actually have been fucking the boy next door under her roof. The last guy in this town she wants me dating.

But wait. Miles can't be in my room. His car's not in the driveway. He's not even home.

Andre and I are on his heels as Jordan races through the kitchen and up the stairs.

Mom frowns, setting down a plate with a tuna sandwich to follow after us. "What's going on?"

Jordan flings open the door to my bedroom.

The room is empty. Everything is exactly where I left it.

"He was in here," Jordan insists. "I saw him in the window."

His eyelids and the skin beneath his eyes are puffy. His face doesn't have its usual dewy, boyish glow. He's exhausted. From partying too much or fucking too many girls or worrying about me, I don't know.

"Jordan, I think you might've been seeing things," I tell him slowly. "His car's not even in the driveway."

"Exactly! He wants you to think he's not here so you don't suspect him." I open my mouth to object, but Jordan cuts me off. "This is getting ridiculous, isn't it? We know who Maddie's stalker is. Why don't we just go look in his room? That's probably where he's got all her stolen stuff stashed."

A wary expression crosses Andre's face. His officer face. "We can't just go into someone's home without permission."

Jordan squeezes his chin. "What about the attic then? That's shared space, right?" he asks Mom.

"Technically—"

"Great. Let's go."

"Jordan, wait—" I reach for him, but he's already beelining for the attic.

He's become so obsessed with his theory that Miles is my stalker that he's completely convinced himself it's true, convinced himself that we're going to find something even though I know we won't.

When he swings the door to the attic open, I'm instantly hit with the reminder of what Miles and I did on that staircase. The memory of his groans fills my ears, the ghost of his mouth and hands all over me, and I try to suppress the ache between my legs.

The steps creak under our feet, and when we reach the landing, the stench of dust and mothballs chokes me. It's probably been months since anyone's been up here. Maybe years.

A tiny sliver of gray light reaches us from the small, lone window. Rain violently splatters the glass and drums against the roof.

Miles isn't here, of course. Just like I knew he wouldn't be.

"What exactly are we doing up here?" Mom clutches her elbows, as irritated to be in the attic as I am.

Jordan pulls out his phone and flicks on the flashlight. He sweeps it over the floor, lighting up boxes of Christmas decorations and forgotten knickknacks and something by the wall beneath the window—

"Wait. Point the light back over there," I tell him.

He does, following the lit path to a small pile . . .

Clothes.

"Don't touch anything," Andre instructs. Officer Jackson

again. He pulls out a plastic glove and slides it on before crouching and lifting up one of the items with two fingers.

The lacy, black thong Jordan bought me from Victoria's Secret.

Bile rises in my throat.

Mom gasps, and Jordan practically growls, "*I knew it.*"

The rest of my missing underwear is beneath the lingerie. Along with my pair of pajama shorts.

My heart pounds inside my chest so hard, it hurts.

A laptop I don't recognize sits beside my clothes, along with a drill.

All the stuff that was stolen out of my room has been sitting right above my head this whole time. While I was fucking Miles on those stairs, my missing clothes were just feet away. Everything I thought my stalker took from me when they broke into our house has been right here.

Turns out no one had to break in. He already lives here.

CHAPTER TWENTY-THREE

OUTSIDE, rain pours and Miles is in handcuffs. Mom, Jordan, and I watch from the porch.

Officer Jackson called dispatch as soon as he found what the drill had been used for: putting holes in the ceiling above our side of the duplex. One in my room and another in the bathroom. Right over the shower.

All those times I felt eyes on me while I was in my room, while I was naked in the bathtub . . .

I hadn't been imagining things. I hadn't been paranoid because I had a stalker lurking somewhere out there.

Miles was in my attic. Watching me.

That's how deep his obsession ran.

I'm an idiot. It's been obvious from the beginning. He was literally watching me at Natalie's party that first night he came back to Beaumont. I saw the evidence myself, and I still chose not to believe it.

I wanted to believe the best in him because I'd been in love with him for years. But I was never really in love with *him*—I was in love with the version of him I made in my mind.

The real Miles lied to me, manipulated me, followed me, spied on me, harassed me, threatened me, stalked me.

He kissed me.

He fucked me.

He lured me. Right into his trap. He made me fall for him. For a lie.

The betrayal makes Jordan's pale in comparison.

I haven't breathed since the flashlight landed on my stuff in that attic, and I don't know when I'll be able to catch my breath again.

I message Natalie and Liv about the news in our group chat and slip my phone back in my pocket before either of them responds. I can't bring myself to field their questions. Worse, I won't be able to bear their silence.

How could Miles do something like this to me? How could he do it to his own sister?

At least he didn't steal her underwear or watch her while she bathed. But he still took photos of her, threatened her.

He's been messing with me since day one. He's known this entire time exactly what happened to Sophie, he knows exactly where she is, and he let me think he needed my help. Let me think he'd help me find whoever was doing this to me, when the whole time . . .

The whole time . . . it was him.

He was sneaking into our unit. Stealing my stuff. Hoarding it in the attic. Watching me shower. Watching me sleep. Watching me change.

I don't want to know what's on that laptop.

Tears brim and slip down my cheeks. We let him into our home. And then I let him into my body and my heart.

Now, he fights against the handcuffs Officer Jackson has him in, while Officer Callahan opens the door to the backseat of her cruiser. His hair is damp from the rain.

"I didn't put that shit in there!" he shouts. "I don't even know where it came from. I don't even know what the hell it is!"

"It's my daughter's clothes." Mom's voice is cutting. "You went into her room and stole them."

"No, I didn't!" His voice is loud, shock turned to fury. He tugs against the restraints, his hair dripping and shirt sticking to his arms, his stomach. Somehow, a traitorous part of me still wants to touch him, even knowing what he did.

Officer Jackson keeps a hand on his shoulder. An attempt to calm him that doesn't work.

My heart aches seeing his hands behind his back. Even though I know he deserves it.

How did I look into those eyes so many times and not see the truth in them?

When no one says anything, when they don't believe him, Miles just gets louder. "He's framing me! I didn't do this!" His wild eyes land on Jordan and my heart leaps up to my throat. "Tell them you did this!"

The heavy weight on my chest is crushing. I survived Jordan cheating on me. I survived witnessing him in the act. I survived our breakup. But this?

This, I won't survive. This is more than heartbreak.

This is soul-crushing.

I fell in love with Miles. I fell in love with my stalker.

He made me believe he actually cared about me. But it was all just a sick, twisted obsession. He did everything he could to terrify me, and then he'd comfort me over the fear he caused.

It's so sickening, my stomach churns.

"Enough," Officer Callahan warns him.

When his eyes land on me, I nearly fall to my knees. No wonder I thought I was in love with him. His gaze is so genuine—devastated and confused and defiant. "Madalyn, don't believe him!" His voice cracks. "He's lying to you!"

Jordan snorts and mumbles, "The guy in handcuffs still thinks you're going to trust him over me."

"Hey!" Liv stomps up from the sidewalk, Natalie trailing right behind her, both of them in sweatshirts with their hoods pulled up to protect them from the rain. Guess they decided to come watch the arrest.

I want to run to Natalie. I've missed my best friend. She finds me and gives me a weak smile but doesn't move from her spot at Liv's side. Even though this is all over, I still accused her girlfriend of stalking me. I got so consumed with my own night-mare that I didn't care about what Natalie's been going through this summer. I don't blame her for needing more time. I just hope we can be friends again before we're apart for four months.

Miles rolls his eyes at Liv's arrival. "Great."

Before anyone can stop her, Liv lets out a guttural scream and launches herself at him.

Officer Jackson gets in between them, and Miles lurches back, but she still manages to catch his cheek with her nail. A small, crescent red moon marks him.

"You killed her! Didn't you?" she shrieks. Half fury, half sob.

My heart stops.

Miles stares at her, jaw clenched so hard it could snap. "No."

A chill trickles down my spine. He still sounds so convincing.

Natalie and Mom hold Liv back while Officer Jackson guides Miles to the police cruiser waiting for them.

Before Officer Jackson gets him in the backseat, Miles shoots me one last pleading look.

I'm not thinking when I lurch toward him.

Jordan grabs my arm, but I yank free and run through the rain to Miles.

I could claw at him like Liv did. Leave another crescent-moon mark on his face with my nail. I could scream, curse, call him all the names that have spun around and around in my head.

But all that comes out is a pained, aching "Why?"

Droplets race down his face in tiny rivulets, falling from his sharp jaw. Before, I would've admired how he looks so beautiful, even in the rain. Maybe more, with his clothes plastered to the smooth planes and hard ridges of his body.

But not anymore.

"I didn't do this, Madalyn." He tries to step toward me, but Officer Jackson pulls him back. "I need you to believe me."

His eyes search my face, waiting for the answer he needs to hear.

An answer that will never come.

"You've believed me before," he reminds me. "Why would you doubt me now? You *know* I didn't do this. I didn't do this to Soph. Or you. You know I wouldn't."

I shake my head, keeping my voice low so only he hears me. "But I don't. I barely know you. Remember?"

He recoils like I've slapped him, and for a second, I almost feel bad. If I didn't already feel so repulsed. I let him in my bed, in my body, and he did this to me.

"Madalyn—"

"I should've listened to what everyone said about you. Everyone tried to warn me. *Everyone.* But you brainwashed me, and I was stupid for falling for it."

"You don't actually believe that." His brows are pulled down low over his eyes. The same expression he wore that first night he returned to Beaumont and asked what the hell happened to me. "You're just saying what everyone expects. Still being the girl you think you're supposed to be. Think for yourself. Listen to your gut. You know I'm not lying. You know me."

I shake my head. "I can't believe I spent all that time telling you that you weren't to blame for your sister's disappearance. You must've had a good laugh about that."

He grits his teeth. "That's not true. You know it's not me."

"I won't be stupid anymore. I'm not falling for it again. I don't know how you could do something like this to me, or to your own sister, but it's *sick*. I won't forgive you for this. Ever. I wish you never came back to Beaumont."

"Madalyn, please—"

"I wish I never met you."

I take a step back, and this time he doesn't try to stop me. I've hurt him, almost as much as he's hurting me.

"I hope you rot in there," I hiss. "Just like your dad. You both deserve it."

A wall slams down over Miles's face.

The book of us, Madalyn and Miles, is finally over. Shut.

Despite everything . . . I'm going to miss those eyes. The ones that remind me of soil after a summer rain. Of warm honey in sunlight.

The ones that seemed to see me like no one else ever did.

I hope it's the last time I see them.

Someone pulls me back. Wraps their arms around me. Jordan.

Once the police cruiser is down the driveway, Miles in the backseat, Jordan shakes his head. "Told you he was crazy."

CHAPTER TWENTY-FOUR

SOMEONE IS STANDING at the foot of my bed.

Was it the feeling of eyes on me that stirred me from sleep, or the sound of another person's breaths in the room?

Or the hand that has a grip on my blanket, inching it toward them. Off my body. Exposing me.

The chill of the night hits my sweat-soaked skin. He is little more than a shadow in the darkness. A shadow that moves. That grins.

That whispers my name. *Madalyn.*

The blanket slithers down my legs. He doesn't want any layers between us when he kills me.

The hiss of his voice, so clear in my ears: *You're next.*

I jolt upright. Turn on the lamp on my bedside table, fumbling with the switch, until the darkness is banished.

No one stands at the foot of my bed.

I press my hand to my heaving chest. *A dream.* It was just a dream. A nightmare.

You are okay. You are fine.

Miles is not in my room. He's in jail.

Still, I play Netflix on my phone. For sound to break up the silence. For the distraction.

And I can't bring myself to close my eyes again.

Miles gets released on bail. Just three hundred dollars was all it took to buy his freedom and my death sentence.

He's staying at his mom's house. He's still in Beaumont.

Mom calls the police department every day, demanding that they lock him back up. That they protect me. But the justice system is not designed to protect victims—it's designed to make them.

That's why, when Jordan asks to get back together, I reluctantly tell him yes. He can offer me the protection I need from Miles, though only until he leaves for California next week.

Officer Callahan calls me to come to the station to confirm the stolen belongings are mine. Which seems like a silly reason to make me drive all the way to Creekview in a flood watch. But it gives me an excuse to curse at the police for letting Miles go.

At a red light, I check my phone. A few texts from Jordan—a photo of a mini fridge followed by two messages.

> For our apartment

> This one's just for beer lol

He's slipped right back into our relationship like nothing ever happened. Like we didn't break up, and the days we weren't together never happened. He doesn't notice the way my smile is forced or the way I shrink away when he wraps an arm around me or the way I want to be anywhere else when we're with his friends. He even acts like I'm still going with him to USC, still planning to share an apartment with him, even though he hasn't actually asked.

I let him think it. And I'll let him keep thinking it until the day he gets on that airplane and realizes I'm not beside him. Because at least by then, I'll be in community college, living in my own apartment, and hopefully far enough away from Miles Mariano that he won't hunt me down and hurt me. Again.

I wish I could talk to Natalie about everything, but I haven't seen her or Liv since Miles was arrested. When I told Jordan I was going to text Natalie about hanging out, he said, "Trust me, those girls aren't your friends. You know they talk shit about you all the time, right?"

I wonder how long they've been talking shit behind my back. Since I started opening up about my stalker? Or earlier?

It doesn't matter anymore.

The windshield wipers frantically *whish* back and forth as I crawl down the state highway through shallow streams of water. When I reach the station, I run inside, the rain hitting me at an angle to soak my legs.

Callahan smacks her cinnamon gum and doesn't bother greeting me. A man with a shaved head intercepts me and holds out his hand. "Detective Dempsey. Thank you for coming. I'll just need a few minutes of your time. Shouldn't take long."

"Why the hell did you let him out?"

The detective gives me a strained smile. "I'm happy to answer all your questions after you answer some of mine. Right this way, Miss Young."

He leads me into a tiny room with nothing but a table, a few chairs, and my belongings all piled together on the table. Along with the laptop.

Before I take a seat, I tell him, "The laptop isn't mine."

He nods as if he already knows and gestures for me to sit. "Miss Young, can you confirm that these belongings recovered from your home are indeed yours?"

I rummage through the pile, even though I want to burn all of it. And I will. "Yes. They're all mine."

"Great. Now there are a few other items of concern I want to go over with you while you're here." He grabs the laptop and opens it. "We found some disturbing images on this computer."

He turns the laptop to me. There's a folder on the desktop labeled *Maddie*.

My pulse starts to race.

Miles doesn't call me Maddie.

Detective Dempsey opens the *Maddie* folder and scrolls. I recognize them all—the photos my stalker took of me.

"I've seen all these. He sent them to me."

Detective Dempsey snaps the laptop shut. "Thing is, he didn't. We got his fingerprints. They don't match the finger-prints on your stuff or this laptop."

"So . . . that's it? The charges are dropped?"

He nods. "He denies the allegation and we've got no other reason to charge him."

My mind is a swirling, jumbled mess. I don't know what emotion to cling to—I'm feeling everything at once. Terror, sorrow, confusion.

But mostly, I feel overwhelming relief. My chest bursts open so light can pour in.

Miles isn't my stalker. He can't have been the one to take my stuff or put those photos on that laptop if his fingerprints aren't on them. He wouldn't have labeled that folder *Maddie*.

I wasn't wrong about him. He didn't betray me. I didn't have sex with my stalker. I didn't fall in love with my stalker.

I should've known it wasn't him. Should've known he was telling the truth when he pleaded with me to believe him. There were too many missing pieces to the puzzle, too many questions without answers.

Why would Miles have written a suspect list if he knew he was responsible? Why send himself a fake text—*I'm okay*—and report it to the police? Why drive me to the police station? Why return to Beaumont in the first place? Why would he have given me a pocketknife if he thought I'd use it against him?

No. A guilty person wouldn't want me to protect myself. They'd want me to be defenseless.

He was telling the truth all along. And when he needed me the most, when he needed me to believe him, I didn't.

I'm the one who betrayed him.

The worst betrayal yet.

"So what now?" I ask, voice barely above a whisper.

"We'll bring in the other people in your house and get their fingerprints." Detective Dempsey leans forward. "And if you have anything you need to tell me, Miss Young, now is the time to do so."

My heartbeat stutters. "What do you mean?"

"If you planted these items in your attic, if you're covering for someone—"

"You've got to be *kidding* me."

Why do people keep assuming I'm faking this? Why the hell would I conspire with someone to pretend to stalk me? For what? Attention?

I'd rather go back to the days before I was Maddie, friendless and alone, than live like this for another day.

Dempsey meets my glare. "I'm not kidding." But when he sees I'm not backing down, he changes his tune. "We need to consider all possibilities. This is your chance to clear the air if necessary."

I stand. "What's *necessary* is your department doing your jobs. If my stalker is still out there, it's not just my problem anymore—it's yours. And if you don't act like it is, I'll make it one."

I don't wait for him to dismiss me before I turn to leave. But there's something else—

"Did you find a ring?"

Dempsey rubs his smooth scalp. "A ring?"

"A ring was stolen from my room too."

He shakes his head. "Everything you see here is what we recovered."

Whoever my stalker is, they still have my promise ring.

Outside, I duck down onto the wet pavement. On our car's undercarriage, where the GPS tracker is still attached, blood streaks the razors.

CHAPTER TWENTY-FIVE

WHEN I ASK where he is, Jordan texts that he's at the country club. I need to tell him about the blood. He's the only person left who can help me track down my stalker.

I navigate the manicured lawns before entering a white building with the air-conditioning turned up so high, I shiver. Tennis shoes squeak across the shiny epoxy flooring.

Liv sits behind the counter. She doesn't smile when she sees me.

I stride up to her. "Do you know where Jordan is?"

Her arms are stretched out across the countertop, her skin free of any cuts or scratches. "No. I don't keep tabs on your boyfriend."

"You must've seen him today," I snap. "This place isn't that big."

"Well, he never comes here, so I don't know what to tell you."

I don't know how I tried to be friends with this girl for so long. She can lie right to my face and not feel bad about it at all. "What are you talking about? He works here."

Liv frowns. "No, he doesn't."

"He's been working here all summer," I insist.

She sighs. "I don't care what your boyfriend told you, Maddie. He's never worked here. I take as many shifts as I can; I'm here all the time. I would've seen him. Why would he work anyway? Rich boy doesn't need a job when he has mommy's money."

She can't be right. Jordan wouldn't lie to me all summer. And working at the country club would be such a pointless thing to lie about.

Except . . . he did lie about cheating on me with Ash. So how can I believe him about anything? Those days he ignored me after Miles came back, maybe Jordan wasn't on a trip with his dad at all. Maybe that whole time, he was with Ash. Or Chelsea.

"Do you hate me?" I blurt.

Liv's eyes narrow. "What? No."

"You've never told anyone you hate me? Be honest."

"No. I've never exactly *liked* you," she admits. "I always thought you were glad Sophie was gone. She went missing, and you walked up to Jordan like it was your time to shine."

I cringe at her characterization of me, the old me, but I can't deny it because she's right. I was glad Sophie was gone. I didn't care that she went missing, and I did bask in her absence. "If you did hate me, I wouldn't have blamed you. I probably would've hated me too." *You know they talk shit about you all the time, right?* That's what Jordan said. He's also the one who told Brett that Liv hates my guts. "The night of Jordan's party . . . did you and Sophie get in a fight?"

"A fight? No? I told you, I was with Natalie all night. Sophie was with Jordan until I saw her leave the basement."

"So Sophie never told you that she didn't want to be friends with you anymore?"

"No? Who the hell told you that?"

Brett. And he heard it from Jordan.

At home, Mom is making breakfast for dinner. I grab a strip of crispy bacon. "You never cook."

Her mouth drops open. "I cook!"

"On Christmas. So what's the bad news?"

She flips a pancake, already burnt on one side. And this is why she doesn't cook. "It's not *bad* news. I just . . ." She sets the spatula down and turns to face me. "I want to ask Andre to sleep over."

"Eww, Mom!"

"Not like that." She rolls her eyes. "I want him to be here more often. To watch over things. To keep you safe."

"Don't you think it's a little early for him to be moving in?"

"He's not moving in—he's sleeping over. And it's not too early for that."

"It's been, like, two weeks. But hey, you're an adult—"

"Actually." She looks sheepish. "It's been a few months. It started after we found the spray paint on the garage."

"You've been dating him since *then*?" I ask. "So that night you got all dolled up wasn't your first date?"

"Technically, yes. We had just been talking before that."

"How did you manage to keep a secret from me that long?"

"I wanted to be sure it would turn into something serious before I told you."

"Wow. I have a stepfather."

She sighs and turns back to the stove. The pancakes are completely inedible now. At least there are still eggs and bacon.

On the counter beside her, two doorknobs sit in plastic packaging. "You got doorknobs?"

Mom snaps her fingers. "Oh! I was going to ask you: Do you have the other house keys? I'm changing the locks."

I fish my key out of my pocket and hold it out to her. "I have mine."

"You don't have the spare?"

I shake my head. "Don't you have it?"

"No, I let Jordan borrow it for your surprise dinner. He said he'd give it back to you after."

Every thud of my heart echoes in my ears. *I got the key from your mom this morning.*

But he never gave it back to me.

He's framing me! Madalyn, don't believe him! He's lying to you!

I didn't listen to Miles.

But he was right.

Jordan has had a key to my house, all this time.

He used it to break in. Steal my stuff. Frame Miles and get him out of my duplex.

Those weren't Miles's fingerprints on my stolen stuff, on that laptop. They were Jordan's.

This whole time, it's been Jordan.

I collapse into a chair.

Jordan.

Jordan, Jordan, Jordan.

Jordan is my stalker.

Jordan was the one watching me from my attic. Jordan was the one following me around town and taking photos of me. Jordan was the one threatening me.

He broke into my house. He stole my clothes and promise ring. He took screenshots from my webcam.

He told me Sophie is dead. That I'm next.

My boyfriend. The guy I was going to follow to California. The guy I thought I would marry. Who promised me forever.

He's the one behind all of this.

Miles was right. I didn't need to change who I was. I didn't need to become Maddie.

That's the worst mistake I've ever made.

I changed who I was to make people like me, to make Jordan want to be with me, and it didn't make my life any better

—it only made everything worse. I changed everything about myself to be the girl Jordan would want, and instead of getting my happily-ever-after, I got a cheating, lying, manipulative, obsessive boyfriend.

I got a stalker.

At last, I know who my stalker is.

A spare key isn't enough evidence, though. It's suspicious, but it isn't enough to prove he was the one behind all this.

I need to find more.

Bile rises up my throat and the words claw out. "He never gave it back."

"That's okay," Mom says, completely oblivious to the tornado raging inside me. "We don't really need it now. Andre's going to help me change the locks later."

The pieces aren't clicking together in her mind because, like everyone else in this town, her mind has already been made up.

Miles is the bad guy. Jordan is the good guy.

But it's always been the opposite.

CHAPTER TWENTY-SIX

MILES'S MOM isn't home. The only car in the driveway is his Mustang.

Dark clouds loom overhead. I knock on the door, knowing once he sees it's me, he'll refuse to answer. But I'll bang on this door until he does. I need his help.

We need to sneak into Jordan's house. They're rarely home and I know the passcode to get in, but with Jordan tracking my every move, I'm sure we won't have long before he shows up. I need Miles there so we can find the proof that Jordan is my stalker as fast as possible and drive right to the police station with everything we find.

While I wait for Miles, I turn off my phone's Location services.

That must be how Jordan's been following me.

I didn't break my phone that night. *Jordan* did.

He smashed my phone and let me think I did it in a drunken stupor. All so he could buy me a new one—act like the hero, the oh-so-generous boyfriend—and put the new phone on his family's plan to monitor my incoming and outgoing calls and texts. To track me using Find My Phone.

How did I not see all the signs?

I rewatch his first viral TikTok for the thousandth time—the one that circulated all over social media and had girls across the country wishing they had a hot boyfriend who loved them that much.

But this time, the increase in pitch doesn't sound like genuine concern. It's forced. The sniff is exaggerated, and when he ducks his head at the end, it's not to hide tears.

It's to hide his flat, dry eyes.

Ones that peered into Sophie's soul as she took her last breath.

When the door in front of me swings open, my own breath catches.

Miles is in a loose t-shirt, the fabric disguising the hard muscle underneath. My knees grow weak at the sight of him. It's been too many days, and I want to drink him in.

But his face is stony, emotionless. So unlike the way he used to look at me. With a half-smirk. With a glimmer in his eyes. With desire. With affection.

All of that is gone now.

The book of us is truly over.

I didn't fight for him. I was the one person in this town who believed him, and then when he needed me most, I let him down. I was the one who pushed him to stand up for himself, who encouraged him to keep telling the truth even when no one was listening. And still, I doubted him, just like everyone else. I let them get in my head, convince me that he was capable of stalking me, and even though now I know the truth, it's too late.

He plants both hands on the doorjambs above my head, revealing the pale undersides of his arms. His flesh free of any wound the razors would've left.

This town spent so long villainizing him, when the true villain has always been their golden boy.

I want to fling my arms around Miles, but before I can move, he grabs for the door. "You shouldn't be here."

I slap my palm against the door before he can slam it in my face. "I know it wasn't you. I'm so, *so* sorry, Miles." My voice cracks on his name.

His face doesn't change. "That supposed to make me feel better?"

I knew this wouldn't be easy. But still, a small part of me hoped he missed me just as much as I missed him. A small part of me hoped he'd understand—that the evidence was staring me right in the face. That the hunt for my stalker made me suspect everybody, including the one person who has been helping me from the beginning.

His black eye is mostly faded now. All that remains is slightly yellow skin around it. On his cheek, there's still a mark from where Liv tore into him with her nail. I reach out to brush a finger against it, but he jerks away.

It makes my heart break.

A tense silence falls between us. So much that I want to say, but I have no idea how to put any of it into words. "I shouldn't have said that about your dad," I manage. "Or you. I'm glad we met. I could never, ever regret that. I . . ."

I want to tell him I love him. But I can't bear to say it when I know he won't say it back.

If he ever loved me, he doesn't anymore.

"Why are you here, Madalyn?" His voice is flat.

"Because . . ." I wring my hands, unsure how I'm supposed to say the words out loud. How they can be true. "It's Jordan. He's . . . the one stalking me."

Miles's stoic face doesn't change. "And?"

Right. He doesn't care what happens to me anymore. But he should care about what happened to his sister. "What do you mean *and*? It's *Jordan*."

"Not like that's surprising. I've been telling you he's a bastard from the beginning. Always thought it was him."

This is news to me. In the months that we've been trying to track down my stalker, Miles never once suggested that the perpetrator could be my own boyfriend. "What? You never said that."

He sets his jaw. "Because I knew there was no way you'd believe me. Perfect Jordan could do no wrong in Maddie's eyes."

In *Maddie's* eyes. But I'm Madalyn, and I'm seeing clearly now. "I need you to go with me to Jordan's house. No one searched their property, remember? The police didn't start investigating her disappearance until after Jordan put a volunteer search together, but they never went to Jordan's house, even though that's the last place she was seen. He put that search together so he wouldn't look suspicious. The proof could all be there."

I can't tell him the other part of the puzzle I'm sure about: that's where we'll find Sophie.

Her body is somewhere on Jordan's property. In a shallow grave or dumped somewhere no one would think to look, I don't know. But I know we'll find her there, and I have to make sure I'm the one to find her. Not Miles.

He won't be able to come back from that.

He shakes his head. "I'm done with you. You can deal with your boyfriend on your own."

The words are a knife to my heart. *I'm done with you.* I bite my lip to keep the tears in. "He's not my boyfriend."

"Not what I heard."

How can I possibly explain to Miles that I was so terrified of my stalker—of *him*—that I got back together with Jordan for protection? That ever since Miles was arrested, I've been playing Happy Couple with the guy I knew cheated on me.

With the guy I now know is stalking me. "I thought . . . I thought I needed him."

"Yeah. That's always been your problem, hasn't it?"

I flinch at the venom in his voice. But I don't object because I know he's right. I thought I needed Jordan. I gave up the real me to be with him, but I've never needed Jordan. I don't need any guy. What I needed was to love myself for who I am, no matter what anyone else thinks of me. No matter who wants to mock what I love or what I look like or who I hang out with, as long as I love myself and do what I love and love the people in my life, that's all that matters.

"Yeah, it has," I agree. "But I'm done with him now. So will you come with me? We need to find proof before he gets home."

His brows pinch down over his dark eyes. "I told you. No."

My stomach drops like lead. If he won't go with me, I'll have to go alone.

He grabs the door again, eyes flat. "You need to leave now."

"Miles—"

His next words come out in a low hiss. "Don't come back, Maddie."

The name is a gut punch. So hard, so painful, it makes tears slip down my cheeks.

"Don't call me that," I whisper.

A raindrop hits my face, mixing with my tears.

Miles shuts the door in my face.

My hoodie is soaked and my Nikes slosh through puddles on the sidewalk that borders Hunter Road. An unseasonably cool breeze pierces through my sleeves and wraps around my bare legs.

Jordan's enormous house looms ahead. The towering stone

and wrought iron fence that surrounds his house no longer belongs to a castle. Now it belongs to a cemetery.

The only car in the Goldmans' garage is his parents' summer Porsche. No one's home.

I breathe a little easier. A little.

Until my phone buzzes in my back pocket.

With shaking hands, I pull it out. This time, I know exactly who's texting me.

Turn around.

But it's not my stalker's number. It's the number from the burner phone that someone used to text Miles right after Sophie disappeared.

My heart thunders and I spin—

It's not Jordan behind me.

Across the street, a white Kia sedan sits beside the sidewalk. *Sophie's* car.

But that's not possible. She's dead.

I head for the car anyway. It's probably Jordan behind the wheel. Even with my Location settings turned off, he still managed to find me. He's the one who texted Miles from that phone number, trying to convince him that Sophie was still alive to throw Miles off his trail.

The driver's side door opens before I can reach it. Someone tall and slender emerges, and the first thing I notice is the pair of pine-green eyes.

Sophie.

CHAPTER TWENTY-SEVEN

SOPHIE MARIANO IS HERE. She's *alive.*

Her once-cocoa brown hair has been cropped and bleached blonde. Somehow, it makes the green of her eyes more subtle. Her Daisy Dukes are smeared with dirt, and she looks so . . . normal. She is less supermodel, more girl next door. Not the picture of perfection that I remember.

Not the dead body in the woods like I suspected. I was right before—she did run away.

Jordan convinced me that she was dead. Maybe so I'd stop digging.

Relief makes my knees weak. Miles doesn't have to bury his sister. He doesn't have to be haunted by the sight of her dead body. He can apologize for not being there when she needed him most.

Sophie is older now. By a year that's somehow ten. But she doesn't wear the years on her face—she wears them in her eyes.

All I can think to ask is "How?"

"I got your texts." Her normally-saccharine voice turns bitter. "I used an untraceable number, just like Jordan taught me."

"But . . . where have you been? We all thought . . ." I don't have to speak the words out loud. She knows what I'm thinking.

"My grandma, Deedee, owns a ranch in New Hampshire. That's where I've been staying. My grandpa . . ." She bites her lip and casts her glance down. "He was like Jordan. She understood."

All this time, Sophie's been in New Hampshire. She's been that close. That Reddit post about seeing Sophie at a ranch with her hair cut short and dyed blonde wasn't a made-up story.

"She didn't tell your parents?" The least Sophie could've done was let her family know she was safe. Maybe then her dad wouldn't have drunk himself to jail, her mother wouldn't have turned against everyone, and her brother wouldn't have spent months blaming himself for her being gone.

"Like I said, she understood. She knew I was safe and that my mom would forgive her. Eventually."

I still can't believe she's really here. I'm talking to Sophie Mariano. Alive and unscathed. "What happened?" I ask. "That night."

She sighs, and I know exactly why it's not something she wants to talk about. I hate talking about it too. "At the party, I went upstairs to change into some dry clothes after you pushed me in the pool."

I cringe. "Sorry about that."

She shakes her head. "Honestly? I'm glad you did. Because while I was in Jordan's room, I found a second phone." Her voice catches. "I found everything—the pictures, the messages, the profiles, the texting apps, all of it. He found me in his room and locked me in his bathroom so no one would hear me yelling."

Oh my god. I can't imagine how terrified she must've been, knowing her stalker had her trapped.

"Then when everyone was gone, he tried to talk me out of

going to the police. I broke up with him, told him to stay away from me." Her voice shakes now. "The moment you try to leave is always the most dangerous. That's when your possessive, controlling, manipulative boyfriend tries to kill you."

She rubs at the back of her neck, just below her hairline. The memory of that night still makes her voice crack.

When I look at her, I see my future. If I hadn't found out about the key, if I hadn't realized the truth until it was too late, I could've ended up like Sophie.

She wraps her arms across her stomach, comforting herself. "He shoved me up against the wall and started to choke me. I tried to push him off, scratched him. None of it was working. Then I kneed him and managed to get away. I got in my car and just . . . drove. I didn't even realize I was going to Deedee's until I got there."

Part of me can't imagine Jordan doing all of that to Sophie. The girl he claimed he loved. The girl I spent so many years being jealous of because she had everything I wanted. Who I spent months loathing while I was dating Jordan because she had him first.

But a much bigger part of me—the part that has finally learned the truth about the guy I once called my boyfriend— knows that he's capable of everything he did to Sophie. And worse.

"But why let your family think you were dead?" I ask. It's the one thing I can't understand.

"You do what you have to when you're in survival mode." The emotion is gone from her voice. "If I came home, I knew he'd kill me, and if I told my mom I was okay, she'd want me to come back. Press charges. But it's Jordan. His mom is the mayor. His dad owns nearly every business in town. There's no way anything bad would've happened to him. Only to me."

She's right. That's why I haven't told anyone yet except Miles. Not until I have proof. Because no one in this town will believe their perfect golden boy is behind this. "So why are you back now?"

Sophie scans the enormous house in front of her. "Because I heard Miles was arrested for stalking. I had to come back and clear his name."

"He's already out."

"I know. Deedee told me. But . . ." Her eyes narrow, and I know what kind of girl she is now—a girl out for vengeance. "I have to prove who the real stalker is."

Yes. We do.

"I just . . ." I shake my head, trying to blink the tears away. "I still don't understand. Why would he do this? He loved me. He loved you."

"Because it's not love." She gives me a hard look. "You realize that, right? No one who loves you wants to hurt you or scare you or track you or control you."

"Or"—I swallow—"kill you."

She nods. "Jordan doesn't have girlfriends. He has obsessions." She focuses back on his house over my shoulder. "And now we go in there and prove it."

"We should call Miles to come help. We'll be faster with three of us."

Sophie finds his number and puts the phone on speaker. He answers on the fifth ring, hesitant. "Hello?"

"Miles?"

"*Soph*?" Her name wrenches out of his throat.

"Yeah. It's me." Her voice is watery. "I'm here. I need you to come to Jordan's house. We need your help."

He's silent on the other end. The only sound the occasional, hissing intake of breath. He's crying.

My heart squeezes. I want to be there to comfort him. Hug him and cry with him that his sister is alive. She's okay, and he'll get to see her again and he doesn't have to hate himself anymore. He never should have.

"Miles?" Sophie asks, her own eyes glossy.

"You're okay?" he manages.

"I'm okay. I'll explain everything when you get here."

He's silent again, and my heart aches for him. "I'm on my way."

Sophie and I don't wait for Miles to show up. We head for the garage and search around the Porsche that sits pristine and barely used in the center.

There, hidden behind some boxes and a dirt bike covered in a layer of dust and cobwebs, is a can of black spray paint.

Even though I expected it to be here, the sight makes my stomach lurch. Makes my skin grow cold. Makes the inside of my head buzz like a hummingbird's wings.

My own boyfriend used that can of spray paint to graffiti my garage and call me a slut. To tell me to die.

I don't want to go inside. I don't want to see the rest of it.

But I have to.

If I walk away now, I won't get the justice I deserve. That Sophie deserves.

I punch in the key code to get through Jordan's front door, and even though I know we're alone, we stay quiet.

"We should split up," I whisper. "I'll search upstairs; you search in the basement."

She gives a single nod. "We need to be quick."

Even though the house is empty, I sneak up the stairs as quietly as I can.

Everything in his room is pristine, as usual. I never considered Jordan's penchant for cleanliness could have been a sign of something sinister lurking beneath the surface. A guy who needs absolute control over every aspect of his life, from his room to his appearance to his girlfriend.

The first thing I go for is Jordan's laptop. The one he planted in our attic was a decoy. This one will have everything he's ever wanted to keep.

The password only takes me three attempts to guess.

sophiebaby.

On his laptop are two folders identical to the *Maddie* folder on the computer in the attic. Labeled *Sophie* and *Maddie.*

I open the *Maddie* folder. There are hundreds of photos of me, most of which I haven't seen. Some I recognize—the ones my stalker sent to me, the same ones on the other laptop.

Others are much worse.

Pictures of me undressing, getting in and out of the bathtub naked. Miles in bed with me.

He was up there. He was in the attic while I was having sex with Miles. And he watched.

I retch but manage to compose myself. I don't have time to puke or cry. I need to find everything he has in this room and take it to the police.

The *Sophie* folder contains similar photos of her. All taken without her knowledge. Some of her smiling, laughing, talking with friends. One of those friends is Liv.

Tears prick my eyes. If I had found this laptop earlier, I would've known she wasn't my stalker.

I stop scrolling before the photos get graphic and click back to the *Maddie* folder.

Natalie and Liv are in some. Standing outside Mariano's with me, walking to the bakery.

In others, Miles is with me. Chatting with me behind the register at Mariano's. Studying with me at a table in the corner. Sitting with me on our roof. Driving in his Mustang.

I take a few photos with my phone. I won't leave here without evidence. Jordan isn't getting away with this.

Not anymore.

There's one more missing piece.

I open the drawers on his desk, and then the drawer on one of his bedside tables. Then the other.

Bingo.

Beneath a strategically placed packet from USC . . . is my promise ring.

Fresh tears spring to my eyes, and this time I can't blink them back or rub them away. Just a couple of months ago, he was handing me this ring and we were grinning at each other like lovesick idiots.

I thought he was the love of my life. I thought we'd be together forever. I thought he was my future.

He is nothing to me now.

The distant rumble of thunder makes me jump, kick-starting me back into action.

I snap a photo of the ring, but when I start to close the drawer, I hear something else rattle inside.

I yank the drawer out until it dips dangerously close to the floor and find that my ring isn't the only one Jordan kept.

Another ring. This one with a peridot birthstone.

I don't remember her wearing a promise ring, but this must be hers. He couldn't bear to part with his final keepsakes, his last piece of Sophie, even in his scheme to frame Miles and get him out of Beaumont.

The door to Jordan's room creaks. Sophie must've found something.

"Hey, baby."

CHAPTER TWENTY-EIGHT

JORDAN TIPS A BOTTLE of Jack Daniels up to his lips, face glistening with a mix of sweat and rain. A flash of his wrist, and just below it, a bright red slash across his skin.

Where the razor blades sliced when he tried to grab the tracking device he planted.

I'm not sure whether I should call 9-1-1 now or try to keep playing his game. Because it may be the only way Sophie and I get out of here alive.

"Find anything good in the garage?" His voice used to send a thrilling shiver down my spine. Now it rakes over my scalp, over every inch of my skin, like sharp claws.

A flash of lightning through the windows behind me, followed closely by a crack of thunder that covers the sound of my pounding heart.

"I don't know what you're talking about." I swallow, trying to keep my voice steady. "I thought I'd . . . surprise you. Be here when you got home from work."

His expression doesn't change—he doesn't buy it for a second. He nods to the phone in my hand. "I had to disconnect your service. There was a problem with the bill."

No.

I unlock the screen. A tiny *No Service* warning at the top.

I shrug and slip my phone in my back pocket. I don't need service to call 9-1-1, but maybe he doesn't know that.

"No problem." I keep my voice light. "We can get it fixed later. So, Liv told me something weird." My heart is drumming so loud in my ears, I barely hear the words coming out of my mouth. "She said you haven't been working at the country club all summer."

Jordan brings the bottle up to his lips again. "Why does that matter?"

My fingers itch to curl into fists. "Because you told me you were."

"But it doesn't matter what I tell you, right?" His eyes are piercing. Dangerous. "You'll believe whatever you want. That's why you're in my room."

Shit. Playing dumb isn't getting me anywhere. He knows I know. But maybe I can convince him I'm here for another reason. "Did you even go on a trip with your dad? Or were you using that time to screw Ash behind my back?"

The Jack Daniels sloshes at his side as he slowly ambles toward me.

I finger the knife in my pocket. My heart is going to burst any second.

I've always thought of Jordan as big enough to protect me. Now I realize he's big enough to kill me.

"I don't know. How long were you fucking Miles Mariano behind mine?"

"I didn't," I insist, but my voice is small.

"Bullshit," he snarls.

I back away, eyes flashing to the cut on his arm as he takes another swig from his bottle. I won't let him control me. Not anymore. "How's your arm feel?"

He stops just inches away. All six-foot-four of him looms

over me. His eyes that once reminded me of a blue sky, of gentle water, now reflect ice so sharp they could stab me.

Thunder booms, the wind screaming and rattling the windows. The power flickers.

"I know you're my stalker, Jordan."

The house falls eerily silent.

His mouth contorts with the rage he's barely suppressing. "I'm not a *stalker*," he spits, flecks of saliva hitting my cheek. I barely resist the urge to gag.

"Why did you do it?" My voice finally breaks.

"I wasn't *stalking* you. I was keeping an eye on you. You can't be trusted. None of you can."

I want to collapse onto the floor. Let myself break down the way I ache to. Somehow, I was still hoping I was wrong. That he'd offer me some proof my stalker is someone else. Someone like Ash or Chelsea. Someone I didn't fall in love with, someone I didn't have sex with, someone whose betrayal wouldn't cut this deep.

I shake my head. "No, it was more than that. You wouldn't have sent all those messages and emails and threats if that's all it was."

Jordan keeps his lips pressed firmly together until he takes another long chug from the bottle.

"You wanted to scare me. You wanted me to . . . to think I needed you to protect me. So you could keep me close. Control me."

"You do need me to protect you."

"No, I need protection *from* you!" I try to step away, but Jordan follows. The walls are closing in, and soon, I won't be able to get away from him. "You wanted to get Miles out of town too. That's why you framed him. That's why you tried so hard to convince me he was my stalker. So I wouldn't have anyone else. Only you."

With every step I take away from him, he takes one toward me. A careful dance around his bedroom.

"I'm all you need." Somehow, he makes his threat sound like a tender, loving promise.

And that might be the worst part of all. How he can sound like he loves you, like he'll keep you safe, when he's the most dangerous person in the room.

Thunder erupts again, lightning flashing once, twice.

Then the power goes out. Plummeting us into darkness.

In the dim light from the flashes between the clouds, Jordan is the shadow that's been following me. The terrifying, looming figure of my nightmares.

"Stay the hell away from me," I warn.

Bravery is not being unafraid. Bravery is coming to your wit's end and having no other choice but to fight.

"I can't do that, Maddie," he says. "I've never been able to do that."

Jordan pauses our slow, careful dance. In a blink, he lunges at me.

I yank the knife out of my pocket.

The blade springs free before I plunge it into his leg.

CHAPTER TWENTY-NINE

THE RAGING storm drowns out Jordan's bellows. My feet pound down the stairs, loud enough that he'll know exactly where I'm headed.

Good. Let him follow me so Sophie can escape. For her sake and for Miles's. I owe them that much. I threw them both under the bus: Sophie, when I told her to run away and didn't care what happened to her, and Miles, when I believed he was my stalker and let the police arrest him.

Even if Jordan catches up with me, finds me, hurts me, or worse . . . at least Miles will still have his sister. He can lose me, but he can't lose her. Not again.

Jordan crashes down the stairs behind me. I sprint through the kitchen and out the sliding glass door, through the pouring rain and across soggy earth, to the woods where I can hide.

He can't kill me if he can't find me.

Twigs and rocks crunch beneath my feet, rain hammering against the leaves and branches high above my head.

But there's another sound.

The slosh of heavy feet against the soaked ground. The snap of anything in his way.

He's injured. I can outrun him. I can get away.

He's not going to catch me.

I'm going to get away—

My toe hooks against something hard and I manage to catch myself before my face hits the mud.

My palms sting, sliced open with tiny cuts now smeared in wet dirt. My ankle throbs and I heave myself backward.

"You just couldn't leave it alone, could you?" he shouts.

I manage to push myself up and hobble on one foot, but the footsteps behind me are getting closer.

Thunder cracks overhead. No one will hear my screams.

Please no. Let me get away. Let me—

Something shoves me from behind, sending me flying.

My body is little more than a feather beneath his palms, and my head hits hard wood. My vision blurs.

He pushes me to the ground, and a gasp barely has time to escape my lungs. A root stabs into my back. My head spins, temple throbbing. Drowning out the pain radiating from my ankle.

I claw at the wet dirt, try to push myself up, get *away*, but he's already on me.

On me, pinning me down.

And this is what I won't escape.

He's discarded the liquor bottle at his side. In his hand is the pocketknife I plunged into his leg. Slick and crimson with his blood.

Now pressed against my throat.

"You stabbed me, you little bitch." Jordan's voice is low. Scarier than when he yells. "I could slit your throat."

That tiny white scar on his cheek glistens under the flash of lightning.

The same shape as the mark on Miles's face after Liv cut him with her nail.

Except the cut she made wasn't deep enough to scar. But Sophie's was.

She fought back. She left her mark on Jordan.

So will I.

"You couldn't kill Sophie, and you're not going to kill me," I hiss. "The police are on their way. I called them before you showed up."

He straightens and drops the knife by my feet. For a second, I almost think it worked. "Nice try. I turned off your service, remember? I saw all your outgoing calls. But don't worry. I'll let them blame Miles for this too. I'll make sure your DNA's all over his car."

Jordan is going to kill me. One last thing he can pin on Miles.

I try to get out from under him, but he doesn't budge an inch. He's too massive, too heavy. An anvil holding me down.

So I spit at him. "And your DNA's all over me."

He rubs the spit from his arm, mouth curdled. "I'll scrub it off."

After he kills me, he will bleach my flesh raw until my murderer could've been anyone.

I grasp for the knife on the ground, shoulder screaming at the desperate stretch for my only hope. Just out of reach.

All I can picture is Mom's face. How she'll fall to her knees when they deliver the news. How heartbroken she'll be when her little girl turns up dead.

Tears drip down to my ears. Snot collects in my throat. Mud cakes under my nails, the only thing my fingers manage to grasp.

I let out the highest, loudest scream my crushed chest can muster. A warbling, choked sound that won't reach any ears except my own and my killer's.

What happens when a girl screams in a forest and no one is around to hear it?

"I'm going to do to you exactly what I did to her," he hisses. "But this time, I'm finishing the job."

His hands grab at my throat. Crushing my windpipe so hard, my vision blurs. The same way he tried to strangle her, to stop her from leaving him. Now to stop me.

He dropped the knife because he wants to watch the life slowly leave my eyes. He wants to kill me with his bare hands.

Hands that held mine tenderly, grazed my hair, tilted my chin for a kiss.

Hands that pulled me into him too hard, held my hips in an iron grip, clutched my arm too tight, shoved me from behind.

Hands that squeeze. That suffocate.

Like they always have.

CHAPTER THIRTY

BEFORE THE DARKNESS TAKES ME, the Grim Reaper materializes. Come to collect my soul after my boyfriend has finished wringing it from my body.

But the Grim Reaper doesn't wait for me to die.

It reaches for the bottle Jordan has been drinking from, and in a dazzling arc, brings it down on his head.

The face above me is far away at first, blurry. Then the dark eyes and hair, the sharp jaw, the soft lips, and the constellation of freckles start to come into focus.

The first face I saw when I closed my eyes. The face I see in my dreams.

Miles.

"Come on." His words are garbled, spoken through water. "We've gotta go."

Sophie stands above us, delicate features distorted with fear. "He's getting away."

Miles leans closer, and I want to reach for him, graze his

cheek, but I can't move my arms. All I can do is blink. And breathe. And stare.

"You—" I try to say *you saved me*, but my throat explodes. Tears burst from my eyes at pain like I've never felt before. Like someone shoved a flame down my throat and burned the inside to ash.

"Take it easy," Miles murmurs, brushing something—mud? Grass? Blood?—from my cheek. "He just tried to strangle you."

"Your throat's going to hurt for a while," Sophie pipes up. "Trust me. Miles, we need to go. Now."

He nods at her, and without another word, sweeps me up in his arms. Sophie leads the way back to her Kia. She opens the rear passenger side door, where Miles places me with aching tenderness, buckling my seatbelt before he climbs in beside me.

Sophie flicks on her headlights and slams on the gas. The windshield wipers *swish, swish, swish*. Doing nothing for the visibility.

In front of us, a single set of brake lights on the road. We're following him.

"What's the plan here?" Miles asks her.

"I don't know," she admits.

I pull out my phone, the screen cracked, no service, but I can still type a note. *What happened?*

Miles's jaw is tight. "When I got there, Sophie said we needed to help you. That he was trying to kill you." His throat bobs. "I grabbed the bottle and hit him. He laid me out and went for his car. He's bleeding pretty good, though."

When Jordan finally notices us following, he speeds up. Dangerously fast for the pouring rain and flooded roads. Water sprays out from under his tires. He barely makes it through the river flowing across the asphalt.

Sophie lets off the gas, tightening her grip on the wheel, and we crawl through.

Still, I'm not as terrified as I was when Jordan's hands were around my throat.

I type another note on my phone. *Thank you.*

Miles doesn't reach for me. Maybe he's worried I'll flinch away from him now. Instead, he scoots closer and tips his forehead against mine. Quietly, so only I can hear, he murmurs, "Sorry I let you go alone."

I type *I wasn't alone* and smile at Sophie in the driver's seat.

I wasted so much time being jealous of her. But Sophie was never perfect. I was just too consumed with my own imperfections to notice hers. Too consumed with what I was lacking, what wasn't good enough about me, why I couldn't be prettier, smarter, funnier, better. And I took it all out on her. I didn't even care that she went missing. I was just happy it meant I had a chance to take her place.

Little did I know, that was the last place I would want to be.

I'm so glad I'm not Maddie anymore. That Miles brought me back to myself.

The next note I type is for Sophie: *Did he give you a promise ring?*

She frowns, eyes glued to his car in front of us and her knuckles white on the steering wheel. "He tried to, last year. But I told him I couldn't take it. We were only juniors. I didn't even know if I wanted to go to college yet, let alone if I wanted to commit to him like that."

At least she had more sense than I did.

"Did he give you one?" she asks.

I nod. A token of what I once thought was love was actually a mark. A label.

Mine.

A promise not to love me or be loyal to me. A promise to never let me go. No matter how hard I fought to get away.

In front of us, Jordan makes a slow right turn. This is the way to the hospital. I wonder how he'll explain the stab wound to his leg, the glass embedded in his scalp, and the three people in the car behind him accusing him of attempted murder.

"Did you get to use the knife?" Miles asks.

When I nod, a corner of his mouth lifts.

Jordan hits another huge stream of water gushing across the road.

But this time, he doesn't make it through.

His BMW spins, the squeal of his tires deafening. Sophie gasps.

Jordan skids off the road, and my heart is in my throat even though he's the last person I should be worried about.

The car flips, the clamor of metal louder than the thunder detonating above our heads. Then it flips once, twice, three more times down the embankment until finally stopping, wheels spinning in the air.

Sophie slows before we can hit the water on the road and pulls over. "Should we go see?" she asks into the silence.

"Might as well make sure he's dead," Miles says.

I never thought I would hope Jordan is dead, but I do. I hope he can never hurt me or Sophie or Miles or anyone else ever again.

When Sophie and I get out of the car, Miles doesn't follow.

"You're not coming?" she asks him.

"Nah." He leans back and stretches out his legs. "Fuck that guy."

Sophie and I make our way down the slick embankment slowly, Sophie supporting the weight I can't put on my ankle. My head spins, the muscles in my arms weak and heavy. But this is worth it.

I have to know—is he alive or dead?

Shattered glass lines the grass. Blood oozes from where Jordan hit his head in the crash. Mixing with the blood from where Miles struck him.

A small smile pulls at my lips when I notice the blood soaking through his jeans, where I stabbed him.

He managed to tie a white cloth around the wound, but it hasn't staunched the bleeding.

His eyes land on Sophie first.

"*Sophie?*" His voice comes out in a croak.

"Yeah. I'm alive, asshole."

When he notices me, his eyes flash again. "Maddie? Help me."

Of course he survived. Guys like Jordan Goldman think they're invincible because the whole world convinces them they are. Even after everything he's done, he gets to survive this.

"Call 9-1-1." He groans. "Get me out of here. I can't get the seatbelt off."

"Good." Sophie stands from her crouched position. "Call or don't," she tells me. "It's your choice." She heads back up the hill. Done here.

How long will he have to dangle before he bleeds out? I hope it will be a long time. But not long enough for someone else to find him.

"Maddie!" he snaps.

Even on the verge of death, he thinks he can yell at me. Thinks he can control me. Thinks he can use the nickname he gave me. The one that reminds him of the other girl he tried to kill.

I swallow the ash in my throat, and even though the words come out in a hoarse croak, they come out. "It's Madalyn."

"Call 9-1-1!" Spit flies from his mouth, his face an ugly red.

I don't recognize him anymore. My first boyfriend. My first time. The boy I thought was my forever.

My stalker. My abuser. The boy who tried to kill me.

He may still be clinging to life, but he's dead to me now.

"Can't." I hold up my phone. The words claw at my throat, but they're worth it. "My service got disconnected."

CHAPTER THIRTY-ONE

MOM AND ANDRE are finally allowed to drive me home after two days in the hospital. The roads are clear of water and the sun is shining. Trees are down, and for some, the power is still out, but I'm excited to go home and start fresh. My doctor cleared me to start college next week, and as long as I'm feeling up to it, I should be moving into my apartment this weekend.

Since I woke up in my hospital bed, Mom hasn't left my side, so Andre spent the past two days scurrying around bringing her coffee and blankets and fresh clothes and sandwiches.

The sight of them together makes me smile.

Everyone's heard Sophie's story now. No one wanted to believe it, but the evidence is undeniable. Jordan tried to kill me, and when he left me there, assuming I was dead, he drove to the hospital. But before he could get there, he died in a car accident.

That's what we let them believe. In a way, it's true.

Jordan always did love twisting the truth.

Mom cried when she delivered the news, apologizing and

lambasting herself for not seeing the signs. The same way Miles blamed himself after Sophie disappeared. So I made sure to remind her that the only person at fault is Jordan.

I haven't seen Miles since Jordan died. I thought maybe he'd be able to put everything behind us after what we went through, but I guess not. I broke us and there's no going back to what we had before.

But I can't let things just . . . end. Not like this. He needs to know how much I appreciate everything he did for me. He needs to know how grateful I am that he helped me see myself the way he saw me. That it's because of him I've found this . . . peace in myself. I'm happy with who I am. I'm happy to be Madalyn. And I don't need or want to be anyone else.

On our front porch, a girl with black hair and a girl with blonde hair wait for us.

Before I'm even fully out of the car, Natalie races off the porch and flings her arms around me.

"Careful," Mom warns.

Natalie gasps and immediately jumps off me. "Did I hurt you?"

I shake my head, even though she did.

Andre manages to convince Mom to give us some privacy, and she squeezes my hand twice and tells me she loves me four times before they head inside.

Natalie tears up and hugs me again. "I'm so sorry I turned my back on you when you needed me the most. When you needed a friend."

"You were defending your girlfriend." Even days later, my voice still croaks. To Liv, I say, "I'm sorry I accused you."

"We could've pushed," Liv says. "We shouldn't have just retreated like that. We could've proved it wasn't me somehow." She shrugs, because none of the answers are simple and there's no use dwelling on what-ifs.

"It's over now."

"Yeah, it is." Liv actually hugs me for the first time ever. Then, just quiet enough for me to hear, she says, "I'm glad he's dead."

The next day, I find Miles's Mustang parked across the street from Mariano's. He's working there again, and since I'm moving in a few days, Mabel told me to take my last week of summer break off and come back for shifts when I'm ready.

I leave the pan of brownies with a note attached on his driver's seat. They won't be as good as those brownies he made for me and Mom, but hopefully he'll see them as the peace offering they're meant to be.

Dear Miles,

You saved my life, and I'll never be able to thank you enough for that. All the brownies in the world wouldn't be enough, but I hope you'll enjoy these anyway.

I'm sorry I doubted you. I'm sorry I let them arrest you. I'm sorry I believed them over you. That's one of the worst mistakes I've ever made. Even though I believed you deep down, I doubted myself. And because of that, I let other people convince me I was wrong about you.

I understand if you don't want anything to do with me now. I'll be moving in a few days, so you won't have to worry about seeing me around town except on the weekends I visit Mom and when I come back on breaks. But who knows? Maybe by December, you'll be somewhere else. Opening your own diner. Even better, please open a bakery. Your brownies are way better than mine.

You're the reason I'm alive today, and the reason I am who I am. You helped me find my way back to myself. And I am so, so grateful.

xo,

Madalyn

CHAPTER THIRTY-TWO

I SIT on the roof outside my window with a stack of books next to me. Mainly contemporary romances, some fantasy romances, and one rom-com that everyone's raving about on TikTok—all of them loaded with spice. All I want right now are books with love and happily-ever-afters. That's what I deserve.

By the time I'm five pages from the end of the rom-com, my eyes are dry and my back aches, but I don't care. I've missed this: the unique feeling of hope that only books can give me. That things are going to be okay. Great, even.

The squeak of plastic makes me jump.

Miles climbs out of his old bedroom window. My heart leaps into my throat.

When he fully emerges, he's got a brown paper bag in one hand and a smile on his face.

I nearly cry tears of joy at the sight of it.

He sits down beside me and sets the bag in the little space between us. He smells so good. Minty and intoxicating. I've missed him so, so much.

"What's that?" I manage to ask.

He nods at the bag. "I brought you a gift." When I reach

inside the bag, I pull out a glossy paperback copy of *Pride and Prejudice*. "Figured you could use a new one."

I trace my finger over the title and sleek cover. "Wow. Thank you." My voice is still a little hoarse, but the pain has receded.

Those two words aren't enough to express my gratitude. Aren't enough to convey how he makes me feel seen more than anyone else ever has.

Jordan gave me jewelry, flowers, expensive chocolate—the kind Sophie always loved. But in all the months we were together, he never gave me a book. He never knew they were my first love, even before Miles.

"That's a thank you." Miles nods to my book. "For helping me get my GED."

A wide smile spreads across my face. "You got it?"

"Yep."

"I knew you would."

"Can I tell you a secret?" He smirks. "I didn't actually need your help. Could've passed that thing in my sleep."

"So you conned your grandma out of fifty dollars a week?"

He shrugs.

"Why?"

He stares at me, the intensity of his gaze making the blood in my veins sing. "Why do you think?"

Please say it's because you've been in love with me as long as I've been in love with you. I swallow. "So you read my note?"

He gives a single nod, lips pressed together.

I hug the book to my chest. "I'm really sorry. For everything. I should've stood up for you. I should've known you didn't do it."

He shrugs. "Dude was a manipulative psychopath. Everyone believed I stole your stuff, not just you. To be fair, it looked pretty bad."

"He convinced people of a lot of things."

I still can't believe it. The reality hasn't entirely sunken in, and I'm not sure it ever will. I fell in love with Jordan. At least, I thought I did. And now he's dead.

Yet I still flinch at every shadow. Still glance over my shoulder.

But I know someday I'll heal from what he did to me.

Miles reaches out to my neck with his fingertips and I stiffen. Try to block out the memory of Jordan's hands reaching for my throat, of his fingers digging into tender flesh.

But Miles isn't Jordan. His touch is gentle, feather-light across the faint bruise still there.

I swallow, the tips of his fingers bobbing with the movement.

The light turns his eyes to warm honey. "You're the bravest person I know."

For August, the air is blessedly cool. Heavenly on my now burning-hot skin. "No. You are."

He shakes his head. "Not even close."

"Thank you again," I murmur. "For saving me."

"We saved each other." He leans closer. So close, I can almost taste him.

Every inch of his beautiful face fills my vision. The dark hair that sweeps over his forehead. The freckles at his hairline, jaw, and the corner of his eye. The soft lips curved into the slightest upturn. The dark eyes that see into my soul—and understand it.

"So you forgive me?" I whisper against his lips.

His breath comes out tasting of chocolate. "Only because those brownies were fucking delicious."

His mouth lands on mine, ravenous and insatiable. Our mouths part, tasting each other like we're each other's first bite of chocolate after years without sugar.

Within seconds, I'm on my back and his hand is buried in my hair, the other sliding up my shirt. "God, I've missed you," he growls.

"It's Madalyn," I correct.

He grins before kissing me again, slipping his tongue in my mouth. The taste of him makes me groan and clench my thighs. I didn't think it was possible to want someone this bad, but I've been aching for him since I lost him.

I don't need him, and I would've been okay without him. But I want him.

His hand slips down my shorts, but I sit up. "We should go inside."

"Aww, you don't want to fool around on the roof for the whole town to see?"

"No, and I also don't want my mother to kill you."

He stands and helps me to my feet. "Inside it is."

We don't get far. We don't even make it to the bed before I'm on top of him. The floor can't be that comfortable, but he doesn't complain. Just hangs onto my hips while I grind against him and yanks my shirt over my head.

He frees my breasts from my bra, tossing it carelessly, and sucks my nipple into his mouth. I clutch at his hair, continuing to rock my hips back and forth over his hard length. I don't know how I went so long without him. How I could've convinced myself to be happy with the little Jordan could give me when I could've had everything with Miles, all this time.

"When are you moving into your apartment?" he gasps.

"This weekend."

"I'll help."

I grind against him harder. "What a gentleman."

He grabs both my breasts and squeezes. "Nope. I have an ulterior motive. I'm not leaving."

"Good. I want you there."

He presses a hand between my thighs, eliciting a gasp from my lips. "I want to be here."

We wriggle out of our clothes in seconds and he moves down until I'm sitting on his face. Another first. His tongue licks and penetrates expertly, making me writhe and whimper and cry out before he scoots me back down his body.

His hard length presses against my entrance before he slowly slides inside me. We groan together.

When I lift my hips and drop back down hard, he squeezes my ass. Finally, I get to ride him as hard and fast as I want.

So I do.

He bites his lip hard while rubbing my clit, both of us getting closer and closer to the edge with every thrust. He pants below me and his heart pounds beneath my palm.

The heart I know belongs to me. Just as mine belongs to him.

He tips his head back and drags in a breath. "You're like the girl of my dreams but a thousand times better."

I smirk. "How am I better?"

"You're real."

Outside Mariano's, Mom and I run into Jordan's parents.

Mrs. Goldman's eyes are puffy. Everything else about her is put together, as usual. You'd never know her son just died.

Rumor has it they're moving soon. Leaving their beautiful home behind, where so many ugly things happened. Mrs. Goldman has already resigned as mayor.

She starts to hold her hand out to me but thinks better of it. "I know you've been seeing a therapist," she says, voice hushed. "We want to pay for your sessions."

She's already pulling out her checkbook when Mom says, "I think that's the least you could do."

That's when Mr. Goldman takes his wife by the arm, jaw set, and leads her away without a word.

It's no mystery where Jordan got his charm.

Part of me wishes Mom had just taken Mrs. Goldman's

blood money. We could use it for all the therapy sessions and medication I'm on now. Klonopin for the anxiety that causes me to clench all my muscles in my sleep, to grind my teeth together. That wakes me in the middle of the night sweating, heart racing, with nothing to do but wait for the terror to subside.

I left my mark on Jordan, but he left his on me too.

Miles is the one who encouraged me to start seeing Marissa, my therapist. She explained to me that when Jordan ignored my attempts to contact him for a few days, he was using a control tactic. He wanted me to feel guilty, to feel like a bad person, to work harder to get his attention, and then feel grateful, clingy, when I finally got it.

I fell right into his trap.

"You were being manipulated, Madalyn. All those times he lied to you, tried to make you doubt your memory, make you think you were going crazy, he was gaslighting you. None of us are immune, but being young makes you especially vulnerable. Girls your age are about three times more likely to be abused by an intimate partner."

She keeps using that word—*abuse*. I've never thought that's what was happening with Jordan. Maybe I didn't want to believe it was as bad as it was. I wanted to believe I was lucky, like everyone told me I was.

He wasn't hitting me. He wasn't leaving bruises.

None that were visible. Not until the end.

Natalie, Liv, Sophie, and I visit the tattoo parlor for one last girls' day before we all head in different directions for college— Natalie to Massachusetts, Liv to Rhode Island, and me to Farmington. Sophie's staying in Beaumont and applying for spring semester at universities to major in psychology.

"I can't believe you're really getting matching tattoos," Natalie says, watching Sophie and me where we sit in our chairs and wincing at the needle whirring across my skin. "Doesn't it hurt?"

"It feels amazing, actually," I tell her. "Like acupuncture."

Sophie laughs, and warmth fills my chest. I wish I hadn't wasted so much time being jealous of her, hating her for things she couldn't control, hating myself for things I couldn't either.

But all I can do is start making up for that lost time now.

A girl with blue hair emerges from the back room. And halts in her tracks when she spots us.

Ash.

I have no idea how she's been handling the news. Did she think she was in love with Jordan too? Was he nothing but a fun time to her? I don't know, but I hope she's doing okay. I want to put everything behind us. We might not ever be friends again, certainly not the kind that gets matching tattoos, but we can at least put the animosity behind us.

Natalie folds her arms, and Liv shifts on her feet like she's not sure whether she'll have to break up a fight.

"Do you work here?" I blurt.

"Um. Yeah." Ash takes all of us in before striding over to my tattoo artist and gesturing for him to vacate his seat, where he's cleaning the small amount of blood off my arm. "I'm taking over."

He shrugs and heads for the back room.

Ash dabs surprisingly gently at the new tattoo on my arm. "I'm glad you're here, actually," she says. "I wanted to tell you . . . I'm sorry."

The apology is physically painful for her. Part of me wants to film this. It may be the only time Ash has ever apologized for anything. I kind of admire that about her, though.

"I shouldn't have posted those videos. I never thought . . . he'd try to hurt you because of it."

"You thought he'd break up with me, right? That's why you posted them. You wanted him to break up with me and date you."

Before, I would've wanted to know how long she was cheating with Jordan. How many times. But I can't bring myself to care now.

"Ha. No. I liked sneaking around with him. That's what made it fun. And I didn't think I owed you anything." Then she adds, eyes flashing up to meet mine, "Sorry."

"He called you 'some random girl.' After you posted those videos," I say. Her lip flattens, like she thinks I'm trying to insult her. "You deserve better than a guy who talks about you like that. Who keeps you a secret."

"Yeah, we all do." She shakes her head. "I'm an idiot. I could've been the one in that hospital." Her eyes grow wide when she realizes what she said. "Shit. Sorry. I suck at this."

"It's okay. Sorry for ditching you."

Silence falls between us until Ash glances between my arm and Sophie's. "So, butterflies?"

Sophie and I grin and brush our arms together to compare our tattoos. Delicate butterflies with one wing a black-and-white outline and the other shaded blue. A symbol of our transformation.

For the girls we were, and the girls we've become.

He tried to break us, but he only made us stronger.

When we leave the tattoo shop, Natalie and Liv race to Natalie's car in the parking lot.

Sophie pulls on my arm to hang back. "The police have finally stopped calling." She keeps her voice low. "I think they're dropping it."

"Our stories corroborate each other. They have no reason to keep questioning us," I tell her. She nods but doesn't look wholly convinced. "Do you think they'll ever find out what really happened?"

Sophie faces me, emerald eyes bright and fierce. "Jordan got what he deserved."

Yes. He did.

"I'm not talking," she says. "Are you?"

I shake my head. "Never."

We fall silent again. Still finding our rhythm in this new friendship.

"Hey!" Natalie shouts to us from where she and Liv sit on her car's hood. "Do you guys want to get ice cream?"

"Hell yeah!" I call.

Sophie smiles. "I love our friends."

Our friends. It's a simple word, one Sophie uttered without a second thought but one my mind clings onto.

I'm not alone. Sophie and I are in this together.

"You're really brave," I tell her. "For doing everything you did. He had no idea who he was up against."

"I'm not brave. I ran away. Bravery is doing what you did—fighting back."

"You got yourself out of a dangerous situation. That's always brave."

We listen to Natalie and Liv cackling together with heads thrown back, all of us enjoying the summer evening air that's finally descending into autumn.

"I'm sorry," I tell Sophie.

"For what?"

"That I didn't care whether you were alive or dead," I say. She doesn't react to my honesty. Not even an upward tick of her eyebrows. "I told you to leave. I wanted you to run away."

"I didn't leave because of you. I left because of him."

I shake my head because I don't deserve an out, even if she wants to give me one. "I was happy you were gone because it meant I could be with Jordan. I could be the new Sophie."

She gives a sad smile. "You got more than you bargained for."

"I deserved it."

Sophie pulls me to a stop, eyes stern. "No, you didn't. No one deserves that."

"Are you two coming or are we leaving without you?" Liv shouts.

Before we start heading for them again, I say, "Sophie?"

I'm still getting used to her with blonde hair. Still getting used to her back in Beaumont. Alive.

My friend.

"Yeah?"

"Thanks for coming back."

Sophie smiles. A girl I once called a queen bee, a prom queen. Royalty. Above the rest of us.

But she is just a girl. The same as me.

A girl with impenetrable armor and secrets she will take to her grave.

—————————

CHAPTER THIRTY-THREE

MILES TEXTS me to meet him at the playground. He wouldn't give any hints when I asked him why, but it's kind of nice being back before I move into my apartment tomorrow.

This playground was both hell and haven for me. I could read on the swings and escape into other worlds—until some kid yanked me back. But I'm over that now. I don't care what anybody thinks of me except the people who love me.

And I have a lot of them now.

When I finally find Miles past the vacant monkey bars and jungle gym, he's sitting on the swings, where I used to plant myself every recess.

A stack of books in his lap.

I grin. "What's this?"

"Since you'll be a college girl soon, I figured you should get a chance to read on the swings one last time," he says. "And if anybody makes fun of you, I'll punch them."

My heart melts. Other than literally saving my life, this may be the sweetest thing he's ever done for me. That anyone's ever done for me. "Good thing there's no one here to make fun of me. Besides, I wouldn't care if they did. I love books and myself, so there's nothing to be ashamed of."

He beams. "About time I got through to you."

I rush over to him, grab his face, and press my lips against his, trying to send every ounce of gratitude I feel through each place our bodies touch.

"This is so sweet," I tell him when I finally pull away. "Thank you."

"In case you couldn't tell," he says, throat bobbing, "I'm in love with you."

My chest squeezes with a feeling I've never had before. A kind of love I've never experienced.

Until now.

I can barely get the words out above a whisper. "I'm in love with you too."

We're kissing again, a tangle of lips and tongues and hands. I'm in love with him. With the boy on the swings. The boy with the books. The boy who saved my life, in more ways than one.

His lips brush against mine when he murmurs, "*Madalyn.*"

Something in me swells every time he says my name. My full name.

Not Maddie, not Mads, not baby.

Madalyn.

ACKNOWLEDGMENTS

I began writing *Always with You* in 2020, and Madalyn and Miles quickly became one of the few bright spots in a dark year. So first, thank you, dear reader, for picking up the book of my heart. Whether you loved this story or not, thank you for giving it a chance. I hope these characters live in your heart the way they live in mine. I hope they can be a bright spot for you too.

To my betas, Kelsey and Lauren, thank you so much for your spot-on feedback! You helped make this book shine.

Thank you to Caitlin F., who read an early version of this book in a single weekend, even though you had to pack. Thank you, thank you, *thank you* for your insightful feedback. This story wouldn't be what it is without you.

Thank you to Caitlin H. for reading an early draft in a *day*! I'm still stunned and honored. Thank you to Mary for being the first to read the full manuscript and for the suggestion about the ending!

To Alex, this book wouldn't exist without you. Thank you for encouraging me to publish this story and supporting me from the beginning. Thank you for your patience and understanding when I spend all night writing, and thank you for helping me through every step of the publishing process. We make a great team. I love you.

ABOUT THE AUTHOR

Harmony West writes dark forbidden romance. She enjoys her love stories with a side of mystery, twists, and spice.

For updates on Harmony West's latest releases, subscribe to her newsletter at www.harmonywestbooks.com/subscribe or follow her on social media @authorharmonywest.

www.ingramcontent.com/pod-product-compliance
Lightning Source LLC
Chambersburg PA
CBHW030144310726
48970CB00005B/1583